SEVEN MINUTES OF CHRISTMAS MAGIC

AN ENEMIES TO LOVERS ROMANCE

K.L. BRADY

LADYLITPRESS

Seven Minutes of Christmas Magic
An Enemies to Lovers Romance

LadyLit Press

11505 Cherry Tree Crossing Road #535

Cheltenham, MD 20623

October 2020

First Edition

PRAISE FOR K.L. BRADY

Winner — Next Generation Indie Book Award for Multicultural Fiction (2010)

Winner — Next Generation Indie Book Award for Multicultural Fiction (2013)

Winner — Next Generation Indie Book Award for Multicultural Fiction (2014)

Publisher's Weekly calls K.L. Brady's work "comic and charming..."

RT Book Reviews calls Brady's work "Hilarious!"... and says she "draws readers in immediately...and propels them straight through the drama, humor and the various twists and turns that will leave you exhausted but satisfied."

"12 Honeymoons had me laughing from the first page. Miki is a hoot, with a smart, sarcastic sense of humor and mouth that won't quit (and gets her in trouble quite regularly)." – San Francisco Review of Books

"I don't know how KL Brady manages to write romance that is equal parts emotional tug and belly laugh. The plot twists keep coming...always with humor...until girl gets her guy and readers get the happily ever after. Fast-paced, this is such a fun holiday read." – Amazon Reviewer

"Cue the Mistletoe! Five Golden Rings is the perfect holiday read."

"K.L. Brady delivered again with Her Perfect Catch. This is a quick but fulfilling romance novel and combines two of my favorite things, football, and love." ~ Good-reads Reviewer

To My Grandma, Katherine Brown
Love You. Always...

CHAPTER 1

 ia

Same Black Friday, different year. This marks the anniversary of one of the darkest days in my almost thirty years of existence. The day after Thanksgiving usually is an occasion filled with joy and fun. Most people look forward to over-spending money they don't after indulging in holiday delights they swore they wouldn't overeat.

For me, it's a grim reminder of the marriage proposal that wasn't and the breakup that now seems more inevitable than I ever believed.

I've barely digested my turkey and sweet potato pie before Christmas-everything overwhelms me. I should've taken the day off to sulk and wallow in self-pity, given the cosmic disasters that are my romantic and professional lives, but alas, I'm too busy and overbooked.

I'm the newly appointed Vice President of Sweet-Hart Cards, and through every fault of my own, we probably are the only greeting card company in the world without a Christmas campaign.

Well, not so much *probably* as we are.

I've managed to do nothing in my short tenure except prove the truth in the suspicions: I'm ill-qualified for my elevated role in the company. Everyone thinks I made a better Creative Director than I will a VP.

Even worse, I haven't been able to replace myself so that I can focus on being a good VP. Can't find the right person. So far, not a single candidate has brought the right combination of skills. We need someone who can drive the artistic vision of the new division of Hart Enterprises with the snark, sass, and class reflective of Keep It Real Cards' union with Hart Cards.

I share the blame with Tessa Sweet, the new Executive Vice President for all of Hart Enterprises, and my BFF. I suppose she entrusted me with creative control over this all-important Christmas collection because I've been with her since Keep it Real's inception. And I'm rewarding her confidence in me with nothing in terms of fresh, innovative, and economical ideas.

I'm stuck. In college, this fraternity guy (a few more than two sheets to the wind) froze a silver spoon in a glass of molasses and bet no one could remove it. An army of his equally toasted brothers tugged, yelled, and yanked, trying to get it out. Well, he was right. No one could. That spoon? It was less stuck than I am. My superpowers are inactivated, leaving me paralyzed and unable to do my job. I've started questioning my abilities, wondering if I have the mettle, grit, and determination to achieve the impossible: develop this Christmas line in seven days, find a new creative director, and mend a broken heart in time to embrace the joy of what is usually my most favorite and cherished holiday.

The scent of cinnamon apples from my burning candles simultaneously soothes and irritates me, like the friction scritch sound of unlined wool as my upper thighs rub together—I blame my three Thanksgiving dinners.

I drag myself out of my U Street duplex and make tracks into the Sweet-Hart offices to meet with Creative. They're a valiant group of writers and artists entrusted with executing a concept I've yet to create—and that I must lead because I've failed to fill a critical slot. I enter the conference room, set the stage, and anticipate the presentations.

"You all know we're behind schedule, and we're all doing our best. But we've got to come up with the right concept. What we've developed so far is good, but not great. This is the inaugural year for the Sweet-Hart Christmas collection. We all know that, for reasons outside of our control, this division's success hinges on this line. We need a campaign that captures the spirit of the season. It's got to be uniquely Hart and Keep It Real. It's got to be sticky and viral to put Sweet-Hart on the map."

"So, I'm having a tough time figuring out exactly what you're looking for," says Destiny, Sweet-Hart's senior writer and copy editor.

"I fear it'll be one of those concepts I won't know until I see it —tough spot. I realize we have to strike the right balance between Sweet-Hart and Keep It Real, you know? Snarky yet celebratory and respectful of the season. What we've got now is either too edgy or too syrupy sweet. We need something in the middle."

Zeke, the lead writer, pipes in, "I know you want to come up with something new, Mia, but we're almost out of time. One option—the safer option—well, we could repurpose the Hart Card campaign from last year, maybe refresh the imaging and use the old copy. We've got, what? Seven business days before these have to go to the distributor? Any later and they won't hit the shelves in time to take advantage of holiday sales. This isn't the ideal solution, but right now, we don't have many options."

Panic seeps in. My breathing's labored. I deflate like a busted animal balloon. That's not how I want to kick off my first year as VP — reusing last year's campaign, one that doesn't even include Keep It Real Cards. Then again, what's the alternative?

Nothing? No Christmas revenue? At least repurposing would meet the deadlines.

"Duly noted," I respond hesitantly. "Maybe some updated imagery and copy. It's not the revolutionary campaign I had planned. It'd help us survive the season with cards on the shelves. Mediocre sales, yes, but a chance to create brilliance another day. In the meantime, we have to plan. We've got to make a splash. A huge splash. Card-Fest and the Winner's Ball are coming up, and we need to make a solid showing, even if we lose, again,"—I shrug— "Let me run the reuse idea by Tessa and Cody and see what they say."

Cody and Tessa now lead Hart Enterprises, the entire half-billion-dollar media conglomerate, including Sweet-Hart Cards (formerly Hart Cards owned by Cody and Tessa's Keep It Real Cards).

"I know it's disappointing, but I don't see what other choices we have at the moment," Zeke says.

"Okay, finish conceptualizing the full collection. Zeke, you'll lead the effort. Once you've got the mockups, send them to me, and I'll get executive approval," I say. "The only good news is that approval should be easy. It's a repeat."

The room quiets. No one's excited about this project, but we're resigned to one simple fact: we're about out of choices.

Zeke asks, "Maybe now we can address the elephant in the room. We're all on edge about the...mole. I mean, we come up with new and innovative ideas, and then our campaigns show up on the shelves as Love & Kisses greeting cards? Is anyone even trying to figure out who's responsible?"

"What I can tell you is this: security is conducting an internal investigation as we speak. Company-wide, from top to bottom. It's been ongoing for several months now. They're examining every aspect of our operations, but it's out of our hands at this point. I've got a gut feeling, and I don't believe the problem is in this room. The culprit's somewhere else in the company. We'll find them, and Cody and Tessa will fire them."

"So, are we taking any measures to keep our Christmas collection secure? Rehash or not, we can't make our sales quotas if Love & Kisses beats us to the racks with our own designs."

"Funny you should ask." I retrieve a brown leather briefcase from beneath the table, pop the combination locks to open the lid, and remove a Surface Pro. "I'm maintaining everything related to the Christmas campaign in this briefcase, on this computer. We'll use this to store the entire collection. I'm sequestering a conference room. Anyone supporting the campaign works there. Zeke will collect your files at the end of each day, and I'll back them up to the cloud.

"I'll attach the briefcase to my hip and keep it with me at all times. The good news is—no long nights, and we're the only ones who know the campaign is in the briefcase. I have full confidence we can keep it safe for the next week. Also, the search for the new creative director presses on. We've got a few interviews next week. We're hopeful," I said, lying my butt off. I'm all but devoid of optimism and in need of a crap load of Christmas magic. "Now let's break up this meeting and get to work. I need to check in with Tessa."

While the team disperses, I ask Zeke to hang behind. The first laptop exchange commences, and I handover custody to him. Once he loads the files and mockups, I'll collect it, lock it away in the briefcase, and remain the keeper of the concept until we ship the final files to the printers and then to the distributors.

A prayer consumes my thoughts, that we figure out the identity of the corporate traitor. It's bad enough we're using last year's line. I'd rather not have Love & Kisses rob us blind using our old campaign to beat us.

For my next trick of the day, I head to Tessa's office to tell her the bad news without telling her the awful news. Back in the day, before the acquisition, when she and I ran Keep It Real, I breezed in and out of her office on whims without a second thought. More often than not, I need an appointment to see my bestie. We both understand that she belongs to Hart Enterprises, and, as Executive Vice President, her time inside the office is neither hers nor mine, not anymore.

I tap on the door frame and poke my head inside. She peers up from the stack of paperwork on her desk and greets me with a smile.

"Mia," she says. The "my girl" in her voice is unspoken but audible to me. "Cody and I were just talking about you. Come in." She waves me inside and gestures for me to fill her guest seat. "How's everything going with the Christmas line?"

I hesitate, hem-and-haw for a second before saying, "Good news, bad news. Which do you want first?"

Tessa purses her lips.

"Fine. The good news is we've nailed down the concept—it's last year's campaign repurposed. We'll get it to the printer and distributor on time. We'll put our heads down and dig in so we can get it out the door next week."

"And for the bad news?" She crosses her arms over her chest, not at all fooled, and narrows her eyes. She's just heard the bad news. This is worse.

"Still no creative director. I never thought I'd have such a tough time replacing myself. It turns out I'm pretty freaking awesome."

"And humble. Don't forget humble," Tessa says with a chuckle.

"I sat through three interviews last week." My horrified expression should tell her all she needs to know about how they progressed. "One guy picked his nose and wiped it under the seat. I invited him to make his exit and then had the custodian glove his hands and throw the whole seat away."

Tessa's mouth hangs open.

"One had never heard of Keep It Real Cards. I mean, c'mon, dude. We're not conducting Google searches before we interview?"

"Lord have mercy," she says. "And the last one?"

"She had the artistic capability of a third-grader, which in this case is an insult to most third graders. Inside her portfolio—stick people. I swear. At least she colored inside the lines. Needless to say, she could use a little more practice, and we need a seasoned professional with new ideas."

"With fresh, innovative, and economical ideas by next Friday, along with our submission for the Christmas Card-Fest Tree Lighting Party and Winner's Ball. Aye aye aye."

At Christmas Card-Fest, US greeting card companies annually deliver the best of their Christmas collections to bring joy to brave troops and win bragging honors. We decorate a Douglass Fir for D.A.D (Deployed and Active Duty) troops in Christmas Cards from all the major suppliers. Each one grants the wish of spouses and children of military personnel who need holiday help—a gift, a bill paid, whatever.

The party begins with the ugly Christmas sweater affair and tree lighting and ends with the Winner's Ball, where they announce the Christmas card campaign receiving the most industry votes. This year Hart Publishing's hosting both in the Executive Conference Center.

Last year Signed & Sealed hosted.

For two years in a row, we've come in second to Love & Kisses—who's "mysteriously" won with variations of unpublished Hart campaigns.

"I received one resume that seems promising. I've scheduled an interview for next Tuesday. In the meantime, I'm pulling triple duty between art, operations, and financials. I'm exhausted, but I'll survive."

"For what it's worth, I'm not worried in the least. I know you'll get the line finished and a replacement candidate. I trust you. You just need to trust yourself," she says. Her shoulders relax, and she leans forward on her desk as the tension in her face releases. "On another note, are you going to the Black Friday party tonight?"

She changes the subject so fast I get whiplash. I deliver bitter fire and venom on my smirk. "Nothing is waiting for me at that party but sadness and humiliation. I'm not going." Our friends Sophie and Brooks, SoBro, throw the Black Friday party every year. It's an all-couples affair, and I've never had a date. I'm usually in the midst of a breakup, and they always claim they'll invite some single guy to stage a hook-up. Three years in a row and the mystery man's had the good sense not to show up. Nothing's gonna change this year, including Tessa's attempt to convince me to go.

"Cody and I have this industry thing, and he needs his plus-one. As a Hart executive, I know I signed up for this; however, Cody concealed some of these commitments in the small print. But you should go to SoBro's. Sophie tells me they've invited a guy—he could be 'the one.' Besides, Dustin's moved on, and so should you."

Can we say disaster? I'm still cutting both of my eyes at her. She knows better than to speak the scourge's name.

"What?" she adds. "You need to get back out there. It's been a minute, way too long."

"No, thank you. I just started peopling again. My breakup with that man couldn't have been more humiliating—or public. Let's not push it."

"Always the excuses with you...how ever factual they may be. Fine. I'm still coming by tomorrow to help decorate, though."

"Don't worry about it." I shrug. "I'd rather you not stand me up again. I'm not sure I can survive any more abandonment. Had I not been fretting over the Christmas collection and the creative director search, I'd have had my decorations finished after Halloween as usual. On a more positive note, your box of ornaments is ready for you to take."

"Christmas isn't Christmas without your ornaments. You're my BFF and tree angel. That's why I'm gonna do better. The newness of Cody is wearing off already, and we'll get back to normal," she says with a chuckle.

"I'll believe it when I see it," I joke. We've been friends for too long for hurt feelings. Things change. Life changes. She's getting lucky regularly. Stuff happens. "It's not your fault we're in the circle of life, and I'm the digested, regurgitated roadkill." I lean over Tessa's desk and offer her a quick sister hug.

IN MY COTTON SNOOPY CHRISTMAS PAJAMAS AT HOME THAT evening, I relieve my attic storage space of mounds of Christmas decor boxes and stack them beside the unlit fireplace. A pile of wood awaits a lighter, but I'm determined to wait until my house is coated in holiday joy before I settle down to enjoy the dancing flames.

The faintest sound of footsteps, and my extreme nosiness, draws me to the window, and I give in to my curiosity. At first, I see nothing, wonder if maybe I'm imagining things. Perhaps it's the universe keeping me alert. I dunno. Then I pinch the shades open.

Have mercy!

One glorious man is standing in a beam of light that surrounds him like an aura. Beneath his Washington football skullcap stands a towering mound of chocolatey goodness with an incredible physique, kind eyes (from what I can see), and a strong jawline.

I forget where I am, who I am.

Drool dribbles out of the corner of my mouth and onto my chin. I'm drinking him in when he, perhaps sensing my presence, turns toward me, and ruins my anonymity.

I release the blinds and flatten my back against the wall, breathless by the encounter, and wonder for a moment if he noticed me. Wouldn't have been tough; my reflects suck. By the time I gather up the nerve to look outside again, he's gone, just like that.

The only evidence of his existence is footsteps in the snow and my pounding heart.

The brief encounter takes me back to a time I've forgotten—

the beginning of a connection, the possibility bubbling in the moments of a first glance. I've missed experiencing this because I've buried myself in work to forget the Dustin humiliation.

From the wastepaper basket, I retrieve my Black Friday party invitation. I should go. Maybe I'll experience the connection again. Also, Sophie and Brooks are my dear friends, and the party might take two or three hours out of my life—max. What's the worst that can happen?

CHAPTER 2

ixon

THEY CALL THIS FRIDAY BLACK FOR A REASON. IT'S THE DAY AFTER Thanksgiving, and the holiday season hasn't quite kicked in yet. It doesn't feel the same now that my father is gone. I sit back and stare at the empty place my tree used to fill on this day in years past. Watching my father set up his train around his tree's base is how I learned to put up mine; he wouldn't allow me to touch his. That and Black Friday marked the commencement of the Christmas season for our family.

It's been six years now, and the tradition feels real, but the thought of continuing without him, along with the drama going on in my professional life, paralyzes me. The fact is, there's not much to celebrate.

My phone rings, and I take the mental exit off of pity parkway. I grab my cell and glance at the screen—a familiar face smiles at me, and the screen flashes. I swipe.

"Hey! There's my favorite lady," I say. "What's going on?"

"Um...," Mom says and then...nothing. She's breathing. I can hear her, but she stops speaking. Understand, if you look up the word chatterbox in the dictionary, it's derived from the words Maxine McCloud. She's never without words, so I know something's wrong.

"Ma? What is it?"

"I'm...I'm in some trouble, baby. I didn't want to put this burden on your shoulders, but I'm out of options. I've got nowhere else to go."

Something tells me this is about money. And I'm unemployed. Next-level broke.

The distress, the desperation in her voice, breaks my heart. I've never heard the sound before. Ever. A pit forms in my stomach, and time stops moving until she explains.

"Are you okay? Tell me."

"I'm fine, Pumpkin. Well, I'm healthy, don't worry about that. No, uh, it's the house. I'm afraid I'm behind on the mortgage."

There it is.

"The house? Behind? But...how?"

"Your dad couldn't live without his man-cave. Since we've been in this house forever, he took out a second mortgage to make the much-needed repairs and renovate. New windows, new roof, a new furnace...and the man-cave. Then, well..."

"He passed away."

"In his defense, he never conceived he wouldn't be here to help me," she says. "Neither did I. We didn't have enough life insurance to cover all the bills. I've been robbing Peter to pay Paul, trying to keep all the debts up to date, but I think I'm going to have to let our home go. The cost is too much, including my piece of mind."

Stunned to silence doesn't begin to capture my state of mind. Talk about thrifty. She could squeeze a buffalo penny until it passed gas. This didn't happen because she's careless or a shopaholic. She wasn't irresponsible. It happened because she's overwhelmed with caring for so much alone, with grief at the loss of my father, and she lost control.

What I cannot do, what I will never do, not as long as I draw breath, is allow her to lose her home.

No matter what sacrifices I have to make.

No matter what compromises I have to make.

We've experienced enough loss for several lifetimes. I won't allow this, too.

"Why didn't you tell me sooner, Ma? I wouldn't have let it get this far."

"I'm your Mama. You're not mine. I'm supposed to be helping you, not the other way around. You haven't worked full-time in a year. What were you gonna do? Break yourself trying to save me?"

"Really? I could've sold my place and moved back home?"

"Oh, no! Not with the parade of women you've got trotting around like prized Clydesdales, horsehair and all. I'd rather be homeless." Her chuckle's weak, and maybe too soon, but she's not lying. However, she might want to get out of the woods before she cuts me up cracking jokes. I'm the one who'll be in trouble if a new job doesn't come through soon.

"Get all your paperwork together," I say. "I'll be over there Saturday, and we'll take care of it. Don't worry about it another minute, Ma. I've got you. The last thing I promised Dad is that I would take care of you, so it's done."

"But, Pumpkin. What about you—"

"Nope. Not another word. It's done. Let *me* worry about *me*. You've got bigger things to concern yourself with. Let's be thankful I'm blessed enough to be in a position to ease your worries."

"How can I repay you for this?" she says, a little choked up. "With you doing this for me. Maybe I can do something for you —help you focus on more important things."

"More important, like what?" I ask.

"Decorating for and celebrating Christmas. It's been six years. Too long! But I'd say we're going to have something to celebrate this year. Wouldn't you agree?"

I can almost hear her smile through the phone.

"Our memories...and our home," she continues. "You know, baby, every day you're an answered prayer for me. Everyday."

"Where would I be without you and Dad? How much have you sacrificed so I could go to college and live my dreams? So, please. This is nothing, a fraction of what you've given me. You don't have to thank me at all...except you could bake me a batch of those cookies."

"Done. I love you."

"I love you, too," I say. "Now, let me get off this phone so that I can make a few calls. But I'll see you, Saturday. Okay?"

"And we're going to raid the attic for decorations and celebrate with all the traditions, right?"

"Of course."

Okay. I'm worried. Really worried. Not about her, about me. If she's in foreclosure, she's got to be at least three months behind on her mortgage, which probably means six months' worth of payments.

Bank account drained.

I need a job I don't have. After being unemployed for over a year, I'd all but given up on trying to find the kind of job I want and quit putting feelers out two months ago. Boy, did I pick a "great" time to change careers.

My heart beats fast; I'm panicked. If there's a way to find some relief, I only know one. So, I kneel beside my bed and pray like Dad always told me to do when I needed help. I'm in need of a miracle today.

Maybe he will call the Christmas guardian angels to my rescue.

After I'm finished praying, I check my email, in the faint hope, something in my box resembles a miracle. There's nothing. But while I'm fixing dinner, the phone rings, and I answer.

To my surprise, I've got one appointment, the first in months, and I'm anxious.

It's at Hart Enterprises, my dream employer.

I'm not accustomed to being considered a candidate for jobs I never applied for but getting my foot in the door seems like too much of an opportunity to resist. I prayed for something more but never expected this.

Part of me feels grateful and blessed. Another part of me feels like I've leaped from the frying pan that is my life and into the fire that is Hart Enterprises.

The problem is I've watched the battle rage between Renee, Regina, and Cody Hart in the headlines for the past two years, and it's been ages since I applied for a position there. Although I've got to believe this is the opportunity I've been waiting for, the question I ask myself is, why me...now? Of all people, I've been called.

Although I've not voiced it, my deepest wish is to become a creative director there. To get hired at one of the largest black-owned media conglomerates in the country would be a dream come true.

It's not only a miracle. It's the mother of all blessings.

The next day, I suit up and tote my portfolio into Hart's hallowed halls hoping to make the impression that will win me the job.

Entering the Enterprises was, for me, surreal. The occasion was sacred because my idols—Brian Sweet and Devon Hart—built Hart from the ground up. Sadly, neither one would be present.

The company had begun to decorate for Christmas and placed multicultural Santa portraits around the lobby walls. The merry men smile at me, reassuring me I'm in the right place at the right time.

Renee and Regina Hart greet me with warm, deceptive smiles and escort me to Regina's executive suite. I see something hidden behind them, but I choose to ignore my gut feeling.

"You've got an impressive resume. American Salutations and Signed & Sealed," Renee begins, "and I see you've worked in marketing for three of book publishing's big five. This is an incredible breadth of experience, to say the least."

"If I may interrupt," I begin. "I'm honored by the invitation to interview for a position, but I'm confused. You're considering me for a job even though I never submitted an application. Don't get me wrong, I'm grateful, but it'd be disingenuous of me not to at least ask."

Renee's eyes narrow a bit but I'm still not suspicious of anything until she says, "Honestly, had you applied, we probably wouldn't have considered you. We need a special kind of person for this role, shall we say, a *niche* set of skills."

Regina nods in agreement. "We've conducted thorough research using extensive, private contacts both in and out of the industry. Your resume alone proves what we suspected—you're more than well-qualified to do the job we need you to do."

"Which is?"

"Well, let's say the task is similar to the one you performed at Keene, Blanchard, and Livingston," Renee says. "And we need skills like the ones you used to force the sale and subsequent acquisition of Bartholomew and Fink."

"I see," I reply. They know my work all too well. At least my identity. If they only understood the kind of man I really am. "I, uh, you may have the wrong idea about—"

"No," Regina said. "We admire your work."

"You haven't seen my work, not the kind I'd hoped to do for Hart Enterprises. I've been on hiatus for a reason; I'm seeking a career change. Thank you for calling me here today. It's been a pleasure, but I don't want to waste your time. With that said," I make a move to stand, and I'm shocked by the response.

"Don't go," they say in unison, holding up their palms to halt my movement. "The task is simple and will be well worth your while. It doesn't cost you a dime to listen, but it may cost you quite a bit if you leave prematurely, before we've had a chance to detail the opportunity."

I sit down. A black Santa's smile seems to disappear into a thin line. He's judging me.

"We need you to collect some proprietary, internal information. If you do that, we can pay you quite handsomely." She rubs her fingers together.

I cringe inside but don't flinch. My better judgment might prompt me to run from the opportunity but not the money. Not now. Helping my mother will drain my accounts.

But their effusive respect for my hatchet work makes me question their motives. They don't understand that the last thing I want to do is leave a legacy of damage that suggests I've created more hurt than good.

I plant my feet solidly against the floor and brace myself to stand. I need the money but not like this. Never like this. My only remaining doubt surrounds the kind of person they'll find to execute their plan if I don't.

"I'm not interested in a temp job or consulting; otherwise, I'd be employed now. My goal is to become a creative director. That's my passion; that's where I bring the most value. I'm here for the opportunity to bring a fresh vision to a company that I respect. If you need to collect information, with all due respect, this is Hart. You're Hart family members and leaders in this company. You'd probably have an easier time than me. I'm sure you can find other ways to obtain the data. I'm an expensive middleman. Again, I appreciate the opportunity."

I stand to leave, calculating the levels of insane I must be to pass up such an opportunity, especially when I'm desperate for money. I'll pay my mother's debt in a few days and regret not saying yes. For half a beat, I consider sitting back down when Regina holds up her hand again and gestures for me to wait. They lean into one another and exchange a series of animated whispers.

When they finally emerge from their discussions, Regina says, "I'd like to make you an offer you can't refuse. If you tackle this assignment and quickly, you'll be more than a creative director. We'll appoint you as Vice President of Creative Operations. As such, you will be responsible for guiding and mentoring all of our designers and writers in brand management, content, media strategy; you name it. From book covers to advertising campaigns, you'll oversee every aspect for us."

I keep telling my feet to move, but they won't. Instead, I find myself returning to my seat and asking the question I don't want an answer to. "So, what's the job?"

"For now, Director of Special Operations. We'll provide more details, but only after you sign a non-disclosure agreement. Obviously, our discussions are highly sensitive, and we need to protect the interests of this company and our own. You understand."

Oh, I understand, all right. The question is, do I care? If I serve as the hatchet man one last time, the fulfillment of my every professional dream is on the other side. There's only one thing I need to know. "The job is legal, right? I mean, I'm not going to jail."

"Of course not," Regina says, batting her hand. "This assignment is in no way illegal. I'm not going to lie, it may tread a thin line around ethics, but we're signing your paychecks, so ethics aren't an issue for us." She shrugs. "We called you in here today based on your past. We believed this to be comfortable territory for you."

She's not wrong. I wish I could say otherwise. I'm very familiar with the ethics line. However, if I were comfortable with breaching it, I'd never have quit my last job.

Just when I begin to have second thoughts, Renee slides a sheet a paper on the desk and asks me to pick it up. "That will be your salary and bonus structure. We'll make it a two-year deal. You can back out at any time. And, yes, we will put it in writing."

I cough, almost choking on the shock. Not only could this money enable me to get my mother out of foreclosure, but it would also allow me to get her so far ahead in payments, she'd never have to worry about where she'd live another day in her life.

"If the offer in writing lines up with what you've told me today, it would indeed be difficult to refuse."

This is the opportunity of a lifetime. How can I turn it down? If I work at Hart Enterprises for two years as the Vice President of Creative Operations, I can write my ticket and work anywhere else in the industry. I no longer have to accept sloppy seconds from anyone, for any reason. It's my dream, but I can't help but wonder if my dream hasn't come packaged in a nightmare.

"Good," Renee says. Then, without a puff of smoke or mirror in sight, she whips out a contract, like a magician pulling a rabbit out of a hat. "We anticipated that you might accept. So, we took the liberty of drawing up an agreement yesterday when you accepted our call."

I want to be offended. I'd strolled in here believing I'd been the one in control. Clearly, I'm mistaken. A quick read through the offer and non-disclosure agreement, and everything seems to be in order, except...

"You can't be serious about this deadline. Seven days?"

"Yes, starting Monday," Regina says. "I wish we could give you more time, but it's out of our control. There's been a development delay, so we're fortunate that we've got seven days."

"And if I can't make the deadline?"

"We part ways...as friends, I hope?" Regina says in a sing-song voice.

"The last question," I ask. "Who is the target?"

"That is the million-dollar question, isn't it? We don't know. A meeting's been set for Monday, and we anticipate that the identity of the person leading the effort will be there. If you choose to accept this offer, you'll find out the identity of both the target and the information we need you to collect then."

They stare at me hungrily, like devils seeking souls to steal. I take a breath, hold it in, and sign my name on the dotted line, offering myself up for slaughter. I'd like to say I've sacrificed only for my mother, but I'd be lying. This is also for me. I nod.

"Welcome to Hart Publishing," they say almost in unison. The black Santa's eyes seem to narrow. He's now glaring at me with disdain, as if he knows I'll be cornering the market in coal-stuffed stockings on Christmas Day. Can't say I blame him.

"I look forward to working with you both." I lie—to them and myself.

They wish me a good evening and send me on my way home to enjoy my weekend. This mission begins Monday morning. I leave with a job, if no dignity, and a way to save my mother, but at what cost? The battle for Hart Enterprises wages on, and I've chosen a side. I've picked my team. I've become a lethal weapon in the war, ultimately pitting me against two men whom I much admire.

It doesn't matter.

This occasion calls for a stiff drink—a large bottle or two of brown liquor. Scotch. One of my favorite U Street haunts, a jazz joint, calls to me. Within the hour, I'm at JoJo's, where I'm a regular. I head to the lower level, where a melodic refrain from a tenor sax smooths the sharp edges of my jagged day.

A line of exposed abs and deep cleavage parade in front of me as I order my drink—until one set stops. She eyes me as if I'm a whole snack, and I return the favor.

"Is this seat taken?" She winks and offers a sultry smile with a lot of teeth—all of them. The room's full of empty tables, but she asks to sit at mine. Her motives are clear.

"It is now." I gesture for her to fill the seat across from me. We engage in a little small talk, and the conversation requires nary one of my brain cells. I realize at that moment, I don't need a chat. I need a connection, and I'm not going to find it here with the abs and cleavage girl whose face is now buried in her cell phone.

Without even looking up at me, she asks, "Can I buy you a drink?"

I down my scotch and slip out of the seat, hooking my coat on my index finger and making a stealthy exit. I'm halfway down the block before I realize I've forgotten where I parked my car. I'm standing on the sidewalk in front of this duplex when I feel eyes on me. A glance over my shoulder reveals a pair of kind eyes (from what I can see) peering through blinds; they quickly disappear. Before I can do a double-take, my phone rings; it's my frat brother, Brooks.

"What's up, stranger?"

"Nixon, man. You coming through? You know tonight is the Black Friday party. Sophie will disown you if you don't show up this year. I mean, come on man, three years in a row? I might disown you—at a minimum, I'll be deeply offended."

"She's not going to try and set me up again, is she?"

He responds with silence and a chuckle.

"Fine, you caught me on the right day. I'm already out of the house. Once I find my car, I'll be over."

"Good, we'll see you in a few."

I shrug my shoulders. Whoever the mystery woman ends up being, she can't be any worse than the cleavage girl at JoJo's.

CHAPTER 3

 ia

I'M SEEKING REFUGE AT SOPHIE'S HOUSE. I'M IN THESE STREETS, AND guilt's sticking to me like static cling. My jaws and eyes tense to the point at which my face aches, partly because I'm cold and the rest because I've been a bad, bad girl. This is not exactly my shining moment.

After sprinting to the peak of Sophie's two-story Georgetown walk-up with her surprise in my hand, I cast a glance over my shoulder to see if I can find what I'm looking for — my breath.

I'm pretty sure I left it down the steps next to my BMW.

Between stealing some yokel's parking spot and running for cover like a banshee, my lungs abandon me. Now I can't catch my breath with a mitt. After reaching Sophie's front door, I poke my fist through the wreath, pound against SoBro's pristine mahogany wood—and skip ringing the dang doorbell.

I need in.

Now.

As I wait for her to answer, I'm shivering, covered in fat snowflakes, and glimpsing the twinkling front porches. I cast shamefaced glances up and down the street like a convict who's escaped with the Hope Diamond.

My biggest fear of the moment is the parking spot I stole—the rightful owner might circle the block again and confront me with the road rage I deserve. Assigning fault to the other driver would be disingenuous at best, dishonest at worst. There's a problem.

It's me.

I'm the problem.

Before I keel over and die of a heart attack, Sophie opens the door. I'm jittery, anxiously ping-ponging gazes over both shoulders, huffing and puffing as if I've just crossed a marathon finish line. Judging from her sideways glare at me, my expression is a startling combination of confusing and amusing. She doesn't bother waiting for me to speak. No, she just snatches me inside like the worrywart she is. Finally, she grabs her box from my hand. Good thing I remembered her goodies. My homemade ornaments are tradition now.

When the door slams behind me, Sophie stares through me as if she can diagnose my predicament with her WebMD vision.

"Are you okay?" She's almost as flustered as I am, and she didn't scale the stairs. "What's going on? Was someone following you? Should I call the police?"

I shake my head, glance out of the window curtains framing the door, and study the snow-covered street as a single set of headlights crawl into view and then disappear. The car doesn't even pause. I breathe a sigh of relief. Maybe my victim has left the neighborhood. "No, I'm fine, fine. I was just...I'm all good. Besides, this is Georgetown, not Afghanistan," I joke.

"Good. Well, I'm glad you made it this year. Third time's a charm." She relieves me of my coat and gives me the once-over while crossing her index and middle fingers as a gesture of hope on my behalf. "And aren't we looking mighty festive?"

She's talking about my sweater. The Christmas Grinch reflects my state of mind more than any fashion profession. If I'm going to hell for my ho-ho-horrible behavior, then let me go down in a burning handbasket, and let the handbasket be draped in garland and twinkly lights while the nose of my fat-hearted Grinch blinks.

Even as Sophie compliments my attempt to take the ugly sweater title, she knows she and her husband will forever reign supreme in this department. It's all but impossible to outdo "SoBro" because, in homely Christmas wear, they've cornered the market. Their evening attire, a thousand holly wreaths weaved in hideous multicolored yarn, takes ugly to new lows. They'll win hands down. With that said, as the black Brangelina of Washington DC (pre-divorce), they're ridiculously beautiful people, so no one will even notice that their sweaters could make human eyes bleed.

"Tessa texted me; today's message was 'M-N-D.'"

My head tilts to the side, and my shoulders shrug. Probably some kind of code for "my BFF's single and desperately alone." I'm mortified by the possibilities of the text's contents. I've considered hiding Tessa's phone, but I'm her ICE, in case of emergency, contact. "Okay, I'm stumped. What's M-N-D?"

"Mia needs date."

My eyes roll. I can't stop them. "Sweet baby Yoda. She's so extra. The only friend in the world who's created special short-hand to pimp her bestie. What am I gonna do with her?"

"The bigger question is: What are we going to do with you?"

I shoot her a suspicious glare, and she rubs her hands together and cackles like an evil scientist who has concocted a mysterious potion.

"Don't worry. We may have a little something-something in store after we've plied you with food and alcohol, of course."

"Oh, no. What?"

"Let's call it a little Christmas magic."

"I hope Christmas magic has a lot of jingle vodka in it," I say with a hearty laugh and then stop abruptly. "And please tell me you didn't do what you promised me you wouldn't do."

"I didn't." Her happy eyes betray the lie. "Except I did."

The deadly stink-eye I shot her could've put us both out of our misery. If only.

"Oh, relax. Come in. You look hangry. You need food."

"Perfect. What would I do if you hadn't invited me...again?" I'm being facetious, and she knows it. Of course, I'd be laid up in my bed instead, scarfing iced gingerbread men with hot cocoa and watching TV Christmas movies.

We proceed through the foyer, all blinky from white fairy lights, and move toward the dining room lined with garland. I exhale in frustration but not over the incidents of this evening.

Not only am I about to endure a dinner at which, if memory serves, I'll be the only single person within a five-mile radius, but I've also got a serious work predicament that may cost me my new promotion. "What I need is an idea for the Christmas line. Imagine that for a second—a greeting card company without a Christmas line on Black Friday."

"Still stuck?" she asks.

"Yep, that's another way of putting it. I've been going with—I'm screwed," I say. "I'm trying to be patient, but nothing ever just comes to me. I always end up forcing things in the wrong direction."

"Please, I've heard this before. The divorce line. The clap backline. Every time you're faced with a challenge, you come through. You deliver like FedEx. Never miss a beat. All you've got to do is trust your gut, which has never failed you before. It's that simple."

"And that hard. Don't forget, we're not Keep It Real, House of Snark, anymore, now that Hart Enterprises has acquired us. I'm not sure if I can pull off this holly jolly stuff, not in time for Christmas Card-Fest, anyway. The last thing we need to do is get beat by our own designs again this year."

"When's the submission due?"

"Next Friday. Seven days."

"Yikes," she says. "But you'll be fine...and, in the end, it's all for a good cause. Well, I can't offer any ideas. But I do have liquid inspiration—some jolly juice. Maybe fun is what you need to get the creativity flowing. You work too much, and you're probably blocked."

"Meh. Maybe."

"And, who knows? You might find everything you need and more right here."

"Everything I need?"

She leads me into the dining room where I'll join the cheery couples, six of them in total—all Georgetown alumni that look as if they've fallen off of a J. Crew ad. I'm an HBCU grad—I'm Nordstrom on my good days.

We're all smiles when I greet everyone. No matter what words have been left unsaid, we all understand the reason we've been invited.

This party's not about dinner.

It's about the *after-dinner* festivities.

The actual objective of this pre-Christmas gathering commences in the adjacent family room after we're too fat and drunk to run.

When I enter and take inventory of the guests gathered, I flash another stink eye at Sophie. She may not fully deserve the hate, but I serve her a massive dose, anyway. I glance around at all the happy couples—and there's not one single man in sight. No one I can remotely claim a pairing with. I'm now the only uncoupled person in the room, standing out like a bail of wheat at a gluten-free bread factory. So, I'm not just solo; I'm painfully solo.

"Hmm. Everything I need? Not likely. But I'll take the jolly juice...and make it a double on the rocks, please."

"Will do. Have a seat. Get comfortable. We'll be serving dinner shortly. My world-famous beef bourguignon."

Brooks, Sophie's better half, greets me with a warm hug,

cheek kiss, and an apologetic expression. I sense he'd rather be watching a game or cleaning his garbage disposal.

"Good evening!" I chirp to everyone as Brooks steps aside and allows me to enter the dining room.

If the ugly sweaters from the nightmares of Christmas past aren't bad enough, lighted reindeer antlers await us at our dining table place settings. Sophie alone goes the extra mile with a matching red nose.

After glancing at my watch, I begin a countdown. The end will signal the moment I can make a graceful, quiet exit without insulting anyone. The current estimate stands at one hundred ten minutes and thirty seconds. That's around when I hope the booze will kick in.

If my acting game's on point, ten minutes before the dead-line, I'll choke on dinner, recover before some hero gives me the Heimlich, and slip out. As I settle on that plan, I remember the choking maneuver is how I escaped last year. No matter. I've got well over an hour to come up with something new.

"It's good to see you all. Everyone's looking so Christmassy." I feel far less cheerful than I sound. My smile is faker than a Kardashian's butt. Someday, I'll find a way to subject SoBro - and all the married couples partaking in this social coup - to the slow, painful deaths they deserve.

I take my seat and offer a few fake finger waves as the crux of my conundrum drifts back into my head.

I'm scheduled to send my Christmas card collection to the distributors in a week. Except I have no Christmas card collec-tion, no concept, no design, no nada.

I'm here because holiday hell with SoBro is better than a blank screen and Tessa's wrath. Besides, it's my job as Sophie's good friend to allow her to lord her blissful marriage over me every so often.

Next to my seat, there's an empty chair. Someone much smarter than I am has bailed on dinner. I'd buck up the nerve to sprint out, but SoBro exits the kitchen with fire-red ceramic cook-ware full of beef bourguignon. They load plates with entrees and circulate savorous accompaniments when the doorbell rings.

My first instinct is to focus on dinner and ignore the new guest's arrival...until I recall the parking incident. My stomach sours. I'll breathe easy when the danger passes, and I'm sure the guest isn't my victim.

"Nixon!" Brooks bellows in an animated tone. I rarely hear him bubble so much. His cheer makes me wonder who the heck this "friend" is. Sophie's never told me about him.

That's when she follows with, "We didn't think you'd make it. Let me take your coat. You're just in time for dinner."

The chances this Nixon guy is the same person as the park-ing-spot guy is minuscule at best. I mean, what are the odds? After thinking about my life and my luck, I decide it's a good time to panic. I hold my breath, fearing the Ghost of Christmas Present has arrived to haunt me.

"Love the sweater!" Soph exclaims.

So far, he replies with silence. Maybe he's smiling. I release my breath and inhale a sigh of relief when Nixon speaks in a voice that can only be described as a sensuous tenor. "I'd have been here sooner, but some jerk hijacked my parking space."

Ruh-roh.

"I circled the block six times and ended up having to park four blocks away to find a space," the sensuous tenor continues.

Shame-heat rises from my chest and lights up the Grinch's nose. My jaws clench and warm up not only from the embarrass-ment now crawling in my skin but also from the humiliation that I glimpse will befall me when he's seated in the empty chair beside me. I gulp hard to ease my angst and remember nobody knows I'm the perpetrator... except me, and I've got no plans to rat myself out.

"Whoever it is drives that black BMW right there," Nixon blabs.

Snitch. He's not laid an eye on me, but he's pointed me out in the line-up of one.

A silence follows, and I convince myself no one's going to mention who owns the BMW—a fact of which most of the visiting couples are fully aware. After all, friends don't drop the dime on friends, and I'm out of here in a hundred minutes and forty-five seconds, anyway.

I'll make my escape, and Nixon will never be the wiser.

I lift a forkful of beef bourguignon to my lips, and it happens. Brooks' voice sweeps in from the depths of hell and hunts me down like the parking spot hijacker I am. "Wait a minute. Hey Mia, isn't that your BMW?"

If he'd been standing within a foot of me, I'd have drop-kicked him and punched him in the throat. *Kaplow!* Right in the kisser.

To make an awkward situation unbearable, the only empty chair at the table is sitting right next to me. I return my fork to the plate and sit forward, stiffening my upper torso as I prepare for the inevitable clash, the moment Nixon realizes the parking spot thief is yours truly.

Footsteps draw closer, and his looming presence disturbs "the force" around me before I lay an eye on him. I resist the urge to turn around but can't stop myself. There he is.

Good Googitty Moogitty!

He stands a glorious six-foot-heaven and appears fashioned from the pure and holy grace of the gods. He's a pearl-clutcher if one ever existed. A quick double-check of the unfazed facial expressions of those surrounding me reassured me that I'd exclaimed at the sight of him using my inside voice.

Our eyes meet, and I conclude he's not only adorable, but he's also a bit miffed. His pinched nose and lips give it away. But if he's half the man he appears to be, he'll forgive me, with kindness, and I'll survive the next hundred minutes in relative peace.

SoBro ushers him to the table and into his chair. "Appreciate the invite," he says. His smile is broad and syrupy. "Can't think of a better way to kick off the holiday season." He glances around the table and speaks to everyone in a chipper tone until he gets to me. "So. You're the one with the black BM—wait a minute. You look familiar."

Yawn. I thought him better than that tired line.I shake my head. "I'd remember you if we met, and I know you'd never forget me. So, I'm all but certain we've not had the pleasure."

And a pleasure it would've been. He's got these glorious broad shoulders and arms so muscular that he'd wrap you up and leave no doubt that you've been held. The wideness of his upper torso tapers like a "V" into his taut waist. He's wearing an ugly sweater and fancy pants—jeans that look as if he took out a personal loan to afford them. All that fabulousness covered up by the wardrobe of a pretentious boob who's trying not to look like one. They probably cost more than Sophie's dining room set.

Instead of stuffing his face like everyone else at the table, he leans into me, close enough for the scent of his musk to waft into my nose and through my tingling spine. In a saltish whisper, he says, "Parties like this are always nice, aren't they? Where else can one meet such considerate, kind, strikingly beautiful people?"

Heeeey! Let me find out. My smile is demure, even a little coquettish. I'm flirting and can't stop myself.

"Any idea what time those people are showing up?"

Oh. No. He. Didn't. Inconsiderate jerk. The nerve.

So, maybe I had that coming. Too bad I'm too ridiculous to admit it—ever. Now, I want to forklift Nixon out of his seat as if I'm a defensive linebacker, and he's a quarterback trying to score from the one-yard line. In light of recent events, my reputation is already suffering. I decide there's no need to add crazy to the mix. So, I grin and bear the insult.

While other guests mutter while holding inside conversations, Nixon and I descend into an all-out battle royale...under our breath and squeezed through tight lips donning fake smiles.

"So, what do you do? Drive for NASCAR?" he asks. "I mean,

the way you zipped in and robbed my parking space, I thought you might be teaming up with Tia Norfleet. I'm relieved to see *it's* okay."

I suppose I should be impressed that he knows Tia's a black woman driving for NASCAR, but I'm not. Instead, I have a question.

"It's?" I respond, "What...it's?"

"Your spine. The way you folded over like a wet noodle when I put my car in reverse, I wondered if the warp speed at which you sped in order to steal my space might've snapped your whole backbone in two."

Deliverance sits on my tongue, aiming a twelve-gauge shotgun, and I'm ready to unload, but an even greater danger eyes me from the other end of the table—Sophie's glare. I'm withering under the knives firing from her thin brown eyes. Instead of giving him the piece of my mind he deserves, I wave the white flag to surrender in hopes of negotiating a much-needed peace.

"Listen, you've made your point with a period and an exclamation. Let's just—"

I stuff my loaded fork in my face and daintily chew as Sophie joins us.

"Are you guys, okay?"

We glance at one another and lie like the good guests we are.

"We were just remarking about this delicious bourguignon, weren't we, Nixon? So, good it makes you want to slap a whole taste bud out of someone's mouth."

To prove the point, we stuff our jaws like chipmunks, as if we're storing food for the winter, and give her the thumbs up.

"Too bad I forgot my Ziploc bags," Nixon quips through unswallowed beef.

Sophie swells with pride. "Eat up. There's plenty." Then she turns her attention to another couple.

We resume the tense tango-in-whisper, except we bring it down a notch as we begin to focus our attention on the dinner party. The real reason we've both been summoned is about to commence, and we're in trouble.

"Well. This was a match made in hell," I say.

"Yep," he replies. "And there's only one way out. We need to plot our escape."

CHAPTER 4

ixon

FINALLY FOUND MY CAR. NOW, I'M ENGAGED IN AN IMPOSSIBLE FEAT: trying to find a decent parking space before Brooks' party in Georgetown. This is the last place I want to be, but probably where I need to be. I'm on a course for destruction—or a date, whichever you'd like to call it.

Same difference.

It's the dead of night, but pedestrians still fill the sidewalks, even with the snow. The most egregious criminal violations in this part of town include squirrel bite reports and drunk and disorderly violations. However, I'm seriously considering murder since this jerk stole my parking space.

The thief was on the prowl. I should've known it when the headlights whooshed from a crawl to a frenetic zoom as I turned the corner. When I pulled forward to reverse and back into the spot, the BMW swooped in and robbed me.

Okay, yes, the fit would've been tight for my Range Rover. A minuscule chance existed that I couldn't squeeze in—but I'd earned the right to try. And I'd plan to do some fancy maneu-vering when that thieving fool ripped off my spot. Then they had the nerve to cower in their front seat so I couldn't glimpse their dirty mug.

Yes, I could've escalated the confrontation to next-level violent glares, but, these days, you never know if a nasty look will end up with loaded words or weapons. Since I'm not trying to meet my maker over a parking space, I pull next to the car, deliver a quick flip of a middle finger salute with all the gusto I can muster within the confines of my Rover, and then circle the block until another spot frees up.

Thankfully, a short time later, the universe rewards my better judgment with an opening several blocks away, which I snap up quicker than one can say "hijack." Now, I'm trudging toward Brooks' place, pushing through icy winds that abuse and punish my face. Snow seeps into my shoes, and my feet squish with every frozen step. My mutters consist of four- and five-letter words that probably are censored by the FCC.

By the time I return to the scene of the crime, the front steps of Brooks' Georgetown home, I'm a volcano on the verge of erupting. Now empty of its rude driver, the offending BMW sits there, parked comfortably, taunting me. Part of me wants to flatten the tires or key the doors, but this looks like a neighbor-hood full of video doorbells, and I'm not going to jail over some nonsense.

Instead, I opt to use my middle finger again, this time to write "Jerk" in the snow on their windshield. The drifting powder might fill it before the offender reads my Black Friday message, but the gesture sure lifts my spirits.

Soon after I knock on the door, Brooks greets me with all the warmth the phantom parking thief robbed from me.

"Nixon!" Brooks says. He's my fraternity brother. We met while pledging at Georgetown. "We didn't think you'd make it."

I'd been lost for more than a year, metaphorically speaking.

But my inability to find myself had nothing to do with the fact that I'd arrived late.

"Let me take your coat. You're just in time for dinner," Sophie adds. Her welcome is as warm as Brooks'.

She need not say another word. The smell of beef and potatoes mesmerizes me. Dinner's the word I want to hear. The stress of searching for a new parking space helped me work up an appetite.

"Love your outfit!" Sophie exclaims. "We thought you got lost." Every year I'm expected to participate in this ugly sweater thing. I'm wearing Santa Paws—a bulldog with a red and white pompom hat.

"I'd have been here sooner, but some nitwit hijacked my parking space. I circled around six times and parked four blocks away to find a spot."

That's when I mention the BMW. Part of me hopes the offender is here, and part of me is afraid I'll ruin the party if they are. I've got nothing nice to say.

Brooks peers over his shoulder and his expression flickers with recognition. "Mia? Isn't that your BMW out front?"

Mia? The nitwit is present, accounted for—and a "she."

Sophie disappears, and Brooks peers back at me. Under his breath, he says, "Really, man? You wrote that on the windshield? I can't wait until you use your powers for good and not for evil. When that happens, you'll be unstoppable."

Mmm-Hmm. I hear him, but I'm listening for a voice, a wicked screech I'm sure will belong to this Mia person. She doesn't respond. In my mind, silence is guilt. I'm going to lay into her.

I've spent four blocks deep in stewed anger, briefly tempered by SoBro's warm greeting, but my eruption's imminent. I'm geared up to storm into the dining room and give her all the pieces of my mind, translated into four- and five-letter words. I've conjured an image of her. In my mind, she's easy to spot—I'm picturing a green witch with the wart on her snout.

My anger morphs into a fiery warmth rising into my neck and ears. My heart begins to thump in angry beats. All I want to do is ream Ms. Inconsiderate face to face as I've done in my mind for four blocks. My eyes narrow with each step I take toward the dining room.

Finally, I turn the corner and see her.

All my words disappear, vanish with my breath.

She is nothing I expect and everything I want. I go slack-jawed for a moment that feels uncomfortable and long. She may be divinity in human form, but she's also thoughtless. Her sweet face stops my feet cold in their tracks and my tongue from flapping.

"Nixon, this is Mia. Mia, meet Nixon," Brooks says, his eyes volleying between us, shining with that match-made-in-heaven glimmer.

"Hi. Pleasure to meet you," she says.

Because her eyes twinkle like the fairy lights in the foyer, I manage to respond in kind. Tonight, the devil's not in Prada. She's wearing a black skirt with like-colored tights that cling to her curvy body and thighs, and calf boots.

Her lips part into a kind, infectious smile, and all those words I'd stored up to unload on her lodged in my throat. We shake, and the mere touch of her hand sends shock waves through me.

Those eyes, there's something familiar about them.

She's an angel, beautiful, thoughtless...selfish, and stunning. The plan to ask her if she learned her manners from wild swine turns to, "Where have you been all my life?" Just like that. At least in my mind.

"I suppose I should take my seat before someone steals it." The words slip out of my mouth without much forethought. Maybe it's because I've lost my senses, and I'm not entirely aware of what I'm saying. She doesn't know it, but I've fallen prey to her, the angel with the shiny coils dangling around her shoulders, the devil who steals parking spaces.

I'm oblivious to how she's reacted to the words I barely

remember saying because I'm too swept up in meeting her. To ground myself, I turn away from her and make small talk with the other couples. They're filled to the brim with mirth and good wine, lots of wine.

"You impressed me tonight," I shift back toward Mia.

"You? Impressed with me? Who says there's no such thing as a Christmas miracle? But I'll bite. How did I manage that feat?"

"The speed at which you folded over in your seat like a wet noodle after you stole my parking space. I thought moving that fast could snap a human spine."

Not even a giggle.

"Not bad. You'd be even funnier if you had a sense of humor."

Ouch.

"But, uh, the point's been made," she continues. "Be like Elsa. Let it go."

"Elsa?" Now she's just being disrespectful, and I'm trying to release the tension with some teasing. The entire incident rests on her shoulders. Maybe I need to remind her. "If I had made my point, you would've apologized. The fact that you barely acknowledge what happened tells me all I need to know about your character."

"Please. It was a parking spot, not your share of the gold in Fort Knox. The fact that you're still clinging to what happened like a baby on its mother's boob tells me all I need to know about yours."

By now, we're going at it. Hard. Everybody's pretending not to listen to us, but they are all up in our business. The last thing I want to do is ruin SoBro's party over a parking space, so I nudge Mia with my elbow, and we play off our dissension when Sophie returns to question us.

"A toast to the gracious hosts." I raise my glass, and Mia joins me. Everyone else follows; we've distracted the bloodhounds from our scents.

We return to our heated whispers when it occurs to me,

perhaps both of us, that this bantering is getting neither of us anywhere. As dinner finishes, we've got much bigger fish to fry.

"Well. This was a match made in hell."

"Tell me about it. Our only way out of this misery is to plot our escape. You got any ideas?"

We barely start hatching our scheme before Sophie announces the first game of the night. The White Elephant game —I think of it as the Truth or Consequences of gifting. Mia won an iPad.

Then we move into a fun game of Christmas Carol Chaos. Lee and Ming, an Asian couple, give the clues to identify a Christmas standard, and we guessed the songs. I receive as my first clue, "Are your ears picking up the same vibrations as mine?" and I rightly guessed, "Do you hear what I hear?"

I win, though not an iPad. No, I'm going home with the second-best gift of the night—a basket of self-inflating balloons. The best prize of all would be Mia's smile, but I'll never confess that truth to anyone except myself in a mildly intoxicated state.

By now, I need a drink—brown liquor in a low ball. But before I get the chance to ask, she and I are paired up in a team for a game of holiday Taboo; we've got to communicate a clue to our partner, yet we're not allowed to give the most obvious descriptions. This means the more teams think alike, the better the chance they have of winning. We're going to lose spectacularly. The clues all center around Christmas themes, which narrow the scope of guesses. Maybe we'll have a fighting chance.

Now we're sitting across from one another, face to face— enemies on the same side. The more points we score, the more we win. I hate losing, and I can tell by her willingness to set aside our differences, she does, too. We lock our gazes on one another, to focus and send and receive clues. But who can concentrate with those eyes, with that face, with those lips? It takes every ounce of my energy to keep me from dissolving in my chair. I want her, but I refuse to give SoBro or Mia the satisfaction of knowing they'd finally picked someone who piques my interest. I refuse to provide the audience with the show they're waiting to gawk at. So, I commit to war.

War is less embarrassing.

The game of Taboo begins, and here we go.

"Blaze." She gives the first clue.

"Fire," I reply.

She glances down at her card. "Pipe," she says.

"Smoke," I reply. There's a long pause as if she's recalibrating her thoughts.

"Up yours," she says with a devilish grin. That's the kicker.

I'm affronted for a hair of a second before I realize it's neither an order nor a request, and the answer comes to me quickly. "Chimney!"

She juts both arms in the air and yells, "That's it!" while everyone around us roars with praise and laughter. I begin to see hope for a victorious end, too. We think alike, probably much more than I thought.

I've got to give credit where credit is due. *Up yours*. Pretty clever. She doesn't fool me, though. The way she barked the words at me, she meant every syllable from her soul.

It's my turn to give the clues, and she winks at me as if permitting me to follow her lead. We've got a winning formula. In a blink, we've evolved from enemies to partners. Her eyes laser-focus on mine, which I find entirely distracting. I almost forget the task at hand, but I clear my mind and glance down at the card.

I read the clue, and I can't say bake, gingerbread, chocolate chip, dessert, or cutter.

The timer goes off, and we're running. My mind churns a bit as I stumble over what to say next. "Sugar," I say as my first offering.

"Chips," she responds.

Wrong answer.

"Chocolate," I offer.

She replies, "Candy."

Then the idea hits. "Bite me," I bark in the same tone she used.

She pauses and stares at me for a moment that didn't seem nearly long enough and replies, "Cookie?"

Now my hands are in the air, and the crowd roars again. We're a hit because we're low-key insulting one another in "Christmas," and everyone's drinking it up like Sophie's jolly juice. When it's time for the next couple to take their turn, they refuse and insist we stay in place.

We oblige.

Now, we're on a roll.

We entertain SoBro's guests with our aggressive Taboo bantering for the next forty-five minutes, hurling insults and calling each other everything but a sweet child of God until we emerge from the challenge and take our thrones as we reign supreme.

We win iPod minis. Man, they give good gifts.

Thanks to our game success, we're the "it" couple, even though we're not a couple and likely won't be.

"Oh, you guys must come to MingMei's Christmas Pageant," Ming and Lee say.

Regardless, it's clear I'm off of my Christmas hiatus, so we're invited to what feels like every Christmas kick-off event through the Rapture—or this week, whichever comes first.

"Don't forget Taste of Christmas," Sophie adds as Brooks cuts her with a severe glare. "That's a U Street jam. Treats and drinks for days. We all go for about an hour, at least those of us without kids."

Brooks injects, "Tessa's already sent out invites for the Card Fest tree lighting and ugly sweater party. It's a big greeting card community thing."

Brooks eyes me. "We usually attend as friends and family of the Hart team."

My stomach sinks as I realize I'll be attending...but not as friends and family.

Mia rolls her eyes and avoids my gaze. I try to focus my attention on the wine and prepare for the next dose of Christmas fun. Mia's starting to grow on me (a little). I kind of regret skipping the previous three years.

Now, I wish we had a song, our song, a slow one. I'd pull her into my arms and dance with her...right here.

CHAPTER 5

ia

During an energetic game of Christmas Taboo, jibing Nixon brings me more joy than I believed the party could deliver. I hate to admit it, but I've slipped up and started having fun. Even more impressive was the fact that after spending the evening at odds with one another, Taboo reveals we're more simpatico than I thought possible.

When I offer "up yours" as a clue for a chimney, and he got not only the hint but also the clue, something warmed beside the cockles of my heart. We crash like two horned mountain goats colliding in a head-to-head crash that'd leave no victor standing. We keep the insults coming for a full forty-five minutes—all in the name of winning—and then it ends.

Now that we're deep into the post-Taboo mingling, SoBro reveals how they turn singletons into couples.

Sophie springs in front of the gift-wrapped closet door to announce the present that keeps on giving. "Since everyone's full of food and booze and too fat to run, it's time for the game of the evening—Seven Minutes of Christmas Magic."

"Great," I mutter in a grumble. The nose lights up on the Grinch, covering my sweater, echoing my grouchy sentiment.

"We made up this game a few years ago. You've got to play to win, but if you play, you win."

Not coincidentally, they masterminded this form of torture at the beginning of the matchmaking spree. Ming and Lee, Joanne and Jason, Avery and Lisa, Marvin and Donna—all victims, or winners, how ever you look at it. This game the secret sauce to their success.

One of the wives yips with conspiratorial glee. "Woo hoo!" knowing she's married and won't be subjected to this relationship waterboarding with Mr. Fancy Pants. No, all the joy to SoBro's world is reserved for this girl right here.

"For crying out loud." I meant to say that with my inside voice. But, judging from the expressions circling, the words roll off my tongue like a Bentley on wax and loudly. *Ooops.*

"Er, what are the rules, again?" Nixon asks, trying to shift the attention from my verbal faux pas. I'm surprised he's not more vocal, given his suffering will equal mine.

"Simple. Brooks and I select two of our lovely guests—or a couple—to enter our well-ventilated closet." Her voice bounces, laden with cheer and wine. I'm guessing the Cabernet Sauvignon. "Inside the closet, you can exchange anything as simple as a Christmas secret or as sweet as a Christmas kiss."

"Grumble. Grumble," I mutter again with my outside voice—this time on purpose. I point at my sweater and blame the squawking on the Grinch. Then Sophie points to the first couple —Marvin and Donna—and they disappear into the closet. They're married, so this is all for show...to make it seem as if this entire game isn't a conspiracy against Nixon and me when we all know what's up.

No sooner than the closet door closes, my eyes dart around in search of a full bottle of pinot, which I spot across the room. With the skill of the Great Houdini and the spirit of my mother, I plan to make it disappear.

By the time the wine is gone, the first couple exits, and I return, muttering expletives. They give off that hippie, flower child, commune vibe, the non-murderous kind. I'm almost certain they're swingers.

That's when Sophie makes the move to end all moves and picks her next selection. "Well, what have we here?" she says in a sing-song voice. Her gaze shifts between Nixon and me. "It looks like two of our guests didn't come with partners."

Nixon looks over both shoulders and says, "Who?" without cracking a grin. Meanwhile, my pinot has kicked in, and I've fallen over sideways laughing in my seat. The realization has hit me that we're not playing the dating game, rather the mating game. And Sophie's not about to break her perfect-match record.

"Come on, you two," Brooks says. He basically follows Sophie's orders. Apparently, Nixon hasn't gotten the memo.

"Good luck with that," he says, confirming this idea will never work. First of all, he hates me. Second of all, the feeling is mutual. Mostly.

We've been snarling at one another like territorial dogs all evening, but I just want to get the magic closet thing done and finished so I can go home and work on my campaign, knowing I will win the good friend participation award.

Nixon's my partner, and a love connection isn't on the program. Oh, he's hot, to be sure, but he put the "etty" in "petty," and part of me doesn't want to end up like the rest of the couples here. I take one more stab at dodging this game, "What are we, in seventh grade?" I ask. "Count me out."

Sophie shoots me a look that may be considered lethal in forty-two out of fifty states. I pin my lips together quickly, recovering from the temporary amnesia that's caused me to forget I will play whether I want to or not. She's got a whole kettle full of tea to spill on me if she so chooses. Before I commit to losing as fast as possible and in spectacular fashion, Nixon speaks.

"I'm not going in that closet. I never win anything." Nixon slides into third with the backup.

"Oh, you will get your butt in there, Nixon. Groan if you want, but my house, my rules." She pauses to wind up for the final strike. "Besides, with this audience of your peers and Facebook friends, I might be forced to let slip a college incident involving a box of Summer's Eve, a jar of kosher pickles, and a One Direction poster."

Annnnnd...we're inside the closet. Blackmail. I didn't think Sophie had it in her.

It's Nixon and me. Me and Nixon. Alone. In the closet of magic.

If this isn't Black Friday, I don't know what is. I feel his presence in front of me and his breath on the high part of my cheek, but I can't see him.

We need more light because only a sliver seeps in at the bottom of the door, giving off just enough of a beam for him to find the flashlight on his iPhone and turn it on.

Seven minutes. We're stuck inside for what promises to be seven of the longest minutes of our lives. This will force us to atone for our earlier parking spot sins.

Well, maybe not so much "our" as me.

Actually, I am "our."

I need to atone for my earlier sins.

"I can't believe this. They've even decorated the inside of the closet," I say. Garland and holiday cards with messages of love cover the walls. Then we both look up to the ceiling and, in unison, say, "Mistletoe."

"You two okay in there?" Sophie's muffled voice mutters through the door. "You're awfully quiet. No one's dead yet, right?"

The background chattering stops, and I break the silence with a whisper. "No. But we're plotting."

We go back to looking at one another, I at him, and him at me. In my mind, we're having a moment, until he speaks.

"This would be the perfect time for a good idea if you've got one."

I'd like to say yes, but I wonder if my idea to get out of the closet is hiding behind the stroke of genius for the Christmas card line.

CHAPTER 6

ixon

MIA AND I ARE INSIDE THE NEAR PITCH-BLACK CLOSET, AND
mistletoe hangs overhead. We're meant to kiss...and I wouldn't
mind, especially now.

I can see her, really see her. A feeling comes over me, one
similar to the moment after I down a shot of fifteen-year-old
Macallan. I'm warm, and the rush of this intoxication sets me off
balance. Her face is kind of sweet. Adorable, really. I'm a little
high on her and this moment to which we're both hostages.

She's mesmerizing, but I'm not sure whether or not we're
vibing or even if I long-term like her, but she's hypnotic
right now.

Her silken brown skin gives off a glow, and her lips are
glossed and thick. She stands so close to me that her body
warms me. I conceal my hope for a kiss behind fabricated
outrage. We've been in the closet for seconds, and it doesn't feel
long enough. Time passes too quickly.

"I know I gave you the blues for trying this line earlier,

but...you actually do look familiar now. Have we met some-where before?"

She is, in fact, correct. We've seen one another before, though only in passing. Her eyes tipped me off. How could I forget them? They pierced me on sight and left an indelible mark. "It'd been a long day. I lost my car."

She takes a few seconds to process before a flicker of recognition widens her eyes. "That's it! You were outside my house earlier today. I wondered why you looked discombobulated out there."

My car wasn't the only thing lost in that moment. Finding the location of my vehicle was the least of my concerns.

I moved through my day, and my life, like a leaf under the force of a relentless wind, in motion without direction, until now. What once was foggy seems more evident. She's "stolen" much more than my parking spot tonight. Standing in front of her, I come alive. I find...myself. The old me. The good me. The one who seizes opportunities for challenges...like Mia.

"It's nice to know you find me so unforgettable," I say.

"Don't flatter yourself," she replies. Her tone is snide, but her eyes are warm, and a twinkle flickers in them. I want to hate myself for liking her so much, but I don't. "After our champi-onship game of Taboo, I thought I should mention that I love playing games with kind, considerate, strikingly beautiful people who aren't small and petty." I bask in the glory of her compliment when she adds, "You got any brothers?"

"I see what you did there." I snap my left fingers, and the sound pops louder in the silence than I expect. "No, I don't have any brothers, but I do know a man very much like the one you described. In fact, you just missed him. He disappeared when some rude, inconsiderate jerk stole his parking space. To make matters worse, she never bothered to apologize."

She clenches her eyes shut as if the message finally strikes the chord that resonates.

"Okay, fine. You win. If someone had, you know, accidentally on purpose slipped into my parking space, ahead of me, knowing I'd planned to park there, it's not likely that my response would be a gracious one. In fact, I'd have gone straight petty and kicked their tires or wrote 'jerk' on their windshield in the snow."

I cough and reply, "Really? Jerk on the windshield? Who's small now? Ridiculous behavior for a grown man...or woman, don't you think?" My cheeks warm from the shame.

"Right? But, unfortunately, I'd be guilty as sin. So, if you do happen to run into him, the good brother, please convey my apologies. I'm under tremendous stress."

"I sense he'd be willing to accept your apology."

"The truth is, I'd been driving in circles for the better part of thirty minutes. In hindsight, I should've ordered an Uber. If I could turn back time and do it all again, assuming I don't know it's you, I'd first curse the day his mother hatched him. I'd mentally flip him the bird. Then, I'd circle the block a few more times until another spot opened. It wasn't my finest hour."

I'm laughing inside if not outside.

"Let's make a deal," I whisper. Little does Mia know she'd been forgiven from the moment she said jerk. "Let's call a truce for the rest of the evening. We can go back to hating one another after the party's over."

"Hating? Oh, no. Now, that would be a shame, wouldn't it?" She offers a hand, and we shake on it. Who knew so many nerves in the human hand could tingle at once?

I wonder what more's in store when she presses her ear to the door and states the obvious. "You know this is a set-up, don't you? This is the third year for me. What's the big year for you?"

"This is the first year I've shown up, the third I've been invited."

"And there you have it. We've been intended for one another. Sophie's matched up everything in this house except Brooks' belt and shoes."

"Tell me about it," I chuckle. "I came for the food, but something tells me I'm going to leave here filled with more than a serving of that beef bourguignon."

"Yeah, a spoonful of regret...with a dollop of hopelessness." We both laugh and louder than we should. The chattering outside the door reaches a crescendo. "And to think I suffered the two previous years alone because you deftly avoided this travesty."

I'd like to be sorry, but I'm not. "Since you're so well-practiced, any ideas on how to get out of this?" I ask.

"Yeah, that's the thing. I may have used up all the good ideas," she says, tapping her lean, delicate finger against her lip. "We could fake food poisoning."

"Hard no," I reply. "I mean, sure we'd make a clean getaway, but we might ruin the party for everyone else."

"True. Hard to be holly and jolly on diarrhea watch," she says.

"I've got an idea! Let's fake our deaths," I say facetiously.

She pauses as if giving the notion sincere consideration. "And, survey says, BONK!" she responds. "Don't get me wrong, the idea's great, but last year," she raises her hand. "You can only get away with death once. Besides, if we both faked it, Sophie would take it as a sign that our souls were destined to spend eternity together, and she'd count another victory."

"Now you're just being difficult. I'm trying here."

"You ready to be buried in adjoining plots?"

We both cackle again. Then her laugh withdraws into a flirtatious grin that curves the corners of her lips upward. My expression now mirrors hers.

"Don't worry," she says. "When I think of something, it'll be brilliant."

"No doubt," I say, unable to shift my gaze from her or blink. "Maybe we can talk about something else, and an idea will come to us. Usually, that's how it works."

"We've got four more minutes," she says after glancing at her watch.

"I suppose we could actually play the game, share a Christmas secret. You first."

We pause for a moment before we sit cross-legged and face one another.

"I'm ready," I say. "Hit me with it."

"Okay. Here it is. Prepare yourself for shock and amazement."

My mind begins to wander, anticipating what she may say. Part of me hopes she'll confess something to break my trance, clip the bloom from the rose, like she hates dogs. Or she eats ketchup on her eggs.

"I've never had a date for the holidays. Not once."

"Stop lying," I reply with a jerk of my head. My gasp draws in all of the oxygen from the closet. She's too smart. She's too beautiful. Then they hit me, the facts as I perceive them. It's the last thing I expect her to say. My response shoots out of my mouth before I can tighten my lips.

This can't be true.

Mixing her divine qualities with a weak man is a recipe for disaster. I suspect this is the reason she's alone. The qualities I adore about her probably drives insecure men insane. I'm unintimidated by everything that is her, and I wonder if she realizes this about me...and appreciates it.

"The holidays have become annual graveyards for my relationships. The bodies are an inch deep and a mile wide. Before and after, I'm single. The excuses are plenty; the good ones are few. The breakups ranged from arguments over ho-ho-hoes to... silent nights when they're boo'ed up with the ho ho hoes."

"Wow."

"Pathetic, right?"

"Not pathetic. Maybe a little sad."

"Oh, no. Sad is worse," she says. "It's funny. I had, you know, romantic, warm holiday celebrations in my mind. I'd imagine myself and my guy laughing together, hanging ornaments and twinkly lights on the tree, listening to Boyz II Men by the fire while sipping spiked cocoa, making out like hormonal teenagers between wrapping gifts...for our families, not for each other, of course. Never happened. Not even once. Hasn't dampened my spirit, though. I'm hopeful, though some might say hopeless; I'm content because I refuse to settle. So, I curl up by the fireplace with my hot cocoa overflowing with marshmallows and watch Christmas movies. Tis the season for wishes and blind faith."

"I'm still trying to wrap my head around you being dateless for the holidays. So, let me get this straight...you've never had a...not even for New Year's Eve?"

She shakes her head. "No boyfriend for Christmas. No kiss at midnight. Nada...wait, there was this one time..."

"Ah-ha! I knew it! You're holding out on me."

"Okay, yes, one time. I was seven and a half. He was eight. He had an afro and a race car set, and he owned roller skates with glow-in-the-dark wheels. I thought he was the best thing since little Michael Jackson. I confess I used him for his race car set. My parents wouldn't buy me one because I'm a girl."

"Indeed, you are," I respond. "I noticed. By the way, all I heard in that story is that you're into older men."

"True...but older men with racecar sets. How old are you?"

"Thirty-and-a-half."

"Ooh, by the skin of your teeth. Older by a year. And how about the race car set?"

"Afraid not, but I do have two train sets."

"Choo—choo!" She whispers and giggles like a shy schoolgirl and her eyes glimmer. Maybe it's the glow from my cellphone light that gives them a beguiling hue, but they're so sweet. I'm enthralled. I'll burn my battery to nothing if it extends this view.

"I love the sound of trains," she continues, "Especially when they circle the Christmas tree. My Grandpap used to set one up. It was my favorite Christmas sound...like a journey. *Chug-gachugga*," she whispers. "So, now that I've shown you mine, it's your turn to show me yours. Judging from your Marine haircut and fancy pants jeans, I'm guessing you have a twisted past filled with raucousness and debauchery."

"You're kidding, right?" I rub my hand against my Tom Ford jeans and wonder how she knows. They look like regular jeans to me.

She presses her lips together and gives me the stink eye. I laugh. The sarcasm went over my head.

"Of course. Honestly, I'm short on secrets…Christmas ones. I suppose the one thing I can share is more of a confession than a secret. Uh, I haven't bought a tree or celebrated Christmas in six years."

She's floored.

"But why?" She's pressing her hand against her heart as if my words have pained her. Her voice slides from low to high, in shock. The ugliness of my Christmas sweater may have suggested I'm a pro at the holidays—but the truth is, I'm no longer the Christmas king I used to be.

"Not even a tree? What happened? Did you convert religions?"

The silence fills with my thoughts, at least in my mind. No words escape my mouth. I've never actually spoken the real reason out loud.

"My father passed away. Six years ago this month. Christmas Day." After her no-date admission, I suppose I feel safe, even comforted, in sharing my family's tragedy with her. "It was sudden, caught us all by surprise. He always made the holidays special for us, my mother and me. So, without him..." I shrug because I'm choked up. The movement in my shoulders helps me deflect, contains the flow of tears and the depth of this lingering sadness.

"This was a bad idea. I'm sorry. I had no...I didn't know."

"It's okay. How could you?" The memories came flooding through my heart and damned behind my eyes. "Every year, he bought a Douglass fir, like five minutes after we threw out the Jack-o-lanterns. Mom would curse him from Thanksgiving to Easter."

She wears a quizzical expression. "Curse?"

"Fresh trees, needles in the carpet?" I say, responding to the look on her face. "She liked to walk barefoot. It was the only time of the year she regularly used four-letter words."

"Ahhh...makes perfect sense."

"He'd set up this model train set. I'm pretty sure it belonged to my grandfather. The antique ones are heavier."

She smiles as if she could envision herself being with us. My mind replays her *Chuggachugga*.

"All year, I looked forward to those days. He used colorful language the whole time he set up the tracks. Lots of bad language in my house during the holidays."

"You mean, like Sophie. Can't you hear her? The silence is probably driving her crazy." We laugh. "But your dad, he sounds amazing. I miss him, and I didn't even know him."

I look down and away. "He once told me that he brought me in the world knowing he'd leave it before me. Funny, he would say that, you know."

"Parents understand death in a way we don't...until we become parents. It doesn't lessen the pain for us when they're gone, but they know. The beauty is that they leave us with this gift, the gift of family traditions, and the joy they bring. Through their gifts of tradition, we're always reminded they were here, especially on days when memories of them seem too distant. We set up the train or bake cookies or watch Claymation movies, and they're close again. I think he'd want you to celebrate, set up the train. He'd probably smile if you cursed a little while doing it."

All these years, I've avoided what I should've embraced. An angel in the closet reminds me of this at such an unlikely time, in this extraordinary place. With nothing but a dim light, and maybe a little bit of this so-called holiday magic, I feel less lost... like I'm becoming whole again. I'm also so choked up I can barely speak. I lower the flashlight to conceal the tears welling in my eyes. "Easier said than done, I think," I say.

"But worth trying," she replies.

We gaze at one another, me fighting my tears, her fighting this connection we've just made. I can tell because she lowers her chin. With the tip of my index finger, I lift it again. We're no longer strangers. Somehow our hands touch, and our lips begin to follow. At last, we indulge in the mistletoe moment. I taste the sweetness of her glossed lips when, with a whispered yelp, she halts the kiss.

"I've got an idea."

I'd been waiting for the kiss since I entered the dining room; now, just like that, it's gone.

Her eyes flash with light. She's had an epiphany. "Mark my words, we'll be out of this misery in T-minus-two minutes. The idea is drastic but, keep in mind, we're taking one for the team, not only for tonight but also for years to come."

There really must be some Christmas magic in this closet if she thinks for a second SoBro's gonna let us off the hook.

"Whatever it is, I'm down. As long as it will teach our friends a lesson."

"This, Mr. Nixon, is a lesson for the ages. They'll never ask us to play again. In fact, we may have saved an entire future generation of SoBro's friends and family."

Her big idea could've found better timing. I was so close to the kiss, the one I've wanted since I laid eyes on her. But this mischievous look in her eyes...well, I want to find the root so I can make it reappear at my will.

"I've no idea what you've got planned, but this innate warped thing happening right now? I'm into it."

My feelings for Mia are as resounding and clear as the chatter outside the magic cloud door, which grows louder by the second. Now that we have an audience, Mia seizes the moment with a performance for the ages.

"Oooh, baby. Oh, yes. Yes. Yes!" she moans. If the sounds of a sexual climax were like a football game, Mia would be in the last two minutes of the fourth quarter. Had I an inkling of the performance she had planned, I may have called a time out. It's too late

K.L. BRADY

now. We're deep into a Hail Mary, and there's nothing more for me to do except stay in the game.

"Mmmm. Sssss," I hiss. "You're so beautiful." If my jaw could drop through the floor, it would be in the Earth's core by now. We're singing a Cherry Poppins and Forest Hump duet.

"Oh, you feel so good," she responds. "Yes, that's nice. Slip it in, baby. Ohhh, you feel so good."

"Mmm-hmm. Mmm-hmm," I say. "Turn around. Let me smack it up, flip it, and rub it down." I'm quoting Bell Biv Devoe because better them than me. Little did I know those would be the words that almost send us over the edge with laughter and threaten to blow the entire scheme.

We somehow manage to stifle our chuckles. Imagining everyone's expressions makes it nearly impossible not to howl. They've placed their bets on us sharing an innocent peck on the cheek and making small talk, not hot butt-naked sex.

By now, Sophie's probably died a thousand deaths. I can almost visualize her squeezing the circulation out of Brooks' arm. On the other hand, he would celebrate with a cigar and a shot of whiskey if she weren't in the vicinity. We won't have to worry about playing this game again. After this performance ends, SoBro will ban us from the house forever.

"Oooh, mmm, big daddy. Mmm, yes!" She begins to pant and bangs her hand on the wall in rapturous beats. "Oh, yes, yes, yes, yes, yes!"

I'm not a bashful man, but the force at which she bangs her hand embarrasses even me. It not only sounds as if we're having sex, but that our passions have become completely unbridled, and we're unhinged. Yet, we've barely touched hands (and lips), and we haven't removed so much as a sock.

"Mmm, oooh, you're so wet." Her eyes bulge, and I shrug. To be honest, I'm a little turned on.

"Giddy up, big daddy. Giddy up!"

We eye one another. There are laughs in our expressions but sex in our voices. She resumes banging her hand on the wall while I moan louder and louder. At the moment of our fake climax, someone taps on the door.

"Everything okay in there?" Brooks whispers.

"Your time's up!" Sophie barks.

"I'm almost there. Five more minutes." I grab the doorknob, ready to explode with laughter—good thing they're expecting our voices to be strained.

"I'm gonna need more time," Mia follows. "Make that fifteen!"

CHAPTER 7

ia

I WONDERED IF AN IDEA WOULD EVER COME, AND IT CAME WHEN I least expected it. Our fake closet tryst sounds as if we're thirty minutes into a porn film, and we've not so much as rubbed elbows, fist-bumped, or kissed...despite the soft lip brush. I'm sure Sophie's died and come back to life three times. A room once bubbling with chatter is now stone quiet. Nixon's and my performance has stunned SoBro and their guests to silence.

But I can't lie.

As I stand here, listening to these sounds erupt from his mouth, the moment is hotter than hot. I could use some ice and a cold beer.

"Mmm...oh, yes, yes, yes," I moan, pouring it on thick. I fear we may be overacting a smidge, but I've got a flair for drama, colorful words, and sounds. That's why I've successfully served as the Creative Director for Keep It Real Cards. Right now, we're serving up the rainbow, and the heat inside this closet is searing.

"Yes! Yes! Yes! Mmm...Oh, yes!"

The farce continues a few minutes longer before our performance reaches its climax, and we climb the proverbial stairway to heaven. The temperature in the closet is now halfway to hell, and I'm ready to strip off the Grinch. Part of that is due to the wine.

From the noises teetering between amazement and disgust outside the door, we may have crossed the line with our performance, even obliterating it with a step too far. We struggle to straighten our faces before we exit. I'm shocked at my behavior, but Nixon's my partner-in-crime, so I feel safe being a little Noel naughty with him.

We prepare to exit, and he grabs the doorknob. Our eyes meet, and we linger in our gazes. I'm enthralled with the moment, with him. Words have been invented to describe men of his ilk. Beautiful. Hot. Sexy. Hot. Strong. Funny... Open. Perfect.

He makes me want to return his parking space and walk four blocks in the white and drifted snow to find another. Rather than walk out of this magical closet, I press my palm against his hand to stop him.

Our eyes meet for a kiss, but we don't.

Instead, it dawns on me that we need to look the parts we've just played. I scrunch my clothes, twist my skirt sideways, and tug a few wrinkles into my tights. Nixon turns his sweater from front to back, loosens his belt, and unzips his fly (but only halfway). We give one another a once-over and thumbs-up before the cellphone light turns off, the door opens, and there's a gasp deep enough to suck the oxygen from every house on the block.

We're greeted by a room full of gaping eyes and slack jaws.

"Anybody got a cigarette?" I belt out, all teeth and grins with my lips stretched from one ear to the other.

"You don't smoke," Sophie mutters, her face twisted into a snarl.

"I do now! Woo!" I'm fanning myself as if it's ninety degrees during a Baptist Sunday service.

"I'm famished," Nixon says. "Where are the snacks? I need a cookie."

"Really?" Sophie says. "You mean, you didn't get enough in the closet? It sounded like Mia was giving away all of hers."

I'm affronted, but only in the most hilarious way. Clearly, somebody's miffed. I usually leave these Black Friday parties feeling hopeless and sad. Today, I feel victorious.

"Seven Minutes of Christmas Magic! My new favorite game," Nixon says as he scavengers for treats. "Can we play again?"

"Noooo!" the Christmas choir replies, including every person in the room except Nixon and me.

Brooks appears ready to give Nixon some dap, but Sophie's narrowed eyes and machete-sharp glares are clear deterrents.

"We need to change the name of that game to thirty minutes of Christmas magic," Nixon said.

"Give or take fifteen minutes," I add before offering a congratulatory pat on Nixon's back. "Y'all picked a big...er, I mean a good one."

Sophie rolls her eyes, but I swear Brooks winks at both of us. We nearly choke with laughter.

"Hee hee hee," Sophie mocks. If anyone could die from stink eye, we'd be goners.

"Don't you mean, ho-ho-hoe?" I quip.

"You're so unfunny," she deadpans.

We're entirely folded over by now. SoBro and her guests stand steeped in disbelief, unsure of what to believe. I haven't let this loose or laughed this hard in years...maybe ever.

"I need a drink...and maybe a nice Christmas nap. Could we —" I point upstairs as if she'd let us anywhere near a bedroom. I'm never going to live this down, and I'm already conceptualizing quarterly apology gift baskets for the next year. For now, I'm relishing at the moment.

"You two should probably be getting home," Sophie says, making a direct order rather than a suggestion. "I'm sure you're both exhausted."

I could take a hint. She hadn't said anything but a word—several of them spoken and unspoken. They say, *Get out of my house now.*

Mission Accomplished.

She doesn't need to tell us twice. We zip around collecting our stuff like elves at Santa's factory thirty minutes to midnight on Christmas Eve. Nixon grabs our coats, and the doorknob barely misses our butts on the way out the door. At the bottom of the front steps, we high-five and congratulate one another on jobs well done.

I'm cut off mid-chuckle when I notice the remnants of snow art on my windshield.

"Well, that's interesting," I repeat the word scrawled in the snowdrift.

"You know...whoever dared to write that is petty and small. I'm just saying. I'd give him a piece of my mind but—"

"One divided by one equals one?" I finish. "Maybe I should ask Sophie to check her doorbell video."

"Oh, that's not necessary." He shrugs. "The culprit probably is long gone by now."

"Mmm-hmm. Long gone. You're probably right. I think we lost him in the closet."

Maybe I should be angry, but I'm too amused. He and I are more alike than I care to admit. "Can I offer you a ride? I mean, to your car?"

He chuckles, hesitates, and then says, "Sure. But, first, let me finish cleaning off your windshield."

"Finish?" I say. "Nice."

A few minutes later, we're off. I pull beside his car. It's time for him to get out, but he doesn't budge. Neither of us seems to want to part. I want to offer him a nightcap at my place so we can talk in front of the fireplace, surrounded by boxes of my unpacked Christmas ornaments and an undecorated tree. I want to offer him something. Ice cream. Rice cakes. My lips. I want him to stay.

We gaze at one another, and our eyes smile more deeply than the cheesy grins on our faces. But we should go our separate ways now. Probably.

"Well, it's been an interesting night." He says, breaking the silence. "You sure know how to do a Black Friday party."

"What can I say? It's a gift."

An awkward silence follows the brief pause because I'm trying to leave space for him to ask for my number, something I haven't offered to a man in ages. I've been so busy working at excelling in my career, I've had neither the time nor the energy to care about any man calling me for any reason, not until this moment.

Now I want all the calls. I want to be that girl whose phone rings at awkward hours and in the worst places because somebody's thinking about me, even when it's not convenient. Now, I'm giving him the "in" to ask for my digits, and his lips are sealed tighter than a submarine hatch.

"Odd though it may sound, I wouldn't change a thing."

"Me, neither," he adds. "Well..."

Questions flood my mind. Did our intimate faux interlude mean as much to him as it did to me? Maybe I'm mistaken; I've been wrong before. Perhaps I don't butter his bread, so to speak. Maybe the connection that I thought existed between us...didn't. Maybe he's got a girlfriend, and we'll leave all the magic shared between us right here...or back in the closet. I'm deflated but manage to keep it together.

He opens the door and fumbles slightly as if he's unsure of what to say or do next. After you've faux-climaxed with a man in the closet, words are hard.

Without my brain's permission, my heart takes control of the conversation and lets him off the hook, relieves him of the responsibility to fill the silence.

"What would you think if I offered to treat you to dinner?" I ask. "Mind you, I'm not asking. I'm just asking how you would respond if I invited you. It wouldn't mean anything...or anything. It'd strictly be an apology...from me...for my appalling behavior."

The corners of his lips turn upward. "Not that you're inviting me because you're not. But if you did, I would say yes. A hundred percent, yes. After all, we shared magic in the closet."

He appears almost as relieved as I feel. We both breathe a sigh. I'm not in this alone, and neither is he. "Okay, then maybe we won't go to dinner," I reply facetiously. We *are so* going to dinner.

"We probably shouldn't," he adds. "I'm so glad we're not going. And I'm relieved you didn't ask. Given our earlier clash, I wasn't nervous about asking—at all."

He was nervous.

"I agree...on all counts."

He breaks in with the truth allowing us to take a small step forward. "I wanted to ask for your number, but after you've faked an orgasm with someone in the closet, it's like, where do you go from there?"

I cackled before butterflies took my stomach hostage and flapped around in my gut. Our similarities had become unnerving. "Exactly. Where do you go?"

Timing's everything. I want to date him soon...like yesterday. I decide to play it cool. I refuse to seem too desperate, too anxious. He needs to know that he'll have to wait when it comes to dating me. Good things come in time, and the best things come with patience. No matter what he says, I won't agree to any date before next weekend. Seven days. Not one day sooner.

"I've got a lot going on this weekend. Family stuff," he says. His eyebrows scrunch as if his mind is churning. "But, if it's okay with you, how about we don't meet on Monday...for dinner?"

A self-satisfied grin stretches my lips, and I prepare to play it cool. I've got a plan, and I will not stray from it. Seven days. If I'm overly eager, I'll seem desperate, and we need more time to get to know one another. So, I'm turning down his invitation for now, and I'm at peace with my decision. However, I blurt out, "Monday sounds perfect!"

Yep. No backbone whatsoever.

I'd have stopped them if I could. He passes me his phone so that I can punch in my number, and I return it to his hand: our fingers touch and my body quivers.

"Thank you. I won't text you the details."

"Please don't." I'm smiling, so he knows what I mean. I turn so many colors I could double for a bag of Skittles, and I'd like him to sample the rainbow. Only one thing could transport me from Cloud Nine to heaven—a kiss. A sweet sensuous Christmas kiss, the one we failed to share in the closet.

He leans in again, but our lips don't touch. He just gazes at me, drinks me in, really. I sit there, silent, willing.

He slips out of my car and into the night, cleans off his windshield, and starts his car. We wave at one another as I pull off and leave him behind.

I crawl through the next few blocks until I hit M Street and turn onto Pennsylvania Avenue. His eyes, his everything, takes me hostage.

I'm still smiling. I can't stop.

No, the night wasn't perfect...but those final moments with Nixon came so close. Almost.

The night was filled with Christmas magic. All I missed was the kiss.

CHAPTER 8

ia

THE LIGHT OF THE NEW DAY FILTERS THROUGH MY BLINDS, CUDDLES me like a warm blanket. I'm buried beneath mounds of comforters, and the chill in the air can't reach me.

Last night feels surreal, like a dream. I'm delirious, hungover from my seven minutes of Christmas magic with Nixon. I open my eyes and roll out of bed, more alive than I've felt in months. Well, at least since my public humiliation with rusty Dustin.

It's only the second time in my life that I've been so drawn to a man and yet simultaneously wanted to punch him in the throat. Sums up my entire relationship with Dustin in one broken nutshell. This is different.

Nixon's body's on my mind. The touch of his fingers has imprinted in my skin. I can still feel his fingers wrapped around my hand. The sounds of his moans echo in my mind and drown out all useful thought, so no hope exists to engage in any semblance of productive activity today. After all, I've got scads of tree and home decorating to do with my knick-knacks and thingamabobs.

A mere seven hours have passed since we last spoke, but it feels more like seven days.

Body parts south of my neck wish he filled the empty space in bed beside me. Instead of wasting the day away in my thoughts all day, I roll over to check the time on my phone. To my surprise, a text buzzes in.

Nixon: Good morning, Mia. This is Nixon. I'm sending this to avoid reminding you about our undate on Monday. Also, sending this to verify that you didn't give me the number to Pizza Hut.

Me: Good Morning. This is Pizza Hut. Can I take your order?

Pause.

Nixon: Uh?

Me: Kidding. Nice of you to text. About time. If I were waiting to hear from you (which I wasn't), it would have been impatiently.

I'm in disbelief.

I hit SEND and cackled, stared at my phone. His reply took a moment too long—and doubt set in. No way would I send another text without an answer. No sooner than my toe hits the floor on my trek toward the Keurig for a hot cup of sanity and humanity, a text pops in.

Nixon: What are you wearing?

Me: Really? Last night you proclaimed smacking it up, flipping, and rubbing it down...and this morning, all you've got is what are you wearing?

Nixon: Funny. But I'm serious. Are you decent? Clothed?

Me: As opposed to indecent? Nekkid? Of course, I'm decent.

Nixon: Good. I couldn't wait for our undate. So, don't come to your front door...and definitely don't open it when you hear the knocking sound.

Knock. Knock. Knock.

Me: ???

I have questions but not for long. Before I can inhale a full breath, a doorbell ring closely follows a series of knocks.

Panic sets in.

Nixon's here? At my door? Sure, we'd briefly spotted each other before the party, but I can't believe he committed my address to memory.

I flitter around the house as if someone set fire to my feetie pajamas, scuttle into the bathroom, brush my teeth, tease my hair. When I look near-human, I give my house a quick once-over. After thanking the heavens all appears to be in decent shape, apart from the undecorated Christmas tree and mounds of unpacked decorations, I zip to the door to open it.

"Breakfast!" Nixon sings. He greets me with a warm smile, dangles bags full of goodies in my face, and says, "I know you've got plans. I promise I won't keep you for long, but I couldn't wait until Monday."

He probably thinks his pledge to keep our visit short is a relief. It's not. The only promise I want him to make at this moment is to stay.

"You're here. I can't believe it." My excitement is genuine. I step aside so he can enter the door and point to the kitchen island so that he can rest the bags.

My home's open design makes his path clear. Following on his heels, I smile and bounce with every step, waiting for the chance to relieve him of the bagged delights emitting the scent of warm, fresh-baked bread and dig in.

Truth be told, he looks way better than the bread smells. If last night served as any indication, he probably smells way better than the bread, too.

Daylight only confirms he's all-season fine and with little effort. His bulky sweater broadens his shoulders, and he's sporting another pair of fancy pants jeans—black today. At the door, I noticed Timberland marks from his boots imprinted in the snow. He's five gold teeth and a Mercedes emblem from being a Hot 100 rapper.

Lawd Hammercy. He's sexier than I can handle without much-needed assistance from coffee and carbs.

He rests the bag on the countertop and tightens the top so I can't see inside. "No peeking. It's a surprise. Besides, I'd like to serve you...I mean, if that's okay."

Serve me? Okay? I went straight Scarlett O'Hara, dramatically pressing my hand against my heart and saying, "Little ole me?" I dragged it out an eked out Southern Belle. Every part of my being crying out, "I dooo de-clare!"

I'd like to serve you...if that's okay. His words were noteworthy due to my memory of the last time a man spoke them to me—the twelfth of never. Men look at me, and they see confidence, ambition, independence; they don't see "serve her."

Nixon's the first man to see me as a woman in need of a man who takes care of her once in a while, a woman who needs love. I'm basking in the spoiling because it's a miracle, a once-in-a-lifetime moment of kismet, as I point him to the powder room just beyond my short hall so he can wash his hands. When he disappears, I commence my happy dance that includes a riveting combination of the Cabbage Patch, Running Man, and the TikTok.

I reach into the upper cabinet in the kitchen, pull down my new West Elm terra-cotta low bowls, and set them on the granite counter. By the time the coffee mugs come out, he's gliding back toward me wearing a broad smile and rubbing his hands together, eager to feast. I inhale steam rising from the goodie bag, and my stomach growls.

"I hope this is okay," Nixon says. "I mean, showing up on your doorstep unannounced and uninvited. It's just after last night..."

"What?"

"Magic. Seven whole minutes," he responds.

"Nixon, you brought coffee and carbs. Of course, it's okay. Plus, I kicked the other guy out the backdoor while you were in the bathroom, so the coast is clear."

I wink, and he starts to laugh. Then he hesitates. "Wait...you're kidding, right?"

"Of course!" We chuckle, and I bump him with my elbow like a crushing schoolgirl. Now, we're both off balance. "So, what's on the menu?"

He pulls out a seat for me and pushes me to the breakfast bar, where we eat. The barstools are positioned at a comfortable distance, so I prefer to eat them there. He says grace before we eat, holds my hand.

While my eyes are clenched shut, I freeze-frame him—this moment—in my mind, so I never forget how a gentleman treats a lady. Tenderness fills his every gesture, pushing chilly bumps through my skin. Then he places his hand on my arm—electric shock waves rock my world. He situates my low bowl and a mug in front of me and begins to plate my goodies and pour coffee.

"You know what today is, don't you?" he asks.

I shake my head, but in my thoughts, I reply, *The Best day of the year? Most romantic moment of my life? Date of the century?*

"I'll give you a hint," he continues. "As of yesterday, the Christmas season's officially commenced, right?"

I nod, curious at where he's going with this.

"So, we can consider this your first holiday date, right? After you confided in me, I was determined to be the first."

I squeal with delight...at least on the inside. Butterflies fly blindly against the walls of my gut. Thank goodness my outside voice doesn't betray my gushing. "Wow, I'm impressed. Somebody's been paying attention in class."

"Honor roll student, all day, every day. I pay close attention to everything. About you," he mutters almost indiscernibly, but I catch it. "That's why I also brought"—he reaches into a second bag and removes the contents—"Coffee and hot cocoa. If you look inside—extra marshmallows."

"Keep this up, and you're going to get a gold star for perfect behavior. You might even make student of the week." *Student of my life.*

"Not bad for a beginning, right? But I'll warn you now; I'm an overachiever. A week isn't nearly enough."

I'm now in awe of him as I give serious consideration to the question: is it too soon to propose marriage? With swiftness, I conclude that I'm high on pheromones and the scent of bread. His cologne, if he's wearing any, isn't helping. Maybe that's his natural man-scent. Whatever it is, I'm intoxicated, and I've not had a single mimosa, which I need. I could use several. They'd give me legitimate reasons to feel this loopy.

"So, what do you do?" He takes a seat and plates his breakfast.

"Oh, no. I call foul. You cannot ruin this perfectly sweet moment with shop talk." The last thing I want to remember right now is Sweet-Hart—the only card company in the country that doesn't have a Christmas campaign due to my utter failure. Last night served as a beautiful diversion but failed at its single task: to help me drum up ideas for this year's line. I'd hoped for some semblance of a spark...and I got one, just not one related to saving my job or producing a card line.

Not that I'm complaining...much.

Nixon's presence in my life during the holidays will get Tessa and Sophie off my back. Who am I kidding? It doesn't bother me that I'll probably receive a few more party invites...but now to couple's soirees. Keeping it real, I want to be asked, but I don't actually want to attend. I'm glad Nixon is here. I've been missing him, and I didn't even know he existed before Black Friday.

"Okay, then. Let's talk about last night." He takes an audible gulp, sparking my fears about what he's going to say. Maybe he's turned off because I went too far. I consider interrupting him when he says, "I can't get what happened off my mind."

See? I knew it. "You mean our performance? I'm sure SoBro will forgive us someday."

"Oh, I know they will, but that's not what I'm referring to.

I'm talking about you and me...that we happened. That I woke up this morning and there was only one place I wanted to be. Now I can't believe I'm here."

"Well, it's been so long since I wanted that...someone here. And now there's you. They say this is the season for miracles and magic. I'm beginning to believe it's true."

"That seals it for me."

"Seals what?"

He sets down his coffee, then mine, and sweeps me into an embrace that speeds my heart and stops my breath. His mouth covers mine, and his arms are home to me. I've never, at once, felt so overcome with joy and fear. By the time I lose myself in the kiss, at the moment, in him, it ends.

My gloss leaves his lips shiny. He wipes them on a napkin, which he reluctantly sets on the counter. "Now that we've gotten that over with, I can think straight."

That makes one of us.

He glances at the mini iPod I won last night. It's sitting on the other side of the kitchen counter. "I'm not a game player, per se, but you play a *mean* game of Taboo."

"*Mean* being the operative word, I suppose," I say with a laugh. "You got a few licks in there. I left a little bruised but not broken."

"No bruising. I'll have you know I only spread joy and good tidings."

"And sarcasm. Now, isn't that better than a Christmas card."

I'm ecstatic, but fear creeps in. Nothing this good ever lasts.

A shoe will drop. The only questions are when and how hard.

CHAPTER 9

$\mathcal{N}$ixon

MIA'S KIND OF AMAZING. WE'VE CONNECTED IN WAYS I DON'T FULLY comprehend, and our two-hour chat over breakfast feels more like two minutes. I'm happy to lose myself in the moment.

Monday's looming pressures fall away, along with the stress of transforming into my alter ego—the hatchet. It's a necessary evil I wish the mortgage and meals didn't require.

As she and I talk, I try to shift the conversation toward work. I want her to know me, both sides of me. I wonder if she can like, maybe someday grow to love them and understand, for legitimate reasons, they exist, side by side, the romantic and the hatchet. But she's taken work talk off the table, making it difficult to discuss.

Since my mother's raised me to clean up my messes, I wash and dry the few dishes we've used. Between cups and bowls, I survey her home, and all of its openness, to get a sense of her style and priorities.

Right now, it's clear Christmas is king.

I'm blinded by jingle joy: a Santa penguin cookie jar and a multicolored Santa Snoopy. On the mantel sits two angels with stars on their gowns as if they've fallen from heaven. Add to that, boxes and boxes of what look to be handcrafted ornaments. They're visible through the clear plastic storage containers, arranged neatly on trays. Some sparkle with glitter. Some appear hand-painted in green, red, blue, and gold. Except for the packs of decorations, her home nears immaculate. She catches me in the act of snooping and says precisely what I would expect Mia to say.

"Take a picture. It'll last longer." Her laugh is like music. I remove the towel from her hand as she attempts to help me dry, and she meets my gesture with the stink eye.

"Mia. I've got this," I speak gently to avoid offending her. After all, she didn't have to let me inside, but I can tell she must be used to playing the boss and is suffering minor internal conniptions from her loss of control. "Looks like you've got a lot of Christmas magic around here."

She cranes her neck and examines the holiday spoils stacked against the walls. "Yep. More than seven minutes' worth. You're looking at about ten years of joy and good cheer."

"This must be a special time of year for you."

"It's...tradition, the one time of year that I feel closest to my parents. Maybe because I miss them more now than ever."

"Your parents. They're—"

She nods and shifts her glance toward her feet, which now rock her. "Car accident. Two years ago. And I'm an only child, so..."

"God, Mia. I'm so sorry." Her expression crushes my soul. All I want to do is wrap my arms around her and protect her from whatever's hurting her. I know first-hand the despair from the loss of a parent—or both—may be too deep, even for my arms to console her.

"It's okay. People close enough to see all of *this* tend to think I go a little Christmas crazy. But all of this is my mom.

You'd have loved her. She was so amazing. Drove my dad to lay heavy on the spiked eggnog around the holidays if you know what I'm saying. But he willingly served as her curmudgeonly minion for hire. His superpower was twinkly light displays. He had a special knack and no fear of heights. Every year, we lit up the block...almost literally. The best I can do now is hang a few strands around the first-floor windows. I don't do ladders, neither for most good reasons nor any bad ones."

Her admission sparks a chuckle.

She's more resilient than I am. Or maybe she's lived with her loss for longer. I'm not where she is in terms of finding holiday joy in the midst of pain, but, for the first time, I want to be. I want to find a way out of this depression and into the twinkly lights with her.

My heart breaks for her.

"I want to stay and help you decorate. I wish I could, but my mother's expecting me. It's the first time in six years. She's finally ready to return to Christmas crazy...or something like it."

"Well, that's cause for celebration. It's not easy," she says. A sadness behind the sparkle in her eyes intensifies as she stares into mine and reads my compassion like the morning edition of *The Washington Post*. "Don't. Your pity's no good here. Besides, this is my favorite time of the year."

I don't doubt what she's saying, but she doesn't understand that I don't want her to. I glance at my watch. "I hate to leave, but..."

"No worries. Help is on the way."

"Help?" A weak bolt of jealousy flashes through me. We're not even together-together, and I'm wondering if another man will substitute for me. "Not the guy you kicked out before me, I hope."

"Absolutely not," she says. Her smile is wide and genuine. "He's coming back later tonight."

A brief flash of envy surges through me before she continues.

"I'm kidding. My best friend's coming by to assist...as she does every year."

"How about you save something...so that I can help when I come back?"

"You assume that if you return, I'll let you inside," she says with a wide grin. "I have an idea, assuming, of course, you'll join me for our office holiday soirees this season. How about we swing by the Jingle Jumper...together?"

"Isn't that the ugly sweater store?"

"Exactly."

"It's one of my mom's favorite stores."

"With the party coming up, I'd really like to win this year."

"Sounds like a plan. You tell me when you're ready to go, and I'm there."

"I'll grab your coat." She changes the subject, but her smile says, thank you. "Also, there's something I'd like to give you. In appreciation for the wonderful treats you brought."

She puts space between us with quick steps, reaches into one of her cartons, and pulls out something I can't quite see from one of her many trays. "I hope you like it," she says as she conceals it behind her back.

Standing in front of me now, she hands it over. "A train?" She's given me an ornament that looks like an engine in the likeness of a frosted gingerbread cookie. The detail is so incredible I want to bite it, but the sentiment isn't lost on me. She remembers our earlier talks, the train, the tree, my dad. I'm almost choked up. "Thank you. This is amazing. Where'd you get it?"

"I didn't get it," she says. "I made it."

My head jerks back and the surprise pushes me back a stride. I need to balance myself. "You? Made this?"

She shrugs. "Sure. I make all of my ornaments...you know, when I'm not concealing myself from the paparazzi and crazed fans...or hijacking the parking spaces of unsuspecting victims."

I laugh before her words spark my next epiphany. "Wait? All those boxes. You...made those?"

"It's kind of my thing, the perils of being raised by a crafty Christmas crazy mom. Every year I come up with a theme and create a new collection. Sometimes I share the old ones with people I care about. Mostly I store them."

"I can't accept this. I mean, I want to, but...it's special to you...and I don't even have a tree. I doubt I'll get one."

She presses the gift into my hand and tightens my fingers around the edges. "It would mean so much to me if you'd keep it. Consider it a peace offering. As for the tree..."

She lays the hint on thick, pauses, and waits for me to agree, but I don't. I can't, especially not right now. "I'm running late. I'm sorry."

"Thank you...for my best holiday date yet," she says.

"It's your first holiday date," I reply.

"But it won't be my last, I hope."

"To verify, we're not going on an undate Monday, right?" I ask.

"Absolutely not," she replies.

Good thing I haven't invited her to join me for the visit to my mother's place.

Her smile was so wide she probably couldn't fit through the door. She stands to her tiptoes and presses her lips against my cheek. They touch me like sweet soft, perfection.

Once her heels return to earth, I look into her eyes, resisting every urge to kiss her again and again and again. If I do, I may not leave. I still haven't quit, and Monday can't come soon enough.

"I should go."

She looks as disappointed as I feel, but the moment dissipates into winter air before I can wallow in the sadness of my departure. Monday is coming—the worst and the best of the day, probably in that order.

. . .

.L. BRADY

FOR NOW, I MAKE MY WAY TO MOM'S HOUSE WHERE THE HEAT IS boiling, and her greeting is as chilly as she is. She's wearing one of her twenty Jingle Jumper sales specials. Her round brown eyes are as kind as her heart and her tongue as sharp as a set of Ginsu knives. I've recounted my evening at SoBro's, most of it. She's aware of Mia's existence, but she wants to know more than I want to share. Apparently, my well-earned reputation precedes me.

"So," she says curtly, eyeing me as if she's caught me with a fresh copy of Hustler. "Is she bony or bonier?"

The line of women I've paraded in front of her explains the reason for her harshness. A cursory glance might suggest that I have "a type," and that type almost always comprises shallow high-maintenance, modelesque vixens who refuse her Christmas treats. This fact couldn't be disputed, at least not before I've eaten 'lunch.

"I'm still trying to figure out why every single one of the women you bring in here looks like she needs half-a-dozen snacks and a whole attitude adjustment. You never missed a meal growing up. in fact, you come from a long line of meal eaters, yet somehow manage to date the hangriest heifers east of the Mississippi."

"C'mon, mom."

My mother consistently overspills into two areas: blunt opinions and unsolicited advice. She sounds ungenerous, but, if I'm honest, she's not wrong. Despite the undue focus on my undersized exes, she's neither shallow nor fat. She also isn't passing up anything that resembles a rib or slice of cornbread if a plate slides by. The point she's attempting to emphasize to me is that every single one of my exes would.

"Mia's not like them—at all. You'd like her. She's Christmas crazy."

Why I've mentioned Mia to her, I don't know. It's not like we're a couple. I've known her for five minutes, and we've dated once. Now that I think about it, for the first time in a month of

84

Sundays, Moms doesn't exactly ask about my romantic life. In fact, she merely questions what I've been up to, and I forget to lie. Part of me understands I need help coming off the Mia high, and, I'm an instant addict, so I can't do it on my own. My mother offers the kind of grounding only someone who's changed your diarrhea diaper could.

"We didn't even like each other, not at first."

"Did I ask you anything? You told me not to pry," she says flatly. "But since you brought up the topic, do you mean to tell me she didn't swoon at the sight of your million-dollar jeans or fall to her knees and kiss your feet in standard fashion?"

I shake my head. "Swoon? Not even close. As a matter of fact, she stole my parking space."

She glances at me and folds over laughing. "I like her already. I'm guessing she apologized after making you squirm a little."

"Eventually. But she did most of the squirming. You'd have been proud of the guilt trip I laid on. Then we waged a war of words for the ages. Head to head. Hermano to Hermana. She's a scrappy one."

"Mmm-hmm. You always did like them scrappy," she says. "You know, I fought with a man like that back in the day. Talk about sparks flying? *Humph.* He and I together were like a detonator to an explosive. *KABLOW.* Never a boring moment. He kept me on my toes, and I liked it...most of the time."

"Wow. What happened to him?"

"After dating him briefly," she said with a sly smile, "I married him. Pushed you out two years later. After—"

"Thirty-six hours of labor on the two coldest days in DC's history." I'm mocking her. She's shared this account thirty-seven thousand times if she's told me once. "How can I forget? Besides the fact that you'll never let me."

"I'll never let you forget or live it down, but it was mostly your father's fault."

"Yuck, Mom. Ew. Back to Mia," I reply. "She and I joined forces to defeat SoBro once and for all. No more matchmaking.

I'm about 99.9 percent certain we put an end to the dating game, and we may never be invited to another Black Friday party."

"Sophie and Brooks." Her head falls back in laughter. "They get an 'A' for persistence. You've gotta love 'em. So how did you and Mia torment them...or do I want to know?"

"I promise you do not want to know. Mia is, let's say, creative. The important part is—we escaped Georgetown single. And, in a unique and interesting twist, we started as enemies and parted as friends."

"Humph. That really is new and different."

"I woke up and delivered breakfast to her this morning. Then served it."

"Breakfast? Wait that means she eats?!"

"Really, mom?"

"And you delivered *and* served?"

I flash her a cold stink eye, and somehow my eyeballs miraculously remain in my head.

She surveys my face and smiles. "I'm not only looking at you...I can see you. Something's different this time." It's mother-vision, more potent than Superman x-ray vision. She senses what I'm not ready to reveal to anyone, including myself.

"So, we should get started on those decorations, huh?" I ask, trying to divert the conversation.

"I see what you tried to do there. It's okay, Sweet Pea, you and I...we've suffered a lot of loss over the past couple of years, and you've suffered more loss than your father."

She's referring to Tami.

"But the thing is...it's okay," she says.

"What's okay?"

"Moving on. Living again. Loving. Your dad would want you to. I want you to. I'd just like you to find someone who isn't chronically hangry."

She stands, and I follow her to the coat rack. "You get the ladder. I'll get the lights," she orders.

I salute, click my heels, and march. "after we pick up the tree, right?"

"Yes, we do. We'll need to run down to Mack's now," she says. "And then maybe we can grab two."

"I see what you tried to do there." She may be ready for a Douglass, but I'm not. I appreciate the thought, but no tree, not this year. "Just one for now."

"You don't have to pretend with your mama, Pumpkin. If you can't afford it, you can just tell me. I know your funds are tighter than PeeWee's pants. I mean, since you're out of work and all." She's got jokes...and I laugh because she's the funniest person I know.

"That's how little you know," I say. "Black Friday came with more than a date. I got a new job."

She eyes me through slits. My occupational choices haven't exactly left her brimming with pride over the years. Starting with my two years at Keene, Blanchard & Livingston, where they hired me to engineer a company break up. It went according to a *plan,* if not *their intent.* At Bartholomew and Fink, I set up an acquisition that led to the layoff of 1,000 people. I, and many executives, made a killing—but the deal proceeded in a way that no employee (and no executive) expected. I've never been the man they expected me to be.

I've served as a useful gun for hire. Ten years of my career have passed, and I'm ready for a change, especially with a new job.

I thought Renee and Regina sought me for my passion and commitment to bringing the best greeting card products to consumers. Receiving an offer from the company founded by Devon Hart and Brian Sweet only compounded my excitement and joy. It turns out I was wrong about Renee, Regina, their motivation, the job—everything.

On the upside, my foot's in the door. Now, I have to decide how to use the opportunity with which I've been gifted while doing the job I've been hired to do. Like a gun for hire, I'll load and fire no matter how many people it hurts. My dream, whatever it is, will have to wait.

"You're not involved in another hatchet job, are you? You had to wear sunglasses and a cap for a year after that last one. Your father and I gave you the tools to rule the world, and you want to be a tool."

"Ouch. Harsh much?" I'm not sure how to answer her question without lying—or worse, telling the truth.

"Hey, if your mama doesn't tell it like it is, who will? Help me understand something, though. We sacrificed everything for your education, and raised you to forge your path, positioned you to do what you love and love what you do. We wanted you to earn a living while never working a day. In your last job, you worked ridiculous hours, and I'm almost certain I've never seen you truly excited about what you do, not since the Signed & Sealed days. Explain."

I shrug.

"I dunno, Mom. Maybe I'm lost. You know, like how you always miss the left at the McDonald's going to my house? Somewhere, I missed a turn, and I'm living an unfulfilled life. I've absorbed so many jabs and uppercuts in the past six years. I'm a little punch drunk and made some bad choices in my state of delirium."

"That last part especially—bad choices. Every time I read the headlines, it's about a court fight at Hart Enterprises. Why you'd insert yourself into that unholy mess, I don't know."

"They made an offer I couldn't refuse. I accepted the position because I've always wanted to work for Hart. In actuality, what's clear is that I've leaped from the frying pan that is my life, into the fire that is Hart Publishing."

"Who are you telling? You used to talk about Hart so much I thought you'd changed your name."

"I'm in it now. I'm gonna shoot my shot. You and dad also used to say sometimes you've got to wade through the weeds before you can get to the clearing."

"I have one question, and then I'll leave it alone."

"What's that?"

"I'm not gonna see you headlining the five o'clock news, am I? I don't have bail money if they haul you off to jail."

"No, I mean, it's not easy, but no one's arresting me. Not without a fight."

At least not anytime soon, I think.

Her eyebrow arches in a perfect curve. "If you say so."

"You only need to worry about one thing: it pays well enough for me to keep you in ten-foot Douglass firs."

"Well, then, you really can't turn it down, can you?" she says with a chuckle. "Speaking of Douglass firs, are you ready to go?"

"I was born ready."

"Mmm-hmm. Thirty-six hours of labor on two of the coldest days in DC history."

CHAPTER 10

 ia

Drool all but slides down the corner of my mouth as I watch Nixon disappear into the distance. After delivering the date of my holiday dreams, he bid me adieu and left nothing behind except his Timberland tracks in the snow, warm memories of my first holiday date, and a big puddle of Mia mush.

He engaged every one of my senses in an intoxicating slow wine. To my eyes, he's a shiny black 1969 Mustang Mach 1. To my ears, he's Miles Davis in a Quincy Jones arrangement. To my tongue, he's honey butter on fresh warm bread. To my touch, he's satin and silk. To my sense of smell, he's sandalwood and leather.

I blink hard three times and pinch my arm before allowing myself to believe this morning isn't a dream. Nixon's as real as the happy pouch in my stomach. I flitter into my bedroom to take a shower and dress in my coziest bulky sweater and yoga pants. Then I connect my iPod to the Bluetooth speaker and turn to Soul Holiday. Each year, I put that song on repeat while unloading storage boxes filled with ornaments, bobbles, and Santa figurines, signaling the beginning of my most favorite time of the year.

After stabilizing most perfect Douglass Fir in the stand and watering generously, I open the storage boxes containing my newest themed ornament collection.

Last year's centered around trains—inspired by a Metro subway driver I dated for a hot minute. The year before that—cookies. No man is attached to that theme; I just remember being hungry all the time. The year before that—sports. My guy played second string on a semi-professional football team. He pursued me and his dreams with all the passion of a walnut. He lived a second-string life with equal effort and preferred women who needed saving and walked two paces behind him.

This year's theme? Christmas love—a twist that can only be considered irony given my SoBro party find. This year's designs are doubles—two turtle doves, two Santa hats, two candy canes, etc.

My decorating approach is layered and begins with lights, lots of the twinkly variety. I'm wrangling with a twisted, knotted strand from the box when the doorbell rings. I bounce over, peek out, and see two of my favorite people in the world, the Christmas Calvary's arrived. Nodding my head to the Sounds of Blackness rhythms, I smile as I fling the door open.

"Surpriiiiiiiise!" the choir sings.

Tessa holds up a large bottle of orange juice, and Sophie, two bottles of Moët. Mimosas. Part of me had hoped Nixon would be on the other side, but I'm facing the next best thing.

I'm not at all stunned to see Tessa. Now, Sophie, on the other hand, well, shock is putting it mildly...especially given my performance with Nixon the night before.

"Happy holidays." I raise my voice so they can hear me above the music. "Come in. Make yourselves at home. You're just in time."

Tessa annoys me because she's so striking with her China

doll eyes and supermodel hair. Even in jeans and duck boots. The better half of SoBro, sleek and merry, is no worse with her holly jolly high-fashion that looks designed by Marc Jacobs.

They enter, remove their snowy boots, and hang their flaky coats on the rack. We hug, and I relieve their hands of the bottled happiness they carry.

"Mimosas on dec," I say. "I'll prepare the glasses and mix the drinks." The inquisition's about to commence. The cocktail ingredients have arrived in the nick of time.

Tessa's the first out of the gate.

My glasses barely hit the granite counter before I hear Tessa call out, "So, I'm not naming any names, but I heard someone in this house attended a little Christmas shindig last night, hmm?"

"Subtle, Tess. Real, subtle. You and Sophie the Snitch," I reply, "What have you been told?"

"Nothing, really," Tessa begins, "except that you may or may not have had relations with a stranger in the closet."

"Yeah!" Sophie adds. "For someone who claims she doesn't bake, sounded like you were giving up the Christmas cookies."

I'm not sure whether to laugh or be insulted. Unable to restrain myself, I snort and almost choke. "First of all, he wasn't a stranger. I knew his name, first name."

"And?" Tessa responds.

"And nothing. What happens in the closet stays in the closet. And I'm going to keep it in the closet."

Balancing the glasses on a tray, I sashay back into the living room to deliver the mimosas, and their suspicious glares burn through me.

"What?" I say in response to their expressions. Then I laugh and join them on the couch, where we sink in the cushions to get ready. The gossip begins.

"Fess up," Sophie says. "I think after everything you put Brooks and me through, we deserve an explanation."

"I don't need an explanation," Tessa says. "I just need the scoop, the 4-1-1, the grimy details."

"Fine. I'll tell you, but first, we need to toast."

"To what?"

"To Sophie and Brooks who give the best Black Friday parties east of the Mississippi. To Tessa and Cody and the successful union of Keep It Real Cards and Hart Enterprises. Cheers!"

"And to Mia," Tessa says. "The new VP of Sweet-Hart Cards and our ride or die, friend, who, despite her best efforts, will not escape confessing her sins. So, she may as well get with the program."

"First—the rules," I say, "Sophie, no names, not until, I'm really certain this, whatever this is, is going somewhere. I don't want to jinx it by claiming him too soon."

After waiting in silence for her to respond, she says, "Fine," and seals her lips with a zip.

I smile. "So...uh, Alex and I..." They can tell by my twisted expression that's not his real name. "We didn't even like each other at first."

"She thought he was cute," Sophie says.

"Hey, I'm telling the story here." I give her the stink eye. "I thought he was cute, but he wore fancy pants along with his bad attitude. In his defense, I may have accidentally stolen his parking space—on purpose."

"Ohhh, she reveals the truth," Sophie turns to Tessa. "But we need to rewind really quick. First of all, she came running in my house like she was being chased by a serial killer hunting women wearing Grinch sweaters."

We all laugh.

"Yeah, after Alex arrived, it was a slog of a beginning. We cursed each other for an hour. Quietly."

"Quietly? Umm, no," Sophie says.

"Will you let her tell the story?" Tessa asks.

"Thank you," I reply to Tessa. "Anyway, SoBro starts the Christmas games. You know"—she nods—"They paired us up, and we started steeply uphill before things took a turn for the better. " I walked Tessa through the Christmas games and our Taboo glory. Then we arrived right back where we started. The closet. "What can I say? We went inside, and we stayed for seven minutes."

"Fifteen," Sophie corrects me. "Not just fifteen minutes, but fifteen of the longest minutes of my whole life."

"Fine, fifteen! We shared a few Christmas secrets. I won't divulge them, but I will say he surprised me. I learned some valuable life lessons. Namely, you can't judge a book by its fancy pants."

"Mmm-hmm..." Tessa says, and then covers Sophie's mouth. "Okay, fifteen minutes pass, you're out of the closet. What's next?"

"We're summarily given the boot, kicked out by our hosts." I jokingly glare at Sophie. "Then, we leave together. I drive him to his car and drop him off. We exchange numbers and make dinner plans."

"Well, hello!! Dinner? Where are we going? More importantly, what are you wearing? You better wear a dress," Sophie says.

"He doesn't care. If he didn't mind the yoga pants and sweater I wore this morning, I doubt slacks versus a dress will make a difference."

"Wait a minute." Tessa gives me the once-over. "Whatchu talkin' about, Mia?"

"He left not long before you guys arrived. Brought me breakfast this morning...and cleaned the dishes."

"Let me find out!" Sophie says as she glances back at the kitchen. It's pristine. "See, you totally buried the lead."

"It's not my fault y'all we're so focused on the closet you missed the trees. He brought me baked goods and hot coffee. If he had brought a preacher, I'm pretty sure I'd have married him...or at least asked."

We all fold over laughing.

"In all seriousness, it was one of the sweetest moments I've ever experienced, especially during the holidays. But I dunno. All seems a little too untrue to be good."

Tessa's expression goes serious. She switches to the seat next to me and holds my hand. "Mia, you went through a tough break-up with Dustin...and, let's face it, all the others. You deserve romantic; you deserve sweet...you deserve happy. Maybe it's not too untrue to be good. Perhaps your time has come."

"And Lord knows you've paid your dues...like ten times over," Sophie adds. "Whether or not this ends up being forever or for now, enjoy the journey. Allow yourself to be courted and wooed. And whatever comes of this experience, you'll have enjoyed your time."

"You've got a good point. I'm going to let it flow, relax, and let it be whatever. It'll last, however long it lasts."

"Now that sounds like a plan, and a good one," Sophie says.

"In the meantime, let's finish these drinks and wrap up the decorations. If I'm going to be fully inspired to pitch this new line Monday, then I need my house drowning in Christmas this weekend. You guys ready to decorate?"

As we transform my home from Christmas blah to Christmas crazy, I begin to wonder what surprises Monday has in store—and hope I don't come to regret the thought.

Surprises.

CHAPTER 11

ixon

I'VE TAUGHT MY NEPHEW COMMON CORE MATH, GONE NINETY-SIX hours without telling a single lie, canceled carbs for six months, dove cage-free with sharks in the Bahamas, bungee-jumped from the Rio Grande Bridge, and not a single one of those challenges was more difficult than going forty-four hours without calling Mia.

I left her place ozone-high, but I managed to convince myself to follow man-rules—two days of silence between each date. That way, you don't seem so, you know, desperate, pressed, and eager. I'm trying to give off vibes but not the desperation ones.

In forty-four hours, I've drawn one significant, life-changing conclusion: the guy who made "man-rules" is an idiot. From this point forward, the only rules I'm following are my own. Mia doesn't strike me as the kind of woman enticed by overly eager men. I decide to play it cool, so she'll think I'm unaffected.

As evidence of this, my declaration is to text her this morning after I'm fully suited up for work, and now it's almost time to grovel and hope that I haven't ruined us with my ridiculousness.

Though I've failed in romantic relationships, I'm winning at the good son thing.

My mother's house looks and smells like Christmas. Takes a day and a half to finish, but we hang lights, decorate two Douglass firs (both hers), and overdose on Motown Christmas songs and cookies. Mom pulls out the old Temptations vinyl and spins them a few times on Dad's old lift-top record player cabinet; it's now about twice my age. It stores all his old records on one side and plays records and static-filled radio on the other. My mom plays the same song over and over and over again.

The night's not silent, although I wish it were. I could go the rest of my life without hearing this again, but the song makes her smile, transports her to a happier time when she shared the season with Dad.

After our devastating loss, the air is filling with life; we're breathing again, living again, not just going through the motions because we're expected to move on.

And yet nothing I've done feels complete.

Mia.

I've ignored my heart following the man's rules. I want to talk to her, I should've called, but I didn't. No, instead, I left a wordless void of doubt and uncertainty between us.

Now I wonder if she's angry with me. If not, is it because she's with someone else? Does she think I'm dating?

Now, I want to text her, but I'm afraid she'll ghost me or worse, banish me to the friend zone. I turn toward my phone and begin to move toward it — and the screen lights up. My eyebrows scrunch. Who would be calling me at this hour? It's early... I glance at my cell and hold my breath for a second.

Mia: So, what are you wearing?

I fold over laughing.

Me: A navy blue suit, a guilty expression, and the biggest apology ever.

Mia: Sounds like the perfect outfit for someone who didn't call me yesterday.

Me: I'm sorry. But you know how it is. I hope?

Mia: Silly, man rules. The woman's version would've told me not to return your call had you bothered to phone me.

I chuckled to myself. Her honesty was as refreshing as her humor.

Me: Glad I got Mom's Christmas decor squared away...but I missed helping you. Hearing your voice.

She shares two emojis, first a blush. Then she blows a heart kiss. I return the latter, anxious to repeat what happened in her kitchen on Saturday.

Me: We're still on for tonight, right?

Mia: Absolutely not. *smiley face* In fact, I haven't thought about it one single time this weekend.

Me: Me, either. I'll text the location. Hoping to find something near my new job.

Mia: New job? Congratulations! That's cause for celebration. I expect a full report over dinner. They're lucky to have you. Wish I had someone like you on my team right now.

Me: You do. I'm on your team.

Mia: Same here.

Me: Wish we could play hookie.

Mia: *sad face* It's your first day, a big day. And I've got to save my job.

Me: You'll do it! Give out some ornaments. It worked for me.

Mia: Can't wait until tonight. Gotta zoom.

And just like that, she did what I thought impossible: eased my mind. I'm a stranger venturing into the foreign land of Hart Enterprises. I don't know how I'll be received, especially given my mission. But I've got to do this. I'm almost out of money. Since solving my mother's mortgage problem, my financial future depends on it.

· · ·

Headquartered a stone's throw from DC's bohemian scene, Hart Enterprises features a grand lobby that intimidates, overwhelms, and calms all at once. The marble floors and palatial glass windows echo the trickling water coming from the fountain. I breeze by guests, dismiss the sidebar lobby chatter to focus on the drizzle and drip that relaxes my nervousness.

A buttoned-up receptionist with a tight hair bun greets me as I approach, welcoming me as I scan commissioned portraits of the Harts illustrious founder, his kids, and two Sweets, Brian Sweet and his heir apparent, Tessa. The newspaper fodder doesn't do justice to their distinctiveness.

As she looks at me, the receptionist dons a warm smile and kind eyes, even if they're on the hungry side. She's serving me a look that says if she had a knife and fork, I'd be the first, second, and third courses of her three-course meal. "Good morning!"

My tone's upbeat. "It's my first day, and I was told I need to stop here and get a badge and an escort?"

"I'll be happy *to take care of you*" is what her lips say.

I hear, *I'll eat you.*

"What's your name?"

"Nixon...Nixon McCloud."

She scans the screen as her fingers scurry across the keyboard. Then she comes to a halt. "Oh, here you are," she says. Her tone takes an abrupt shift from sweet to brusque with a heavy dose of side-eye. "So," she barks. "You...you're working for Ms. Renee and Ms. Regina?"

I nod hesitantly.

Before my eyes, the bloom falls entirely off the rose. The warmth she once exuded transforms into a deep frost.

I've received warning sign number one. I'm not even looking at the Santas.

"Yes. I'll have their receptionist come down to pick you up shortly. I'm busy. She'll set you up with a new badge and temporary Wi-Fi passwords."

Talk about a change of heart. Thirty seconds before she finds out who I'm working for, she volunteers to escort me, and now she's yanked the offer from the table like an old wig.

"Thank you." I have questions, but I don't ask. Renee's and Regina's reputations clearly suffer in the translation. Unfortunately, we all speak plain English.

I'd more than suspected their shady operations after last Friday's meeting, but now I question whether I've gotten myself trapped in a web from which I can't escape without going broke.

A phone ring jars me out of my thoughts. The formerly friendly receptionist picks up and soon shuttles me to a back elevator, expresses me up to the C-suites, and, as the door opens, my new bosses greet me—both of them.

Besides their haircuts and night-and-day pant versus skirt suits, it's hard to tell them apart. Two sides of the same coin.

A dark, ominous cloud seems to follow me, and I sense something wrong, very wrong, but I smile, trying to keep my expression as upbeat as possible. "Good morning."

"Well, well, well. Aren't you looking cheerful this morning?"

They wait for me to exit and then lead me to the executive suite area. "Hey, it's the start of the season. Plus, I'm excited about the new opportunity," I say

"Great attitude. Keep it," Regina says. "You'll need it for your first assignment with Hart. Let's go to the office and discuss." She glances at her watch. "We're pushing it, running out of time."

"I'm excited about this new opportunity and to find out what's in store." Stone cold lie. The closer I get to finding out the details, the more I question my fortitude...and sanity.

"You'll be working against...I mean, with someone from the happiest place on Earth," Renee says in a droll tone. Then she adds, "Hart Cards."

"Let's go and talk over the next steps," Regina says as she glances at her watch.

I follow them inside the executive suite. They allow me to enter first and give me the once-over, like a Grade A chicken inspection, making sure I'm up to the task, I presume. I want to tell them I'm an executive, not a gigolo. If I even get the hint that this is that kind of party, I'm out.' Until then, I play the game.

The truth is I'm only aware of some of what the assignment entails, but it's clear I'm about to find out the rest.

We enter the office, and I take a seat. "So...about your assignment."

"You've been a bit mysterious about what you need me to do. I can't help but be a little curious."

"You're not nervous, are you?"

I shook off her question with a shrug. "I'm never nervous, not when I know exactly what I'm doing?"

"Good because your assignment isn't a what...it's a whom."

"I'm sorry, what?" My head jerks backward, and my eyes scrunch.

"That didn't come out well. What I mean to say is someone at Hart Cards is leading this year's Christmas line. Your job is to identify that person and disclose the line's details before its delivered to the distributor. Are you still on board?"

My face breaks. She hinted that the assignment would be a challenge—not a person. But I'm here, at Hart, my dream company (if not my dream role). Becoming a creative director is within my grasp. I'm only one task away.

"I see," I begin. "Yes, of course, I'm still in." I don't have a choice.

They balance the conversation between them like a practiced, coordinated team.

"So, we have good and bad news. The bad news is Hart Publishing and Hart Cards are two separate business entities, so we don't have ready access to their information. Operations keeps our systems compartmentalized. The good news is we both leverage shared services, like printing, across both divisions, to save on overhead costs. My brother, Cody, plans this meeting every Monday to address the upcoming schedule. So, today's the day."

"Later, they'll have to discuss the Christmas line, and you'll find out who's leading the Christmas design. They're behind schedule by a few weeks; so, whoever's overseeing the project will have to move very fast."

"Okay," I say, "Well, I'm on it."

"In the meantime, we'll let you take some time to familiarize yourself with your office and settle in before the meeting."

Regina orders her secretary to escort me to the opposite end of the hall, my suite's there. I'm grateful for the distance. Regina's secretary glowers at me as if to say the only reason she marches to orders is that she needs the check.

I focus on collecting supplies and getting my network accesses, and email set up at my desk. By the time I'm finished setting up a password I'll never remember without writing it down, the twins are at my doorstep.

"You ready?" Regina asks.

"Of course."

They lead me to the other side of the building. We reach a conference room where a handful of people busy around. I catch a vague glimpse of Cody Hart, recognizing him from the newspaper articles. He's taller in person. All of my years in the industry, and I've never been this close.

A familiar voice, a woman, calls everyone to take their seats; the meeting's about to commence. I quicken my steps to no avail because the twins chatter in the doorway and block my path. But, the voice—that voice. I've got to know who's speaking.

Finally, I enter the door and survey the room. I see Cody, Tessa, a few women, and a man before the voice's source becomes visible. My knees weaken.

It's Mia.

I can't believe it's her. I see her, but she doesn't notice me, not yet. She's talking to Tessa and Cody. After glancing at the clock to check the time, she finally spins her chair around and notices me—and her eyes nearly bug out of her head.

Then the introductions commence.

"Good afternoon," Regina says. "Everyone we'd like you to meet Nixon McCloud, the new Director of Special Operations. Nixon, this is everyone."

"It's a pleasure to be here," I say, trying to keep from glaring at Mia. "I look forward to meeting you personally and working with everyone."

"If we could go around the table and introduce ourselves?" Renee adds.

They begin with Ms. Tessa Sweet, the Executive Vice President of Hart. Cody Hart, he's the CEO. We continue with key staff before we reach her. Finally.

"Hi, I'm Mia Copeland, the Vice President of Sweet-Hart Cards. I'm serving as the lead for the Sweet-Hart Christmas line, which will consume our resources for the next two weeks as we prepare for Card-Fest and the Winner's ."

Wait, what? I reply in my mind. If I wasn't sitting down, I might have fallen. Mia, the woman of my dreams is my target. To help my mother and keep my job, I'll have to destroy hers.

CHAPTER 12

ia

Today is Monday, and it's already left of ridiculous. The heel broke on my favorite shoe. I've spilled coffee on three shirts because, apparently, I can't find the location of my bottom lip. I put liner on one eye before the tip broke off and fell down the drain. So, I look like I've taken one jab in a heavyweight bout and lost. I vow to switch to pencils; they're much more reliable.

I've failed to step up and be the VP Tessa needs me to be, and my day shows it.

First, instead of this creative new Christmas campaign that I promised Tessa upon my appointment as Sweet-Hart Cards VP, I'll be finalizing the refreshed retread to make my deadline. I spent the weekend stewing over the Christmas line, trying to will a new idea to materialize. My little magic closet escape idea gave me false confidence. I'd hoped to conjure up a concept at least as ingenious as the one Nixon and I used at SoBro's party, ending the practice for all Black Friday's to come.

After Sophie and Tessa helped me decorate the tree and my

house, I spent the rest of the weekend half thinking about Nixon and wishing he'd do the thing he'd apparently refused to do—text me. I half review cryptic emails discussing the new images for the old line while keeping our ideas secret from the mole. Someone in the company may still be divulging proprietary Hart campaigns to Love & Kisses Cards.

The team's pitched several, but they don't strike the right tone for the first Sweet-Hart Line—which is half Keep It Real Cards and half Hart Cards. We need sweet AND snarky, not OR. Unless some miracle happens and I think of something major, I'm screwed.

I'd scrap the entire line this year except for the fact that we need the revenue. Suffering these losses after this mole sent our campaign ideas to Love & Kisses, we can ill-afford to go an entire Christmas season with no holiday line.

Retread or not, this collection will bring in some much-needed revenue, and the minute we submit these files to the printers, we will complete the Card-Fest Party and Winner's Ball preparations. So, we will do what we must until we can do what we want.

Secondly, I've not yet found a Creative Director replacement. I'm beginning to think the skills I have in mind are figments of my imagination.

The only good thing about this day is that it will be over in about ten hours, and Nixon will be there to greet me at the end of it.

I wonder when and if he'll call again as I conduct a hopeless review of resumes. My lack of creativity only compounded my frustration about not hearing from him.

One thing this weekend has taught me is that I love men, but I hate their stupid rules. Women have stupid rules too, but at least most of us have sense enough to ignore them when our emotions whip up us into a frenzy over a new guy. Men march on in blissful ignorance and don't call.

I can't control all the confusion swirling around me, but

there's one problem I can solve right now. Eventually, I give in and text him. I shouldn't, but I do, beginning with a familiar theme.

Me: So, what are you wearing?

We exchange light banter about man-rules until I decide to forgive him. I share two emojis, first a blush. Then I blow a heart-kiss, anxious to repeat what happened in my kitchen on Saturday. He returns the latter.

Nixon: We're still on for tonight, right?

Me: Absolutely not. *smiley face* In fact, I haven't thought about it one single time this weekend.

Nixon: Me, either. I'll text the location. Hoping to find something near my new job.

Me: New job? Congratulations! That's cause for celebration. Expect a full report over dinner. They're lucky to have you. Wish I had someone like you on my team right now.

Nixon: You do. I'm on your team.

Me: Same here.

Nixon: Wish we could play hookie.

Me: *sad face* It's your first day, a big day. And I've got to save my job.

Nixon: You'll do it! Give out some ornaments. It worked for me.

Me: Can't wait until tonight, but gotta zoom.

On my way to work, I grab the briefcase containing my job security, all the files we'll need to send to the printers so we can get the Christmas line on the shelves. It may not be inventive, but we'll take advantage of the season and bump up our profit margins. I'm meeting with my creative team to explain why we're using the old concept and get everyone on board. After enduring a few inevitable smart-aleck comments from the peanut gallery, I'll discuss resourcing with the executives and operations leadership.

The Cruellas, Renee and Regina Hart, the co-Executive Vice

Presidents of Hart's publishing division, will be there jockeying for priority on the printing calendar.

Keeping it real, the twins were Bitter Bettys before Hart Enterprises acquired Keep It Real Cards in a multi-million-dollar deal. They've since grown exponentially worse. The more Cody's true passion—Sweet-Hart Cards —flourishes, the more they seem determined to spark its downfall.

Book and card sales tend to increase this time of the year, so it'll be interesting to see who comes out on top of this argument.

The news of my retread line certainly will come as a relief to the Devilment Twins—and probably even a source of eternal joy for them, making my position that much more precarious.

Tessa and Cody are my friends—outside the office—but it's business in Hart's hallowed halls. If I'm not profitable and pulling my weight, I may not even have the option of returning to my position as Creative Director, especially if I find the replacement. Even worse, what if I end up working for the person that I hire? This made the creative director pick even more critical than I thought.

After changing my blouse for the fifth and final time, I bundle myself up in my coat, hat, and scarf, grab my briefcase, and head into the office. It's going to be a long day, but at the end of it—Nixon will be waiting. Finally, I have someone to lift me up when I'm down, and I'm almost certain to be down.

MY TEXTS WITH NIXON START THE MORNING RIGHT. FOCUSING ON our exchange, I'm not walking into Hart Publishing this morning, I'm gliding in, with a rhythm in my steps, and the grace of a ballerina, as I sing good morning to Mabel, who eyes me suspiciously.

First up is the team meeting; sitting here reminds me of why some animal mothers eat their young. It's to put the little rug rats out of their misery or to prevent them from inflicting suffering on others in the future.

Sitting in front of my team and telling them I'm not good enough to come up with or decide on a new line from the material they've presented over the past two months could only be worse if, right this instant, I was hit by a semi-truck, and then it backed over my mangled corpse...twice. As it is, I won't be eaten or put out of my misery. Not only will I have to endure this mess, but I'm also leading it.

"I know it's cliche to say this, but it's not you; it's me," I begin. "Going with last year's collection is no reflection of the quality of your submissions, which are all sublimely Hart Cards. The problem is we must find a balance between the existing Hart and Keep It Real lines and then combine them to make Sweet-Hard cards. The failure is not yours; it's mine. The fact is, I know Keep It Real Cards better than anyone here except Tessa. I've worked with her literally from the day she conceived the company. My problem is my muses are on a Christmas bender, and the blended concept hasn't materialized."

Zeke stands up and looks over his shoulder before turning to me. "It's disappointing, but I think I can speak for all of us when I say that we understand. We've been blocked. We realize we can't summon your muses on your behalf, but I'm sure many of us are wondering how this will impact our performance reviews."

"It won't. This is on my shoulders, not yours. I've made certain that Cody and Tessa understand you've done your jobs. But turning in a campaign was more critical to sales than submitting a new one. Our profit margin impacts end-of-year bonuses, so submitting nothing's not an option. Therefore, we'll reuse our concepts from both Hart and Keep It Real, keep them separate, and live to innovate another day."

Folks around the table nod. No one looks particularly unhappy, but they don't look happy, either. I can relate.

"Today, I'll meet with leadership to discuss the printing

schedule, but we're down to six days, so the earlier, the better. That way, we can prepare for the Christmas Card-Fest submission, the big Christmas Party, tree lighting, and winner's ball—at least if Love & Kisses wins this year, they won't beat us with our campaign." I tap the briefcase. "I can't wait to put this one behind us."

Destiny asks, "So will there be any changes to our work schedule?"

"We'll be working some overtime to prepare for the submission, and then we can enjoy the holidays. Let's just dig in for now."

A choir of groans sounds before I release everyone to return to work. I'm carrying the briefcase, keeping it with me no matter where I go. The mole will not defeat us.

The meeting's gone a little longer than I expected. I glance at my watch. It's about time for the executive session with Hart Publishing. I head toward the conference room and run into Tessa on the way.

"So, have you heard the news?" she asks. Whatever the update is, she's apprehensive. Her forehead's tensed, seemingly with worry.

I shake my head and tighten my fingers around the briefcase handle. Tessa doesn't look like she's about to deliver any good news.

"The Devilment twins have hired a new stooge." Her eyebrows arch and lips pinch.

"Voluntarily? Doing what?" I ask, immediately wondering what kind of nightmare human being would work for them.

"Director of Special Projects," she says.

"Special projects?" I repeat. "Hmph. Maybe we could check out the resume. It'd be a coup if we could sign them to work as oue creative director."

She and I both chuckle.

"Who is it?"

"Don't ask me the identity or what the job entails. I have no idea," she says. "But what I don't know is how anyone could work for them? Especially now, after the war in the papers? Make no mistake about it; they're up to no good. A scoundrel. Keep a close eye on them, that's all I'm trying to say."

"Message received. Loud and clear."

"When have they ever hired anyone with useful experience? Rarely ever. You only need to ask Cody. And everyone with an ounce of talent and integrity ends up quitting."

"Useless or resigned. That's a pitiful combination."

"I know I don't have to remind you, but your most important mission is to protect the Christmas line. It's no coincidence that Hart Card lines have been leaked and later published by Love & Kisses cards. This year, more than any other, we've got to keep our proprietary secrets, secret. This is Sweet-Hart's inaugural Christmas line. Who knows if we'll ever pick up steam if we're not successful this season, right?"

"Well? I can't lie; it's not the innovative, fresh and economical collection I hoped to deliver, but it's good, it will sell, and it'll get us past Christmas Card-Fest. We'll be in great shape come Valentine's Day. Absolutely. You can bank on that."

We turn the corner into a long stretch of hall and enter the meeting room at the end. I take my seat in a chair opposite the door. Renee and Regina usually sit near the exit because apparently, their brooms can't breach the force-field of positivity. I tend to keep plenty of distance in case there's a threat that the evil rubs off. I dip under the table to situate my briefcase next to me, and when I sit up, my eyes bulge out of my head.

It's Nixon. My Nixon.

I'd rub my eyes in disbelief, but I'd spend the rest of the meeting looking like Rocket the Racoon.

What the heck is he doing here?

I'm confused by his presence and can't connect a single dot that lands him here. His wide eyes and obvious attempts to avoid looking directly at me suggest he's as shocked to see me.

Not five seconds after he enters, Renee and Regina follow,

and they all find spaces to sit right next to one another. How cozy. He's sandwiched between them like fresh prosciutto and mozzarella between two pieces of moldy Wonder bread. The scene begins to unfold. He's with them, on their side, and my mind can't execute the mental gymnastics necessary to understand how this happened.

One thing I'm sure of, he's not been deceived into siding with the wrong team. Anyone with half a brain can read a headline. What the twins have been trying to do to Hart Enterprises has been plastered all over the news for years. No, he's a smart man. He's willingly accepted a job with the witches, so who or what does that make him? A flying monkey? And if I, in my soul, believed him to be a good man, an honorable man, then what does that make me?

Wrong. Just when I'd started to believe my instincts were back on track, but it's clear they're off by a mile.

"Before we officially begin this meeting, we'd like to introduce our new Director of Special Projects, Nixon McCloud. Today is his first day."

"Welcome," Tessa says, following Cody. She's painted a smile on her face as fake as Destiny's acrylic nails. "Let's all go around the table and introduce ourselves. We'll start with you, Nixon. I'm sure we'd all love to hear a little bit about your history."

He smiles widely and scans the table, allowing his gaze to linger on me for more than a few seconds before he moves on and begins to talk about his work history. "My most relevant positions were at Signed and Sealed and American Salutations, where I supported art, creative direction, marketing, and brand management. I've also worked for three of the five major New York publishers in various capacities. I'm excited to accept this position with Hart Publishing, and certainly, I look forward to working with all of you."

When he says, "all of you," he looks dead at me. He can just turn his head in the other direction. He and I cannot exist in the same space when he's working for the Devilment Twins.

We complete our trip around the rest of the table, and everyone's been introduced themselves. Now, it's my turn.

"Good morning," I say, trying not to look at him, but my heart's paying no attention to my mind. "My name is Mia Copeland, I'm the new Vice President of Sweet-Hart Cards, and this year I've got the pleasure and responsibility of leading the creative direction for Sweet-Hart's Christmas line," I turn to him. "Sounds as if you and I will be going head to head early and often, vying for printing priority."

Everyone chuckles, but when he hears me announce my position, his eyes bulge a little. I'm sure he's stunned that I technically outrank him.

Then Tessa goes for the jugular. Her words spring from her mouth like a cobra attack, straight with no chaser. "So, Director of Special Projects. Sounds like a new position. Exactly what do you do?"

Translation: We all know your position is make-believe. What in the Devilment Twins are you doing here?

Renee prepares to answer because she's usually in control, but in a move that seems designed to demonstrate he's nobody's puppet, he presses his hand against her arm to hush her (his boss) and then begins to speak. I sit there stunned as I expect Renee or Regina to stand up and fire him on the spot. Instead, they listen.

He hems, haws, and hesitates as he explains. "Among many things, I'll be working with big-name acquisitions and helping to focus on delivering better care and attention to our celebrity authors."

Everyone at the table seems satisfied with his answer. I'm not.

Try as I might, I can't pretend I'm not impressed by his background. I mean, with his killer resume, he should be a creative director, not some "special projects" minion for Renee, which begs the question, why not? If I'd gotten to him first, he'd be announcing his position with Sweet-Hart cards today, not the travesty to humanity that is Hart Publishing under the twins. As it stands, he's working for the enemy, for evil personified. Willingly.

Sure, I like him—liked him. But how could I be so wrong about the character of someone who felt so right? Now we're working in the same building, and I can't get away from him. Oh well, he may work here, but that doesn't mean I have to see him.

"Nixon will be overseeing the printing schedule for the late January and February title, so he'll need to coordinate with Mia," Regina says. Then she goes on to explain his role in helping to organize Hart for the tree lighting, the Card-Fest party with ugly sweater contest, and the Winner's Ball on behalf of the publishing arm.

Tessa and I nod in agreement. Isn't that rich? As much as I'd like to, there'll be no avoiding him or ignoring his presence. How can I do this? How can I forget our time in the closet or the fact that he brought me breakfast? We'll be in each other's faces, at least until I submit the files to the printers. The only way I'll survive this with any semblance of sanity is to finish this project as quickly as possible and move on.

Paying attention for the rest of the meeting becomes a challenge. All I want to do is stand and run, so I can think about how great and wonderful he and I had it for two days. Instead, I wait until the end, and everyone disperses, including Nixon. I'm hoping that he returns to the lair with the twins, and I can return to my office uninterrupted and figure out how I'll spend the rest of my career avoiding the man I thought I'd fallen for.

No sooner than I exit the office and head down the hall, he's there in my face. I've nowhere to run, nowhere to hide. The confrontation's inevitable. We've got to do this sooner or later. Better now than later.

"What are you doing here?" I ask in a loud whisper—the words kind of fall out of my mouth. I'm hoping he doesn't offer some ridiculous and obvious response, but my hopes are quickly dashed.

"I mentioned that I got a new job. I work here," he says. "You do, too, by the way."

By now, I want to punch him in the face. He knew exactly what I meant. I purse my lips and scorn him with my sneer. "Given the current state of our, whatever this is, and the fact that you and I now work together, I think we should call off our dinner for tonight."

"Why? We work in separate divisions. I'm neither subordinate to you nor vice versa," he says—his voice all but cracks.

He actually has the nerve and gall to appear wounded...and to sound affronted. "The only difference between the man you texted this morning and the one standing before you right now is the location of my employment."

"And your supervisors. Let's not forget those."

The halls are busy as people pass us and give us sideways glances. Thankfully, we've been ordered to coordinate with one another, so our interaction doesn't set off alarm bells.

"I understand needing a job and money. What I can't believe is a man of your intelligence has so little discernment that you can't see the character of the people who hired you."

"I can't believe the woman who came up with that brilliant idea in the closet could be so shortsighted and closed-minded. Have you liked every boss you've worked for? Probably not." He had me there. Before Tessa, the answer was quite the opposite. "But you did what you had to do to pay the bills," he continues. "I'm still the same guy who brought you breakfast and washed dishes, and kissed your lips," he whispers. "Don't you owe it to yourself to try?"

He went there. All the way. He's breached the wall, but he's not managed to bring it down.

"Do I, Nixon? Do I really?"

"Listen, I've got to get back to the office. As much as I want to keep seeing you, Mia, I'm not going to beg you. But nothing that happened today changes how I feel for you. Meet me for dinner. I'm still going to text you the location. I'll be waiting for you. If you show up, then I'll know we're going forward. If you don't, I promise I won't bother you again."

He rubs his hand against my arm, which sends a wave of chills through my body; then he turns on his heel and walks away. What can I do except stand there and watch him until he disappears down the hall?

Turning on my heel, I walk in the opposite direction, a fitting move for our end. At first, we were on opposite sides of the same table. Now, we've set off in entirely different directions. As I disappear, I mutter, "Don't hold your breath," as if I'm unaffected.

I'm only lying to myself. As I head back to my office, Tessa's voice calls out to me, and I clench my eyes shut.

"Step into my office," she says. I can hear her excitement to gossip bubbling beneath her calm exterior.

I walk inside, and she closes the door behind me. "So, what did you think of Nixon?" Then she takes a seat.

She wants to dish on Hart drama. I want to bury myself under my desk.

Okay, I should come clean about what's happened between Nixon and me, right? I mean, not only is Tessa my boss and best friend also, but her entire business is at stake if he turns out to be a scoundrel.

"I'm not quite sure what to make of him," I say, it's the truth, just not the whole truth. I try to work up the courage to confess, but the words stop in my throat. Besides, any burgeoning romance between us will all be over by dinner, and I'll have alarmed her for nothing. "He's certainly qualified, which is new and different for the twins."

"True. But I can't help but think there's something more to this situation than meets the eye. You two will have to collaborate while coordinating on the publishing schedule. I need you to keep watch."

"Excuse me? You want me to what?"

"Keep an eye on him," she says. "You've got the best gut

instincts of anyone I know. If he's shady, you'll be the first to catch it."

Ugh. Gut instincts. Depending on mine is what got me into this mess. My gut allowed Nixon into my house...and my heart. Now, she wants me to stick close to the very person I'm trying to avoid. She doesn't know Nixon is "the guy," the one I fawned over this weekend for giving such excellent holiday date. If my gut had a nickel's worth of valuable instinct worth trusting, I wouldn't be in this predicament...nor would I be so conflicted.

What am I gonna do now?

CHAPTER 13

ixon

OF ALL THE PLACES TO WORK IN ALL THE WORLD, I ACCEPTED A JOB at Mia's company. I'm back in my office at my desk and awestruck by what's transpired this morning. Not only is the woman who's turned my life upside-down employed at Hart Enterprises, but she's also well aware that I'm working for Renee and Regina—the bane of Sweet-Hart's existence.

With each moment that passes, the twins' reputations circle deeper and more quickly into the drain and appear to be earned. They're poorly regarded, not just for the way that they behave, but how they treat those around them. Not that they are overtly mean. They are dismissive and elitist, which may be worse.

I'm already second-guessing my decision to work here. I'm not filled with warm and fuzzies about my choice. Yet, I can't help but believe that my mother's financial struggles and this opportunity have intersected for a purpose beyond my under-standing. Everything happens for a reason. Perhaps the truth will become apparent in the days and weeks to come.

Right now, one thing is sure: I couldn't allow my mother to foreclose, and I'm on the verge of destitution. My money is in struggle mode, at least until I figure out my next right move.

I SPEND THE AFTERNOON GETTING SPUN UP ON HART PUBLISHING, researching the intranet to comprehend the lay of this land, and begin preparing my strategy. Then I locate a private restaurant down this street and around the corner from headquarters and reserve an intimate dinner table for two. I glance at my watch and am relieved it's almost time to leave. Just as I begin to shift down from overdrive, who should appear in my office doorway?

"Sorry for being neglectful today after the meeting," Regina says. "We've got a lot of work on our plates going into the Christmas season. How's everything going? You doing okay?"

I nod. "All is well. I've just been getting myself up to speed on operations, current projects, and such."

She walks inside, shuts the door behind her, and takes a seat. "Good. You'll need a solid understanding when dealing with Mia. She's a tough nut to crack, but I'm sure that if anyone is up to the task, you are. What's your next step? Do you have a plan?"

I smile and nod before replying, "I'm using today and tomorrow morning to really get up to speed on company operations. That way, when I sit down with Mia, my presence won't strike her as suspicious. She's cautious and maybe even a little skeptical when it comes to unfamiliar faces."

"She is. Understandably so. She's lost two campaigns to Love & Kisses in as many years, so she's justified in being guarded. Getting the details on the Christmas line won't be an easy feat. You will have to gain her trust very quickly, or she'll never let you get close enough to get what you need."

"Any ideas?" I ask. She may not know Mia as well as I do, but she does know her professionally.

She shrugs and stands to leave. "That's what we hired you to figure out. Do whatever you need to do as quickly as possible. Personally, I don't need to see how the sausage is made. It just needs to be cooked and sitting next to my eggs when I'm ready for breakfast. You understand me?"

"Loud and clear," I say as she departs and closes the door behind her. Then I mutter again, "Loud and clear."

I want to gain Mia's trust but not to ease my betrayal. I begin to question whether I can separate my heart from my mission and accomplish the job I need to finish to stay solvent. My bank account is empty, but my path may cost me my heart.

WITHIN THE HOUR, I ARRIVE AT THE RESTAURANT. THE CLASSIEST, most Christmassy spot I can find. I picked it from the web for the tall decorated Douglass fir, the garland, and white lights, and live holiday music to keep her in the spirit. The ambiance is soothing; it'll help calm an angry soul, but I paid for a private dining area in case it proves ineffective in the calming area. Thanks to my reservation, the maître de seats me promptly, but I slide him an extra tip to ensure he greets Mia by name and escorts her to me. I want her to know she's special to me and hold this debate in isolation. The last thing either of us needs is for the twins to spot us.

The mahogany wood stands in perfect contrast to the soft yellow walls. For our viewing pleasure, a rainbow of shapes comprise the abstract contemporary jazz art peppering the restaurant.

If this ambiance doesn't take her mind off of our game-changing troubles, nothing will.

I hope she likes it here as much as I do.

My server returns, and I order a double scotch neat, my tall glass of calm. I'm too excited, too nervous, too anxious, and ill-prepared for this conversation, which I predict is headed south before we even get started. After hanging my coat on the nearby rack, my drink arrives, and I sip and wait. Sip and wait.

❄

ALMOST TWO HOURS AND THREE EMPTY GLASSES LATER, I'M READY to give up. She's not coming. What started as wonderful could've been the dream of a lifetime. Now it's been snuffed out before we truly began. I plan to lick my wounds when I get home. For now, I'll order a meal to go and chow down at the house, just me, my humiliation, and I.

As I wave over the waiter for the final time, he freezes and turns toward the door, then shifts back to me, holding up his index finger. My forehead scrunches in confusion as a curvy silhouette glides in from a distance.

It's Mia.

At last, she's arrived, and she comes thoroughly irritated. I'm as happy now as I will be when the alcohol wears off. She shortens her stride as she approaches the table, and I stand to greet her.

"You look beautiful." The alcohol lubricates the words that might otherwise stick in my throat.

"Really?" She gives herself the once over. "It's the same thing I wore to the office."

"You looked beautiful then, too." I ease over and pull out a seat. "Please join me and let me help you with your coat." I remove and hang it on a nearby hook before sliding back to push in her chair and then filling in my own.

"A gentleman to the end," she says. I hear more warmth than sarcasm to my relief.

"The end. I hope that's not your plan."

She inhales deeply and locks her eyes on mine. "I wasn't going to come."

"I know." I lean forward and reach out for her hand. She reciprocates the gesture at first, placing her hands inside and gripping mine. Then she lets it go and returns my hand to the table. She's withdrawn, but she hasn't walked away. I'm disappointed but hopeful.

The waiter approaches again, and I ask her, "Would you like a drink?"

"Wine, please," she says. "A Pinot Noir would be nice."

I mouth the words to the waiter, who nods, and then I ask Mia to continue.

"Few things hurt worse than when you hurt yourself," Mia begins. "I'll be honest, when we met, aside from our minor conflict over the parking space, I thought well of you. Quite well, in fact. You seemed to be a good man, a really good man."

"I am," I respond.

"Then you delivered breakfast to me and washed the dishes, confirming you've got a kind heart, and keeping it real, you're not a little bit easy on the eyes." she says with a chuckle.

"That feeling is mutual."

"But I've made the mistake of trusting my instincts before, and my miscalculations only result in heartbreak and depression. When all is said and done, no one ends up crying except me. I just got out of a relationship with someone who deeply disappointed me with a full serving of despair and humiliation. I believed him trustworthy, and he let me down in the worst way, at a horrid moment. Forgive me if my instinct is to duck and run when I see the potential for that to happen again."

"He's not me, Mia. I'm a different man. I may not always be the man you hope for," I say. "but every day, I'm striving to become him. Meeting you is making me want to become him. Doesn't that count for something?"

Her hardened expression softens, but she doesn't give in to me. Not yet.

"I'm not asking you to let down your guard completely, Mia. By all means, protect yourself, but give us a chance. Allow me the privilege of chipping away at the wall with truth and honesty, so someday I can share the space with you. We can take it one day at a time. What do you say?"

"I say...I say..." Her eyes bulge open as if she's shocked or surprised.

Was it something I said? I'm not sure whether to register the expression as good or bad until she grabs my hand, the one she only minutes ago refused.

She's whispering, "Sit..." *something something something.* I can't hear what she's saying, so I lean closer.

"Sit next to me, please." Her voice is clear now. I still don't understand the reason for her abrupt reversal, but I shift modes on the fly and do as she asks. Now is as good a time as any to begin proving myself. I stand up and move my seat directly adjacent to hers. I fall into the role she wants me to play. Had I known she'd agree with it, I would've sat next to her when she first arrived.

Then I grab both of her hands and press them together inside mine. "Is everything okay?"

"My ex. He's here. Right now," she whispers. "Over there...by the window. Don't look."

I start to turn my head, but she presses her hand against my cheek to prevent me.

"Why is it every time you tell someone not to look, they look?"

I laugh hard, more than the comment deserved, and whisper, "I'm reminding him of how funny and engaging you are."

She looks adoringly into my eyes as if she means every ounce of what she's pretending to feel. We may be playing make-believe in her world, but the moment couldn't feel more real in mine. I adore her, so I allow my gaze to linger...until she breaks the trance with her next words, "Uh-oh! He's coming this way."

Before I can speak or react, her lips are plastered on mine in a kiss. At first, it's forced, and then it slips into a sweet fantasy. Her mouth, soft and sweet, dances with mine in a gentle grind that sends my heart swinging and pulse racing. Instinct causes my hand to release hers and find her cheek. I caress it with a tender touch, and the more authentic her acting seems, the more I want her to understand what she's doing hits me in every right way. I want her. I want this. I want us.

After a minute passes in the span of an eternity, our lips part slowly, and my expression feels as hers seems. We're both awestruck. She doesn't take her eyes off of me. Instead, she stares at me as if she's emotionally moved in some way; she's surprised by what has transpired. To me, we've shared more than a kiss. So much more.

She clears her throat with an *ahem*, casts a glance back over her shoulder to scan the restaurant. Then she leans back in her seat as I retreat to my space across from her. My mind is on what just happened. Her mind is somewhere else.

"I'm, uh...looks like the coast is clear. I got carried away."

Let's be clear. I never glimpsed the boyfriend. At this moment, I can't point him out in a line-up. The only thing I can verify to anyone about what happened is Mia kisses the way I've imagined since the moment we met.

"Not nearly far enough," I reply, adding a nod. If we part and she's unwilling to give us a chance. I want my hopes to haunt her.

"Man, I want to believe you," she mutters in a volume, not meant for me to decipher.

"Stay for dinner?" I ask. "Then maybe you can explain to me what just happened here?" She can't possibly believe I'm going to let her off the hook this easily.

"Umm, yes. You deserve an answer, and under any other circumstances, I'd offer you one. I'd gift you with much more than my phone number and a Christmas ornament but—Regina and Renee?" She shakes her head. "I can't wrap my head around that one."

"Mia. You can trust yourself...you can trust me." She's already grabbed her coat and is heading toward the door. I catch her and trail on her heels.

She turns to me as she skitters toward the door. "Thank you for helping me with my ex...situation. Truly," she says.

In the wisp of a blink, she's gone, and I'm confused. Her eyes say she no longer wants anything to do with me, but her voice says she wants to try. I can't press her as much as I'd like. If she tells me to back off, I've got to honor her wishes.

Before I can finish my thoughts, the waiter returns, and glances at the empty seat. "Dinner for one?" he asks.

I nod. "Yes, I'll take the special."

Another one bites the dust. Months ago, Tami...and now Mia. For some reason, this one stings—a lot.

ia

Okay, the dinner interlude with Nixon was supposed to be quick, decisive, and leave no doubt that I'd snuff out any spark between us, according to Tessa's mission for me.

That didn't happen.

Instead of meeting Nixon and telling him that I thought we shouldn't see one another anymore, at least not outside the office, somehow, my lips landed on his...in the middle of a restaurant. Talk about screwing up the plan.

Courtesy of Dustin Wright. I blame him.

It's all his fault...mostly.

Of all the restaurants in the world, he shows up where I'm supposed to be nixing Nixon. Perhaps I shouldn't be surprised— but I am. Sure, he's a creative director consultant at Smythe and Starks, headquartered directly across the street, at least he was a few weeks ago. Word on the street is he's been snapped up by some major firm.

When Nixon texts me with the dining details, I recognize the location. Once upon a time, Dustin and I called it "our spot." Anyway, for that reason, I never expected to see Dustin's face, not after the humiliating breakup. I assumed he'd never have enough nerve to show his smug, fat, arrogant face there, which is why I accepted Nixon's invite.

Then he appears, like Satan himself, chilling with his boys from the office. All of them were dateless. Not me. Heehee. For the guy who broke up with me in a manner that Tyler Perry couldn't write, the optics couldn't be more perfect. Another man's lips on mine. *Mhm. Mhm. Mhm. Sweet. Sweet. Sweet.*

Oh, that kiss!

I'll rewind that moment in my mind over and over again.

I can't even lie. My toes curled back so far; you'd have thought a house fell on me like a witch in *The Wizard of Oz*. I keep trying to convince myself that Nixon and I shouldn't date one another, not anymore. My gut instincts about him being good...about him being "the one" are wrong, aren't they?

Even if I'm right about him, trusting my instincts and hoping he's good means risking my job, Hart Enterprises, and Sweet-Hart Cards, not to mention my heart. My mind, which is winning the argument in a photo-finish, screams that I should run as fast as my size eights will carry me.

The truth is, I miss having someone special in my life, a "my guy" who rings my phone first thing in the morning because I'm his first thought when he wakes. I long for those three a.m. phone calls that drift on and on because we're lost in discovering each other, and all we want to do is talk. I want to be enveloped in strong arms, sip spiked hot cocoa in front of the fire, and listen to Stevie Wonder sing about Christmas somedays and what the holidays mean to us. I want slow walks in falling snow, window shopping for perfect gifts on sleepy Georgetown weekends.

I want to dream with someone. I want to love with someone. And no matter how much I resist it, from the very first moment I laid eyes on him, I've wanted that someone to be Nixon McCloud.

The more I think about him, about the life we could share, the less I'm able to convince myself he's not worth the risk.

So as much as I want to, I can't talk myself out of Nixon.

My mind may be listening to arguments opposing our "relationship," but my heart is giving me "the hand." When moments of confusion arise, there are only two things to do—drink a shot of vodka and sleep on it. By morning, I'm sure the answer will be much clearer.

I AWAKEN WITH BLURRED VISION, BUT MY CHOICE IS CLEAR—I STILL want Nixon. He's my first thought when I awaken.

Nothing has changed, not my feelings, not my desire, and certainly not my heart. As I stare at my phone, I'm willing it to ring and hoping he's on the other line. He's the first person I want to talk to…but he's not the first person that calls. No, the first voice I hear belongs to a familiar friend.

"So…I heard there was a dinner?" Sophie asks.

"Yes…and I called it off. Not dinner…the beginning of whatever we'd started. He's great, wonderful even, but he works for Renee and Regina…willingly and without medication. Something's wrong there."

"Okay, I think you're wrong. I mean, wouldn't it be nice to have a plus-one for all the Christmas kick-off events this week? Nixon's amazing," Sophie says. "But, okay, let's say you're right, and he's up to no good. Wouldn't it be better to figure that out before he inflicts any real damage on you or the company?"

"You've got a good point there," I say.

"It's been known to happen."

"Listen, I'm gonna need to call you back."

"What are you going to do?"

"I'm in an impossible situation. As I see it, there's only one thing I can do."

I grab my phone and begin to tap my fingers on the keys.

They instinctively seem to know what I want to say even though my mind doesn't. I want him to know I'm thinking of him, and I hope he's thinking of me. I send up a signal, otherwise known as a text.

Me to Nixon: What are you wearing?

There's a pause that feels like forever. I wait for a sign and receive one.

Okay, it's a text—same diff.

Nixon: A smile. It's a big one. I'm so glad to hear from you.

I breathe a sigh of relief.

Me: About yesterday...

Nixon: No need to explain. You had me at "What are you wearing?"

After a hearty laugh, I wonder how in the world I could even consider letting him go, not dating him.

Me: I'm in such a difficult position, but I can't deny that I kind of like you.

Nixon: Kind of. :) Okay, fine. I like you.

Me: I like you a lot.

Nixon: I've written the same text twenty times. Trying to give you space to think. Glad you didn't wait long.

Me: One caveat. Given our work situation. I think we need to keep this on the hush.

Nixon: ???

Me: Just until we're sure where this is going.

He doesn't answer immediately. Part of me is nervous about how he's going to react to "my proposition," but, as I now assess our predicament, it's the only way we can move forward without causing upheaval and disruption at work. Already I'm risking my job, any modicum of respect I've earned, and Tessa's trust in me.

Yet, my heart says, follow my gut. It's telling me to hold onto him, not to let where we're employed interfere with a relationship that can be pretty amazing...terrific, and I'm following the command.

On the other hand, my mind says, not so fast. Stay on guard. Monitor him like a bad heart. If he's my next Mr. Right, keep him close; if he's an enemy, keep him closer.

Nixon: I'm not opposed to keeping us quiet, but you're not dating someone else, are you?

Me: I understand why you ask, but no. I promise.

Nixon: Church and state.

Me: Work-life and life-life. You can pray everywhere.

Nixon: Okay, fine, but we go fifty-fifty. I'll agree, but only if you give a deadline.

Me: Hmm. Let's say off-the-clock, we do what we want. On the clock, business is business. We "come out" at Card-Fest. The tree lighting. Twin ugly sweaters and all.

Nixon: Complicated, but I'm down.

Me: Good. And for my next trick...

Nixon: ???

Me: Date! Meet me at the corner of First and H Northeast. 6 pm tonight. Be there or be square.

Nixon: It's on. See you then.

It's official. We're treading cautiously in the shallow end. It's hard to contain my excitement, so I happy-dance. For the first time since Dustin, I'm paired. I'm half of a whole, at least we're committed. I'm floating and flying high on the wings of something. It's not that Jeffrey Osborne love, not yet. I'd characterize it as more of an intensifying like and affection.

Suited up and equipped with a smile and a candidate resume for the Creative Director, I'm eager to begin and end the day. Nixon is in for the Christmas surprise of his life. Now, I'm off, dressed in a navy pantsuit with my hair tamed into a standard business bun, heading into the office to conduct an interview. I hope I've identified the winner.

The search has been exhausting, but this resume couldn't be more perfect if I'd written it myself. With a gender-neutral name —A.M. Wong— I can't tell whether the person I'm meeting is a she or he. Tessa and Mabel coordinated directly with the candidate.

I don't care as long as they're competent. Since A.M. Wong survived Tessa's scrutiny, I get the distinct pleasure of conducting the interview and submitting my final decision.

By the time I'm in my seat, Tessa's at my door. "Good morning! You prepared for your interview this morning?"

I spin and smile. "Lord, yes. This search has gone on for far too long. All I want to do is submit this year's Christmas line and enter Christmas Card-Fest for our audience seats at the Winner's Ball. Then we can focus on Valentine's Day and get a head start on next year's line."

"Ah, yes. The reason I'm here to chat. We all know your secret identity is Superwoman, but don't burn yourself out. I'd like you to enjoy the holidays, not just survive them."

"From your mouth to God's ears."

"Right now, our candidate is between consulting jobs. This could represent a bridge opportunity or a permanent opportunity for him, depending on how this project proceeds."

So, she's selected a man. Right now, we're top-heavy on women, at least on the Sweet-Hart side. Infusing the team with a little more testosterone could help jolt our creative juices. I know one thing, if he's handsome, all the women will show up early and dress better.

At the sound of approaching footsteps, Tessa leans backward across the threshold, smiles, and waves. "Ah, here he is now." She leans toward me and whispers. "Fair warning, it's someone we both know."

My eyebrows scrunch. Unfair warning. She waits to tell me now? My memory might experience an occasional gap in long-term retention every now and again, but I'm positive I've never met anyone named A.M. Wong.

She steps outside my office and extends a welcome greeting: The voice sounds eerily familiar, with eerily being the operative word. Then she says, "Mia's waiting for you. Please, go right in."

After a few muffled steps, a well-known form fills my doorway.

Dustin Wright. No one so irritating or ruthless should be that fine. I struggle to center myself and catch my breath for a moment. I couldn't be more flustered if Santa Claus showed up smoking medical marijuana, reading Jet magazine.

"What the hell are you doing here?" I say, before mumbling, *no pun intended*.

"Mia, I'm surprised at you. That's no way to greet an old friend...or a new employee." Like a ball of lime green slime, he slinks over to my guest chair, a place he won't be for long, and takes a seat.

I always thought that if Satan appeared before me, he'd arrive in a hail of fire and smoke, a Cuban cigar, red skin, black horns, and a menacing sneer.

I never thought he'd show up wearing the greyish blue Prada suit (that I bought him), spit-shined shoes, and a Clorox-bright toothy crap-eating grin. His eyes are so deep and chestnut brown, I'm immediately transported to the Appalachian Mountains.

Yet, here he is—the devil in the flesh. Thank goodness I'm expecting someone else.

"Well, at least I know you won't be staying for long. We both know you've got commitment issues. Thirty seconds, which is all I can endure of you, should well-exceed your limits. I'm waiting for Mr. Wong, but it's nice of you to stop by. Please, see your way out."

"I'm Mr. Wong,"

My head jerks back.

"Am Wong. As in I am wrong? " he says. "I thought for sure you'd figure out the clue once you reviewed the resume."

"A mystery. I'm not surprised at all. We both know you're a better game specialist than me. I've never been one for playing around," I say. "Well, it's been real. Thanks for stopping by."

"I can't go."

"Says who?"

"Tessa. She requested my presence as a creative director, not your man. Besides, you may not want me here, but you need me here. I want to help...with the Christmas line," he says. "Whether you like it or not, I'm one of the best in the business. I've not only got the skills required to help you get your line submitted on time; no one hired off the street knows Hart the way I do."

"Is that right?"

"Of course, as you well know. You're a smart woman with a better business sense than most people I know, including me."

"Was that a compliment? I'm so accustomed to soul-crushing demoralization in your presence; I'm not quite certain how to assess this discussion."

A repressed huff locked his jaws, but he choked it down and continued to respond. "The fact is, you're not going to find anyone more qualified than I am, at least no one available. The market won't heat up until the spring. No one well-qualified quits during the holidays."

I hate him and what he's saying, mostly because he's right. He's worked for Hart marketing, albeit a few years ago, so he knows the business and understands the personalities. His departure was abrupt following Regina's rise to the helm of Hart Publishing, which might be about the only thing that speaks in his favor. By my calculation, resigning was the only thing he's ever done that reflects well on his crappy character. His subsequent nosedive was steep and swift.

A promotion at a local PR firm— and he never looked back. He also never stayed in any position for more than a year, which is why he now consults.

We met during a wayward lunch break at the swanky restaurant directly across the street from his new company. Tessa's executive secretary, Mabel, introduced us. We'd only just begun to build Keep It Real from the ground up, and my job and my status were too small for him. He wanted to be the better half of a power couple, and he got his wish in Penelope Paul. She's the woman he openly dated barely a week after breaking off our relationship...in front of 20,000 people at a Wizard's home game.

My heart told me he was the best thing that could ever happen to me. He was smart. Ambitious. I could appreciate that characteristic in him, a bit of a workaholic, because he very much mirrored me. Our similarities begin and end there. In time, I would peel back his complex layers to reveal a self-absorbed, inconsiderate, arrogant boob who was too cunning and manipulative to commit to any person of reason.

Now, I'm expected to employ him? Trust him? I suppose my new position as Vice President makes me worthy, something he's never been or could be, title or no title.

Regardless of his personal motives, I'm a woman with a job to do, and despite my reservations, he's an option I must consider as a means to a speedy end to this Christmas line dilemma. I consider even a slight revision to the copy a complex task, but we also need a slate of new images for the campaign. Zeke is good, phenomenal even, but he can't execute the vision alone and in time. With me juggling numbers and trying to prepare for Christmas Card-Fest, I need help. A lot of it. I'll recover from the "L" after turning in the Christmas line.

"So? What do you think?"

"I'm out of thoughts. Full of questions. Namely, why are you really here? I mean, really?"

"Truthfully?"

"That would be so unlike you...refreshing."

"I made a mistake with us, okay? The biggest mistake of my life. There's no way I can turn back the clock or recover what we shared. I let you down in the worst way."

"Don't forget, in the worst place. That's not an insignificant detail."

"Yes. Way and place. The worst."

"The absolute worst. Ever."

"Really? Are you finished?" I nod, and he continues, "The fact is, right now, you need help and I'm in a position to offer assistance. I'll step up to the plate if you let me. I'll get you through this. Will you allow me the chance to do that?"

Inside, I'm giving him the hardest glare known since human existence. Outside, I'm keeping cool. I steeple my fingers together and sit back in my seat. "Maybe it's insanity...or desperation. Or both. But we'll give it a shot...on a trial basis."

He's all teeth and gratitude now, no discernible smugness.

"We'll re-evaluate this arrangement after the holiday," I continue.

"Okay. That's an offer I can't refuse." He stands to shake hands on the bargain. He's making his agreement with an honorable woman, and I'm dealing with the devil.

I'm vexed enough that my anger should burn his fingers, but I give in and return the favor. Hiring this man makes my stomach boil with bile.

One thing is certain, witnessing his remorse, seeing him acknowledge the err of his ways, brings me a comfort I've not known since we split. But my gut check tells me to trust him—but only as far as I can throw him—and I couldn't throw him an inch.

At this moment, the stark difference in my instinctive feelings about Nixon versus Dustin becomes as clear as country air. The question is whether I'm right about either...or neither.

I can't fret about it now—time to leave my doubts on the shelf. I've got my date with Nixon to focus on, and, this time, I'm on a Christmas mission—to deliver a healthy dose of holiday cheer to a soul in need.

CHAPTER 15

ixon

I'M AT THE CORNER OF FIRST AND H IN NORTHEAST. IT'S EVENING, and there's nothing in the air except the white of my breath and the glimmer of holiday cheer. City employees finish their day's work, twisting lighted garland around street lamps as I watch and wait. I turn to see her approaching.

Mia.

I can't stop myself from smiling. She radiates a light that brightens my dark places. I force myself to remain calm.

"There he is!" She greets me with amazement in her voice, as if she didn't expect to see me. "I've got a surprise up my sleeve. A little something-something that is critical to our foundation if we're going to take this thing between us to the next level."

"Okay, I'll bite. What is it?"

"Follow me." She grabs my hand, intertwines her fingers with mine, and we stroll in a direction that is new to me but seems routine to her. For the first time in a long time, it not only begins to look like Christmas but also feels like the season, and she's the reason. Decorations dangle from every post, window, and doorway; lights and wreaths alike are strung along the main thoroughfares. The corners of my mouth and spirits lift with every step.

"So maybe we can walk and talk while we're on the way," she says, filling the silence that previously consisted of only footsteps. "Tell me about yourself. What's your favorite Christmas memory?"

This answer is easy, and the memories surface without effort, a reason why I've avoided engaging in seasonal festivities until this year.

"Without question—the hunt for the tree. My dad would always take me to the lot to select a fresh one. My choice. He never cared how big or small or ugly the thing was. He'd always let me choose it, and every tree I picked, no matter how unsightly, was always the most perfect McCloud family tree in the world. At least he made me feel that way, and trust me, Charlie Brown's tree had nothing on the beauts we took home. Check it out, this one I picked, I dunno, I must've been nine; it was missing limbs and had a gaping hole on one side."

"Oh, no."

"Oh, yes. The absolute ugliest tree on the lot. But I was determined to buy it because I didn't want to abandon a tree in trouble. So, dad bought it, and we lugged the monstrosity home and decorated it. Mom said it was so ugly a dog wouldn't even pee on it."

We both stop in our tracks and fold over with hilarity. Her laugh is like music to me, and her smile is fine art. I want to know the secret to keeping it there.

"But with lights and a train, we made the best of it. Boy, she got so mad she had to look at that thing for two months. I think she served Brussels sprouts until March. I hated them. The better my tree selections became, the fewer Brussels sprouts I ate. Lesson learned."

"What'd you guys do about the hole?"

"I wrapped my stuffed koala bear in tinsel and stuck him inside it. It looked like we had a visitor peeking out of the tree," I say with a chuckle. The memories warm me as a chill wind begins to whip up, and we pass a second block. For the first time in a while, I permit myself to smile as I remember days gone by.

"Your dad sounds amazing. Truly."

"He was...is," I say. "Listen, I don't mean any harm, but it's getting cold out here. I'd much rather be spending time with you by a fire than out here in the cold."

"Don't worry. A warm fire is on the agenda, but we've got an important stop to make first. It's just up here around the corner."

Before we turn the bend, she stops me and tells me to close my eyes, and then guides me a few more steps before she says, "Okay. Now open them."

My eyes open along with my heart. What a few days ago might've left me feeling conflicted an angry now only fills me with joy.

"Winterfest?" I say. I know this because the word "Winterfest" is spelled in a giant arch of white Christmas lights and almost blinds me.

"Yes. Isn't it great?"

MIA

A part of me fears I may be overstepping my bounds, a move that could potentially push Nixon away if I don't play this hand right. One way or another, tomorrow, I have no choice except to get back to work and get this line in shape. Right now, it's time to show him a little of my Christmas crazy.

I drive to H Street, park, and walk to First, and spot him from half a block away as I close the distance.

"Surprise!" I say from behind him. He turns to me and greets me with a half-smile. Despite his presence here, he seems unsure of what to think of what to say."

"I'm here," he says, looking around confused. There's nothing in this area that's noteworthy except the garage and an Ethiopian restaurant, which he points to with a question in his expression.

"No, I've got something much better in my mind, but you've got to trust me. It's a few blocks up the street."

He raises his hands, palms up, in surrender. "I'm here and at your beck and call."

"Just the way I like them," I say, grabbing his hand to lead the way. Uncertain of whether my gesture is welcome, I begin to release him as we get in motion, but he doesn't let go. Instead, he weaves his fingers with mine and clasps my hand snugly but not too tight.

"Where are we going again?"

We talk, and he tells me a Christmas memory. I suppose it's only fate that it centers on trees and his father. By the time the story ends, we're nearly there.

"You'll see, as soon as we turn this corner."

Before we cross the final bend, I ask him to close his eyes. I peer around the corner, and everything is just as I've imagined it would be, the way it is every year. We've arrived at the best part of DC at the most perfect time of the year. Dusk has turned to night, and we're facing a galaxy of twinkly lights.

Now I face him. I've covered his eyes and slowly guide him to the perfect spot. I stop him and say, "Okay. Open your eyes!"

He opens his eyes, and my heart warms at his expression. I realize we're probably at a place where it's tough for him to be, but in my heart, I feel it's the perfect place for him to be.

"Winterfest?" he says, reading the giant lighted sign with bright white twinklies. "Where is this place?"

"Wunder Garten," I reply, pronouncing the "W" with a "V" as I imagine is appropriate for this German-themed oasis in the heart of DC's posh Union Market area. It's like Washington's own gentrified Brooklyn in NoMa, north of Massachusetts Avenue.

"I've never been here before."

"I figured you hadn't. I promise you're gonna love it," I say as we cross the street and prepare to enter. "And if you don't, you'll get the pleasure of me making it up to you. It's a win-win. Besides, there's no better place in the city for German craft beer, chilly cheese dogs, and they've even got a fire with benches where we can make s'mores."

His eyes follow the trail of Christmas lights strung across the fence and light poles with all the curiosity and wonder of a kid visiting Santa for the first time.

"I'm not an easy sell, but I've got to admit, this is pretty amazing, Mia," he says. "Hard to be standing here and not slip into the mood for the season."

"Exactly," I say as I lead him through the archway entrance that looks like a Christmas wreath tunnel; it's lit with multicolored bulbs that increase the sparkle factor. "Full disclosure...one more thing," he says.

"What's that?" I reply.

He leans down and peppers my cheek with feather-light, grateful kisses as we pass through the archway. He may want to take that back when he comes to realize my true motive for this trip.

Now, we're out of the tunnel and inside the gardens. There's a climate-controlled tent, the size of one circus ring to the right, a fire pit surrounded by benches to the left. And directly in the center, all the way in the back.

"A Christmas tree lot?"

He's spotted it. Before he can brook opposition, I attempt to neutralize his arguments.

"Yes. First, it's my treat, and I will not entertain even a hint of opposition." I sound more certain about my chances for success than I feel. "Isn't it great? Best trees in the city. Any dog would be proud to pee on any of these. And, did I mention the tree is my treat?"

"I can't let you—"

"I insist. After all, it's my fault that you need a tree. I gave you an ornament, and you will have no peace if you don't hang it. I'm just saying. I'll be like your mom but serving you dirty looks laced with Brussels sprouts—forever."

He pauses at the moment. "I can almost hear my dad whispering in the wind. Okay," he says. "Looks like I'm getting a tree."

"Of course. Besides, I find men with Christmas trees and train sets to be very sexy...and desirable."

His eyebrow raises.

"More importantly, a portion of every tree sale goes to children toy charities. So, you see? We've got to buy one lest some underprivileged child wakes up without a teddy bear in his stocking. I mean, you don't want to be a Grinch, do you?"

He pauses for a moment that feels like a lifetime. I can almost see his brain churning over the decision.

"Charity, huh?" he says before tightening his grip on my hand in the sweetest way. "Then I guess we'll have to get two. But first, I'm gonna need some beer and chili cheese dogs. I don't know about you, but I'm starved."

The ground is covered with artificial turf so realistic we could curl our bare toes in it. Even in the winter, the gardens and tree lot appear plush and green.

We enter the main tent, the centerpiece of the Wunder Garten, and I gasp with delight at the sight of the ceiling. Curtains of multicolored Christmas lights and decorative balls rain from the rafters as if it's storming Christmas decorations. Rumor says they hang 10,000 ornaments, but it looks more like a million. And if they hung any lower to the ground, you could get lost in them forever.

The tent hosts rows of picnic tables where we sit down to eat after grabbing some food and Mad Elf Holiday Ale. Both of us scarf down our food without much conversation. He has two dogs, and I stick to one. We share a supersized order of fries.

Then we head to the fire pit for s'mores, the dessert before the tree shopping. Plus, I promised him a warm fire.

Once I get him situated, I realize I've forgotten one essential ingredient.

"You want hot cocoa?" I ask. No fire pit visit would be complete without it.

"You want me to get it?" he asks.

I shake my head. "Tonight is my gift to you. All of it."

As I trot off for our hot beverages, I turn back and notice Nixon has drawn a couple of visitors. I don't know who they are, but I'm not surprised. He's attractive, a chick magnet. I know the women are on him like eagles on baby goats. As they see me returning, they scurry off; I resist mentioning them for as long as possible since he doesn't.

After we finish our cocoa, I say, "I noticed you had some admirers earlier. Not that I'm jealous or anything. Just curious."

He clears his throat and smiles. "They weren't admirers. They were looking for the signs directing them to the ladies' room."

"Ah...I see." I ask, "Are you ready for this?"

"As I'll ever be," he replies.

Sick on s'mores, we follow the old-fashioned wooden arrow sign pointing toward the tree lot as if we need it. We can see it, but the nostalgia adds a nice touch. We pass a giant snow globe display guarded by two giant lighted deer. The short trees have twinkly lights. The tall trees do not, probably because they'll be the first to get bought.

We take cautious steps toward our destination. I'm not sure how he'll react since it's been years since he enjoyed this much Christmas in a single outing. He hasn't visited a lot to buy his tree since his father passed.

I pray this is less like scratching the scab off an old wound and more like releasing pain to make way for healing. I'm not sure why I've taken the mantle, but I want him to remember the good his father left behind the way I remember my Christmas crazy mom and my curmudgeon minion dad.

I want him to chill in front of a majestic Douglass fir with the lights off and watch the train circle as the engine *chuggachuggas*.

We're at the tree lot now, and the lights cast a purplish haze along the trees' base. Giant plastic candy canes frame a sign with "The Giving Tree" written in large green letters. If it's cold, I don't feel it. His presence warms me as he scans the decorated trees.

I inhale so deeply my lungs almost burst. It even smells like Christmas. The air is ripe with the scent of pines and firs, and they stand perfectly shaped—fat in the middle and towering over me, if not him. He searches and searches until his eyes lock on what must be a prime candidate. We weave in between the trees until Happy the Elf, or a man dressed like him, steps up to us.

"Can I help you find a tree?" Happy asks while looking at me as if we're co-founders of the Christmas Club. "Oh my. Do I detect a note of Christmas spirit?"

"Oh, no. Not a note," Nixon says. "She's an entire symphony."

I couldn't ask for a more perfect response.

"So now, what are your rules for buying Christmas trees?" Nixon asks me. "I'm sure there must be some Mia standard by which all trees must be selected."

"My only rule for trees is that there are no rules. You should just go with what feels good," I say and then pause. "Actually, I've got one rule. You've got to have fun. But be warned. I can cook the worse pan of Brussels sprouts you've ever eaten in your life."

We agree to split up, select our favorite trees, and then agree to hold a final vote to make the decision. We're on a five-minute timer, and, after a speedy yet exhaustive search, I've settled on one. We return to one another, and both point out our choices.

Nixon grins. "You picked the tallest tree on the lot. I should've known."

I nod. "Of course. And you picked the smallest. Big guys with little trees are like the six-foot-six dudes who walk Chihuahuas. Yes, you can do it, but should you, really? Probably not."

He laughed. "So, how will be we decide?"

"I've got an idea—rock, paper, scissors. Best two out of three. The winner makes the final choice."

On the first try, I'm rock; he's paper—he wins.

On the second try, I'm scissors; he's paper—I win.

"It's time for the last round," he says.

I look at him. He looks at me, and we go for it: Rock, paper, scissors. I stick with scissors to throw him off the scent. He goes from paper to rock.

"I win," he says. Gloats is more like it.

I want to apply some undue influence, so I give him a sad face, the most pitiful I can conjure up.

"Aww...I'm sorry I won," he says with a smile so bright it's got a UV rating. Then he starts singing Queen in a screechy Freddie Mercury, except "I am the Champion" instead.

"Really?" I say with a chuckle. "Fair is fair, I guess."

He takes my hand and leads me toward the scrawny Charlie Brown tree he's picked out and then makes a sharp U-turn toward the one I picked.

"Are you serious?" I say, thoroughly delighted.

"I guess we both win," he replies.

AT HIS POSH PLACE, A MID-RISE WITH A DOORMAN BETWEEN BOUGIE-ville and Georgetown, we squeeze it through the main door. But lugging the monstrosity of nature in and out of the elevator and then into his place proves to be a challenge.

"Good gracious," I say. "If I wanted a workout, I'd have pulled out the struggle yoga DVD. This thing is a beast."

"Hey, this is on you! Why do you think I picked the small one?" Nixon says. "We're almost there.

A few minutes later, we squeeze it through the door and into his house. Before we fall back on the couch, we set it up in an old stand, and he hangs the train ornament I gave him. It looks lonely. No lights except the dimmed recessed one glowing overhead. He turns to me.

"Thank you. I mean, without you, I wouldn't be here."

"Exhausted in a heap in front of a bare Christmas tree?"

"Yes, but in a good way, the best way. I feel like this is the first real Christmas I've celebrated in a long time."

"I'm happy that I inspired you, but we wouldn't be here if you weren't ready."

"Thank you for saving my life, too," he says.

Huh? Was all over my face.

"My mother. I promised her I'd buy myself a tree after I bought her one. Now I won't have to lie."

He leans over and kisses me. I'm no longer in a heap. I'm in a puddle, and I'm not even close to exhausted. If I didn't have to worry about this Christmas line tomorrow, I'd stay in heaven tonight.

CHAPTER 16

ia

I'M HOME FROM TREE SHOPPING, BOUNCING IN THE DOOR LIKE I'M moving on Tigger paws. I couldn't have crafted a better night in a Christmas card. My mind spins like a hamster on a wheel. To be honest, I'd have stayed later if tonight wasn't a school night.

I can't afford to arrive at work in a zombie state. To deal with Dustin and finish this line, I've got to stay alert. He'd like me to believe he's come with honorable motives, and I'd like to join him in that fantasy, but the sound of 20,000 "awwwws" ring through my mind and remind me of who he really is.

I change into pajamas and try to settle down my thoughts to no avail. All I can think about is Nixon's naked Christmas tree. So before I crash, I visit my storage, an attic space too small for anything bigger than ornaments and pull out what I never thought I'd part with—the train ornament collection I created the year my parents died. I'd not considered giving it away, but I hear my mom saying, "What good is it being Christmas crazy if only you can see your insanity? You're not bringing joy to anyone letting your creations languish in the closet."

What good are any of my collections saved over the years past doing anyone really? They're stored in the dark recesses of my home, like monuments to Christmases past, when they should be offering joy to people I care about, people who matter to me, people...like Nixon. I wonder if it's time to gift them, all of them, and allow them to bring others as much happiness in receiving them as I have in making them. After all, I've got enough to open a store.

I dunno.

What I'll do for now, saving one tree from nakedness, will have to fill me with holiday joy. I pack up a few Knick-knacks along with a wad of extra lights and garland and pack them in a spare storage container. These will find their new home sooner than later, especially now that they will be displayed appropriately. Until I make the crucial delivery, I'll dream about my date with Nixon, holding his hand, making s'mores by the fire pit, and playing rock-paper-scissors for the power to pick the Christmas tree.

I'm exhausted and should be in bed asleep, but my mind resists. I replay the evening in my head in endless loops before my cellphone vibrates. It dances across the table, and I stare at it in disbelief. Everyone who means anything to me knows not to call after eight o'clock. It's after ten. That's when I realize it must be someone who doesn't know better. I find the couch, snuggle beneath the Chenille throw, and prop up myself with pillows. Then I grab the phone as if it's a winning lottery ticket.

"Hello?"

"Uh, yes, ma'am. I'd like to order a pizza. A large Mia-lovers, please?"

It's Nixon's voice, and I can almost hear him smile through the phone.

"Excuse me, sir? Did you say meat-lovers?"

"Mia lovers. I said what I said," he responds with a chuckle.

"I should mention this isn't Pizza Hut."

"It's not?" he replies

"Nope," I answer. "Now, what are you wearing?"

"Gratitude cloaked in a smile for creating such a beautiful evening," he answers. "I had so much fun. Now I can't sleep. Too wound up. I never go out on school nights. Look at you, already a bad influence. What are you doing up, by the way?"

"Thinking of you."

"My mind is still in your Christmas clouds, and I'm sitting here looking at my new tree. I can't thank you enough for—"

"Pushing you into buying the biggest tree on the lot? And then donating the one to that family looking at the Charlie Brown tree you really wanted?"

"I wouldn't call it a push, more like a little nudge, a much-needed one. I thought you could join me in a little glass of wine before bedtime. A toast to a wonderful night...and I think it would help us both get a good night's rest."

"Mmm. Good idea. I wish I could join you, but you won't believe this. I'm fresh out of wine. Drank it with the girls when they came over to help me decorate this weekend after you abandoned me."

"Abandoned? That's harsh. But you're wrong about being out of wine. Look outside your door."

"You're here?" I say, hoping he hasn't turned into a full-out stalker. Plus, I'm stripped down from a Rolls Royce to a Hyundai; I'm not dressed for company.

"Of course not," he says to my relief. "But I did have a delivery dropped off at your door about thirty minutes ago. Door Dash. I asked them to leave it near the bushes, so it was tucked away safely."

"You did?"

The biggest smile seizes my lips. I run to the door with the phone still in my hand and spot a wine bag wrapped with a large golden bow. The bottleneck pokes out of the bag, and I read "Pinot." I don't know whether he bought it at random or whether he knows he's picked my favorite...but score for Nixon. I all but skip into the kitchen after kicking the door shut with my feet.

"You're amazing," I put him on speaker and rest my cell on the counter. "Let me pour a glass, and we'll meet on our respective couches in two minutes."

"See you then."

Tessa bought me an electric wine opener two Christmases ago. She says every woman needs one at that critical moment. I've never really understood what she meant until now.

In a blink, I'm back on my couch and snuggled beneath a warm blanket with a satiny sheen that glows from more than the twinkly lights on the tree. After a few sips, the tension releases from my shoulders and my mind relaxes. A few more sips and we've both reached the zone, judging from our increased chattiness. We both begin sharing everything, yet I'm sure we don't share enough—at least I don't. He makes a good start.

"So, you want to know my favorite Christmas memory?" he replies to my question, one I may not have asked if the wine hadn't loosened my tongue a bit.

"I want to know you." I reply, "Everything. Favorite Christmas memory included."

"My crossroads Christmas, I think I must've been about nine. If my dad hadn't done what he did, I might not have turned out to be the man I am today..."

"Wow, what happened?"

"A little snot happened. That's what. Me. I was horrible. I had every gift I could ask for, but, instead, I chose to dwell on the one I didn't get...I don't even remember what I asked for now. That shows you how unimportant and insignificant it was. Anyway, after opening presents, I spent half the morning belly-aching and whining about whatever the thing was my parents didn't give me. Finally, my dad had heard enough; he erupted like a volcano...a maybe once-a-year occurrence, if that."

"He didn't..."

"He sure did. After chewing me out, he packed up every single one of my presents as my mother looked on with more pride than I'd ever seen. He made me get dressed, and we were off."

"Where'd you go?" I'm sitting up in my seat, and my wine glass is empty. The story is gripping.

"To the homeless shelter in DC, where he made me give away every single gift. I mean, he made me pass them over with my own hands."

"Holy moly! You must've been beside yourself."

"That doesn't begin to describe it."

"And you were nine?"

"Yep. I'm not sure how my dad resisted punching me in the face for all the crap I talked from the back seat. But when I saw the kids' faces as I handed the presents over, they lit up. They were so happy, appreciative, so grateful. When I noticed, I stopped being angry and started smiling at them...and soon with them. The moment transformed me. It was then I learned the true power of giving."

"Wow, what an amazing lesson at such a young age."

"That's my dad, though. Those kids had nothing and what I gave them meant everything to them and nothing to me. From then on, I'd always give away half of my Christmas gifts. Voluntarily. I started choosing gifts for other people."

"Wow."

"Mom and I still serve meals every Christmas. Now it's tradition. So, what I once considered my worst Christmas turned out to be not only the best that year but also the best of my life...although, I must say, this one is quickly climbing the charts."

What could I do with that story except smile? He'd not only learned the true meaning of Christmas; he was living it. Every moment with him, talking to him, confirmed I'd made the right decision in giving him a chance.

"So, what about you?" he asks. "What's *your* favorite Christmas memory?"

"I dunno. Yours will be hard to top." I pause to consider the question. "I'd say this one's climbing the charts."

"No fair. That's cheating."

"It's true." I shrug, but he can't see it.

"I don't have a 'meaning of Christmas' story because we had humble beginnings. Tradition always mattered more than gifts because we didn't have a lot of presents. We appreciated everything because we had so little."

"Wow. That's surprising," he says.

"You mean because I seem to have it all together?" I reply. "I'm probably overcompensating for all the things I never got to have as a kid. But each Christmas was special because we always knew we were one unexpected bill or expense from not having anything at all. After my parents died in the accident, I learned that Christmas is a gift and not guaranteed. Each one matters, each one is more precious than the last, especially when you can share the day with the ones you love. I feel even more blessed since they're both gone."

"You're amazing. I've honestly not met many women like you...or any for that matter."

"You mean, poor?"

"No, silly." He chuckles. "Humble, grateful, kind-hearted. You know inherently what most learn the hard way. Christmas is so much bigger than things. It's about the tradition and those whom we share them with, you know?"

I smiled again—this time from the inside. I never would've believed Mr. Fancy Pants thought so deeply or cared so much.

"Wow. Look at the hour," I say. "I don't need to remind you this is a school night. We should probably go to bed."

Then he sings a melodious Christmas tune. His pipes floor me. He belts out *Someday at Christmas* in a tenor that makes the hair on my arm stand on end.

"Now, that's what I call a serenade. What a voice."

"I don't want to hang up," he says.

"So, what are you suggesting...we sleep together?"

"Can we sleep together?"

In bed, in our respective homes, he instructs me to lay my phone on the pillow beside my head and turn on the speaker. Then he sings me to sleep.

The next morning, I awaken in the same position that I drifted off...with a smile on my face.

My phone has disconnected, but a text message sits on my screen.

Nixon: I sang until you snored. Don't worry. You weren't full out calling hogs. It was cuter...and snuffly. See you soon. :)

Snuffly? I don't snore! I mutter before folding into a deep laugh. Then I bounce into action on a natural high. I almost look forward to what the day has in store...until I remember what else awaits me at the office—an unfinished Christmas line and my ex-boyfriend, Dustin.

I'VE SEEN BOATS, BALLOONS AND FEATHERS FLOAT. I'VE EVEN SEEN A root beer float, but I've never actually floated myself, not until today. Sounds of Nixon's singing still echo in my mind as I enter the Hart Publishing lobby.

I feel transparent as if everyone can see straight through me as if I'm exposed to the world. A week ago, I couldn't possibly be further from it. If my smile isn't a give-away, my outfit is; I'm wearing a dress—and a little black one at that. And when I say little, I mean my knees are showing. It's little for someone who spends ninety percent of her office time in pantsuits, a detail that's missed by absolutely no one. I'm eyeballed from the lobby to my office. Tessa can't seem to resist unleashing her curiosity monster on me.

"Well, well, well," she begins, "don't you look spiffy this morning. What's the special occasion?"

I shrug. "Nothing. I'm just wearing clothes. I've been known to show up to work dressed for the office from time to time. Why do you have to make a big deal out of it?"

She's giving me a harsh squint, and she's paying me in full. I try to make tracks to my office, but I'm not fast enough in these cute boots. She catches up to me, follows on my heels, and closes the door once she's inside.

"Mmm-hmmm. Who is he?"

"Who is who?" I say coyly. I'm being facetious; she and I both know exactly what she's talking about.

"Don't play with me. I know enough of your college secrets to embarrass you into your next life. Don't make me unleash the beast."

"You and Sophie with your idle threats."

She and I stare each other down. If I didn't think her serious before, she's scary enough to believe now.

"Okay, fine. I think...maybe I've found someone."

"Whaaaaaat!" she exclaims, bounding into my guest seat. "I thought there was something different about you. You're glowing."

I palm my cheeks. They're warm. "Really?"

She nods. "Do tell. I need more."

"I met him...at the Christmas party."

"Hold up! This isn't closet dude, is he?"

"Yes," I clear my throat and say, "Alex. It turns out he's not nearly as annoying as I thought. He's wonderful. We may, in fact, be dating—officially."

I go onto tell her about tree shopping and the subsequent late-night phone call about everything and nothing. I'm motivated less by my need to share the details and more because I'm reliving and remembering what a special time we spent together.

"He sounds amazing, but you've been awfully secretive about Mr. Mysterious. This Alex guy. Who is it?"

I tighten my lips and puff out my cheeks. "Well?"

"Come with it, Mia. You never keep secrets from me."

After a moment of hemming and hawing, I say, "Okay, I'll tell you, but you've got to promise not to say anything to anyone. Also, I need you to keep an open mind."

"Open mind? He's not half-wolf, is he? Or worse, Dustin."

"No! Of course not. Now promise."

She nods and holds up three fingers in a Girl Scout salute. "Promise. Open mind, and I won't breathe a word."

"Fine...Alex is...Nixon."

"Wai—min," she says, her words run together to the point it's hard to distinguish one from the other. "Nixon. Nixon?"

I nod and smile.

"Why?" she says, sounding genuinely confused.

"Why not?" I say in a voice that's on the border of bark and bite.

"Mia, I can tell you think he's amazing, but you don't need to take my word for it; look at his work history? Google him and see for yourself the pile of dead bodies he's left at every company for which he's worked—I did my research. Maybe you should consider doing the same."

"That's not who he is...maybe it's what he's done in the past, but I know, in my gut, that's not who he is, not anymore."

"Wrong. He's not what he says. He's what he's done."

"He's changed. Trying to be a different man, a better man for himself...and for me."

She huffs. "I hope you're certain about that because there's more on the line than your heart if he turns out to be the man his record has proven him to be. This company will survive Nixon no matter what kind of man he is. The question is—will you?"

"Will I?" I need to do some mental gymnastics to let that slip by for the sake of our friendship. "I understand your concern, but he's changed. You'll see."

"For all of our sakes, I hope you're right."

Just as she sweeps herself out of my guest chair and office, Dustin enters—a one-two punch in the gut. Between Tessa's seeming lack of faith and his face, I don't know which is worse.

"I wanted to let you know we're done with the images. Zeke

had already completed so much work that it only needed a few of my finishing touches."

"Thank you," I say, truly grateful. "In a week loaded with craziness, this is a welcome repose."

"I've been working in the conference room since I started. Maybe you could give me a private tour and show me to my office? I always get turned around."

He's more full of crap than a Christmas turkey. I stand to meet him at the door so that I can escort him out of it. Instead of retreating, he walks toward me. As I'm about to tell him that his office is in the opposite direction, he leans in to kiss me.

My eyeballs bulge out of my head, and I don't know whether to dodge him or activate the vomit reflex. Before I can lean back, I hear a light knock and a voice crawl out from the confusion.

"Uhh, I'm sorry. I should come back later," Nixon says. As quickly as he speaks, he disappears.

I press my hand against Dustin's chest. "If that's the reason you accepted the job here, you wasted your time, and the offer is no longer on the table. This is a place of business, not your little den of sin."

He puts his hands up in a surrender position and backs away from me. "I'm sorry. I stepped over the line. I promise it won't happen again."

"See to it that you never do that again. Ever!" I growl. "Go to the receptionist's desk and speak with Mabel. She'll get you settled in an office and help you set up your systems. You and I will talk tomorrow."

He leaves the room, and I collapse in my seat. I'm going to catch up with Nixon in a minute. My gut is telling me I need to make another call first.

CHAPTER 17

ixon

I<small>F GOOD THINGS NEVER LAST FOR LONG</small>, I <small>SUPPOSE IT STANDS TO</small> reason that amazing things disappear in no time at all. Yesterday, I lost all hope to be with Mia after she learned Renee and Regina hired me to work at Hart Publishing. To make matters worse, Mia glimpsed my "admirers" at the Winter Garden. Except they weren't admirers—they were Renee and Regina, warning me not to associate with Mia outside of work hours and reminding me they hired me to complete a mission. Then they pushed up my deadline.

Her disappointment at learning that truth about me could only be matched by mine when I caught Romeo McPuckerface leaning in to kiss her square on the lips—in her office, no less.

I didn't stick around to witness what happened next. Why would I subject myself to that? So I could replay the moment and relive the nightmare over and over again in my head? No, thanks.

On the other hand, maybe I should've watched. Perhaps, if I

had stayed and allowed my eyes to linger on the misery, I could walk away with no regrets and never look back. I could categorize her as undateable and file her away in a drawer never again to be opened.

Instead, I'm left with a mystery—is she or isn't she "the one"? With my emotions boiling over, I'm confused about what to do next. I'm outside myself right now and can't get a grip on what I'm feeling. This isn't me. I'm the game master; I don't get played.

Yet, she played me.

Wish I could say I quietly returned to my desk, but my attempt to play it cool and hit an unaffected pimp strut sounded more like a three-year-old stomping after a tantrum.

I pace around my office for a minute before I glance at my phone screen. I only wanted her to call me so I could ignore her, but she played me again.

Probably wouldn't.

You know what? I'm done. I'm through thinking about what happened, and I'm done thinking about her.

I decide to give her the silent treatment, and I'm not asking for her reasons or excuses or anything else she chooses to offer.

I turned my focus back to my mission.

The time has come for me to double down. I'll get my hands on the Christmas line and quit this company. Then I'll never have to see Mia, Renee, Regina—none of these conniving women ever again. Carpet tracks from my nervous pacing cease at the office window. I look outside, and the snow is old, brown, and melting. Funny how everything seemed so bright and fresh yesterday, uplifting my spirits. I'm ready to leave for the day and lick my wounds when a voice calls out, "Nick McCloud!"

My reaction isn't immediate, but no one calls me Nick except my fraternity brothers.

"Nick!" A man calls out again.

The sound crawls over my shoulder and jolts me out of my thoughts. It can't be. I excitedly spin around.

"Kyle Anderson?" I say. He's indeed my frat. We attended Georgetown together, although he was a couple of years ahead of me. We exchange dap and the secret handshake. Because I started school when he had nearly finished, I built closer relationships with the younger brothers, but he served as one of my most influential mentors. No doubt, brothers for life.

"Man! I thought that was you! I saw your name on the new employee roster and wondered if that was *a brother* or *my brother*. Glad to find out it's the latter."

We both laugh and take our seats.

"Good to see you, man! This is a nice surprise. How did I not know you worked here?"

Kyle shrugged. "You know how it is, man. We're on adult time now. We get busy with life. You married yet? Wife? Two and a half kids and a dog?"

"No on all counts. I narrowly escaped Tami. We came closer than I'd like to admit, but she wasn't the one. Well, she was 'a' one, but not 'the' right one."

"Same here," Kyle says. "Narrow escape. My job keeps me busy. I lead operations here. I make sure everyone gets equipment connectivity, whatever's necessary to get the job done, so of course, your orientation paperwork came across my desk. Technically, I'm Cody Hart's right hand."

"All right. All right. That's what's up, man. Congratulations."

We exchange small talk and play a quick game of catch up. Parents, deaths, the latest happenings with mutual friends like Brooks and Sophie. It's not long before we circle to the question weighing most on his mind.

"So...Renee and Regina, huh?" he half asks, and half declares. "How did that...happen? I mean, we're boys, man. It's been a minute, but I know you. I can't see you taking a position working for them? What gives?"

"A twist of fate, I suppose. Some might call it that," he says. "Others might call it the Bermuda Triangle. You know...when dangerous, unfortunate things intersect."

Kyle laughs, and I proceed to tell him about my unemployment situation. "Before Hart, I'd been out of work for almost a year. Moms got into a little bit of a financial jam. Pops passed away, so, you know...I did what I had to do."

"Ahhh...say no more. It's up to you."

"Exactly. I guess you can say I'm doing what I have to do until I can do what I want to do."

"Understood. You've got to take care of Moms. Is she still making those cookies? The chocolate ones with the red and green sprinkles? We used to swarm like locusts when your Christmas packages came in."

"Yeah. By junior year she started sending enough for everyone. She's still making them. Gave me a fresh batch a couple of days ago. Now that I know you're here, I'll bring some into the office and let her know you stole mine."

"Oh, man! I'm gonna hold you to it," he says, making a move toward the door. "I've got to head back to my office, but we need to hang out soon. We do holiday happy hours every Wednesday down the street and around the block. I'll make sure you get an invite."

"Sounds like a plan."

"And let me know if you need anything...at all. You know I've got your back."

"Uhhh..."

Kyle stops dead in his tracks and waits for me to continue.

"Maybe there's one thing you can help me with," I say as if my request is a second thought when this is the sole focus of my attention. "Do you...do you know anything about Mia?"

"Mia Copeland? The V-P of Sweet-Hart Cards?"

I nod. "I'm uh...well, you know, Tessa and Cody have asked us to work together on some projects...collaborate." My face must reveal that there's more behind what I'm saying than the words coming out of my mouth.

"Mmm-hmm. Collaborate. I'm with you."

He reacts to an expression that's apparently giving me away

dead to rights. He not only steps back into the door, but he also closes it. "So you want me to tell you more about Mia. Interesting. Out of everyone at the company, I'm surprised you asked about her."

My eyebrows scrunch. "Why do you say that?"

"As I said, it's been a minute, but you've always had...shall we say...a type. Now, don't get me wrong, Mia's great, but she's not *your type* if you get my drift."

"I'm asking for professional reasons."

"Mmm-hmm. Professional."

"Really, Kyle?"

"I'm not sure what you expect me to say. She's private, but she's good people."

Now I'm dishing out the stink-eye like timeouts in a toy store. I'd be affronted if he hadn't spoken the stone-cold truth. Knowing what I'm supposed to do, I should be asking how to access her system so I can retrieve the Christmas files. I would if I had any sense or real fear of Renee's and Regina's deadline. Instead, I'm finding out about her relationship reputation.

"You know what I'm saying, man."

"I'm not sure what you want to hear. She's a nice lady. Quiet. Smart, spunky for days. Not someone you want as an enemy by any stretch of the imagination. You can't ever take her kindness for weakness. It's funny you should mention her name. She called me not even ten minutes ago."

Ten minutes? I'm sitting up board-straight now. That's about the length of time that has passed between me catching her in the act and Kyle showing up in my office. I definitely needed to hear more.

"Mind if I—"

"She asked about network monitoring," he responds before I can get the words out of my mouth. "I guess her boss, Tessa, hired some new cat to help with the Christmas line, and she's not remotely thrilled with him. In fact, I'd go so far as to say she's angry and doesn't trust him, not even a little bit."

"You think?" A smile tries to squeeze its way into my lips, but I press it back.

"Oh, I know without question. Mia's a little bit of a mystery, except when she's angry. And on the rare occasion someone takes her there, she loses her cool with good reason."

Private. That's something new and different. Tami was the opposite of private. She lived and loved in the open because she always wanted to be seen, to be noticed. And focusing my eyes on her never satiated her thirst for attention, for glory. No, her day couldn't be complete unless she received a thousand likes on an Instagram post. She lived out loud. I'm not mad; it just wasn't the way I wanted to exist. I made the mistake of dating high-profile women when I wanted a quiet life. And talking to Kyle had the opposite effect that I intended. Instead of confirming for me all the reasons I need to stay away from her, he confirms why I need to follow my heart (not my head) and give her a second chance. For some reason accepting her as "the one" is a place I fear to tread, and I'm confident of the reason. That's when Kyle brings me back to reality.

"It's funny we're having this discussion. I always thought she was in a relationship," he says. He ends his sentence with a stinging smile, one that infers he's got Mia on his mind and, in his thoughts, she may not be clothed or engaged in business pursuits. Before I can clamp my trap shut, my mouth speaks.

"Well, don't you get any ideas. Any. None." I made sure I put a period and an exclamation point at the end of my sentence to eliminate any confusion.

Kyle laughs at my expense. Now it's clear to me he made the statement more for my benefit than his own curiosity. Then he follows with, "Oh, it's like that, huh?" and enjoys more laughs at my expense.

"I'll call you for drinks," I say, trying to play it off. Now I'm left wondering what the heck is wrong with me. I'm the problem, not Mia.

My reaction shakes me because I'm worse than wounded; I'm

straight-up jealous, and I can't stand myself for allowing this. The truth is, the situation proves what I'm unwilling to admit to myself: I'm unaccustomed to these emotions.

I've survived relationship failures by remaining a fugitive from commitment. The women I dated were always much more into me than I was into them, particularly since my father passed away. The distance I kept between them and me protected me from the confusion, doubt, and loss of control I'm experiencing at this moment.

Jealousy means more than the fact that I don't want Mia not to be with another man. It means I've invested myself, my emotions, my heart.

I'm not ready, and I'm not about to get ready.

No sooner than this thought flitters through my head, I'm saved by the bell. The workday is over, as evidenced by the staff exodus.

I leave Hart and trek through the falling snow to the annual holiday gathering—A Tast of Christmas on U Street; I've promised Brooks I'd attend. The Christmas funk wraps me like a ribbon on a gift. It happens every year, but today feels different somehow. I'm not the same. Changed already.

As I slosh through slush-covered sidewalks, I hear it. Silence. It's quiet, and I can think straight. Maybe too straight. The absence of sound surrounds me except for a distant tire splash and occasional laughter from couples passing on the other side of the street. I'm left with too much space to think about everything I once had, everything that used to be, everything I still want.

The closer I get, the more I'm greeted with an unending deluge of happy couples frolicking in the snow seems only to deepen my confusion. Since Tami, I tell myself they share something I don't need, something I can live without. Perhaps part of the problem is I'm lying to the world, the universe, and myself.

Even with the spate of bad weather, the turnout is perfect. The street is lit with Christmas luminaries and bright scenes as shop owners give away samples of holiday delights and drinks for the 21 and over set, including hot toddies and Christmas mojitos.

I reach JoJo's, a jazz joint where I'm as regular as Norm at *Cheers*. They're pumping music through the speakers from inside to out, which welcomes me like a warm smile. The trio's tenor sax smooths the rough edges of my hard day. I grab two samples of the Christmas 7&7s made with Cherry 7-Up, one for me and one for Brooks, who's meeting me soon. He called to join me in the nick of time, saving me from my own stupidity and gullibility.

The newly delivered elixir rolls over my tongue to warm my body. My shoulders go limp, even in the cold, a steady parade of deep cleavage and tight abs pass before me until the perfect stack pauses.

She eyes me as if I'm a whole snack, and I return the favor. She's easy on my eyes, and her beauty nearly lulls me into a dream.

Mia who?

"How are you enjoying the Taste?" She winks at me, not even waiting for an answer with her sultry smile. The street is full of male strays, but she's found me. Her approach is not inventive but also not unwelcome.

"Much better now," I respond as she fills the empty space next to me, the one waiting for Brooks. At this moment, I realize I'm old school because how she arrives at my company is just as important to me as the fact that she's here. She's denied me the thrill of the chase, which I now appreciate more than I thought. It energizes me, excites me.

"Rough day?" she asks; however, she says it in a way that tells me she doesn't care about the answer. Still, I'm taken by her pretty brown eyes. They're large and doe-like, innocent—a stark contrast to the long stretches of leg teasing from beneath her car-length coat. They're hot enough to set fire to fire.

"It could've been worse as days go, I suppose." I lean

forward and eye her from toes to tatas. "But it's getting better by the second," I say. I'm not sure where the words come from, but there they are.

Then she seals the deal but not the one she expects. She pulls out her cell phone and begins texting while at the same time asking, "Maybe we can take a stroll down to DC Noodles. I hear they have excellent samples." Doesn't even lookup. Just taps out the message on her cellphone as she talks to me. She doesn't seem to recall she's asked me a question, nor that I've not answered.

At this minute, I learn why she's so different from Mia, why Mia is special. She may not have legs that go on forever (although they're mighty close), but her inner beauty bleeds out.

Mia would care about me.

If I told Mia I had a bad day, Mia would buy me a tree and give me a hand-made ornament. Mia would spend all night with me on the phone, let me serenade her with a carol, and talk about everything and nothing. Mia would look at me, into my eyes, and see me, what I feel, what I need.

"Thanks. But, no, thanks," I reply.

She was beautiful, to be sure. Desperation might lead some to sit there and play second fiddle to her phone. Not me. I think better of myself and someone else.

"Huh?" she replies; I read her lips. Her face is down, but my body is halfway down the block before she knows I'm missing.

One glance over my shoulder confirms my suspicion. Not even a blip from her. By the time she peers up, I'm out of her sight, and she's almost out of mine.

When I reach the next block, Brooks is rushing toward me, looking at me as if I've lost all of my mind.

"Bro! I thought we were gonna throw back a few drinks. Where are you going?"

"Sorry, man. I'll treat you next time. Maybe this weekend. I've got someplace to be. It's important. We exchange dap as I leave, and he stays. Maybe Soph will join him.

I wander up and down the street before eventually stopping at the only place in the city, in the world, that I really want to be. Mia's Christmas lights leave a glow on my face, but the snow on her front steps is undisturbed. She's not been home. Part of me says it's time to go home, but the only part I listen to tells me to sit and wait.

Now, I'm sending a text. I think back on the JoJo girl and her unattractive texting. It's funny how you give your attention to the people who really matter. No amount of beauty or sexiness can distract from the woman who has your heart—and the irrevocable gulf between you can be erased with a long dose of reality and a short walk.

CHAPTER 18

 ia

THE FINISH LINE STOOD IN MY SIGHTS. THE PATH WAS CLEAR. NIXON and I formally agreed to date. Not twelve hours later, he catches Dustin in the act—a full lean-in with an intent to kiss.

Rusty butt's antics have landed me in hot water with the first man I've fallen for since, ugh, him. I'm not sure I can undo the damage. Will it even prove helpful to explain to Nixon that Tessa's decision to hire Dustin smacks of some level of insanity of which I was previously unaware?

Of all the creative directors in all the world, Dustin appears at Hart—via my BFF. Okay, yes, I was a little pressed to finish the line. A lot pressed. I was making progress with the Hart Cards and Keep It Real teams changing to Sweet-Hart, but not achieving as much as I needed, nor as fast.

We needed help, and Tessa did what good managers do for their companies: she found a consultant. For all she knew, Dustin was an evil necessary to deliver the line to distributors on time and return our Christmas profits back to black.

Never mind the fact that I hate him, and she hates him—despises him (or so I thought.) He's the most talented Creative Director on the market right now, a fact of which I'm sure of since I've interviewed them all—and most of their mothers.

My apprehension about Dustin probably stems from fear, paranoia, me wondering if Tessa brought in Dustin to replace me. Maybe I won't have a job when the line gets submitted. Perhaps her desperation is less of a reflection of concern for her company and more of a reflection of her loss of faith in me and my ability.

Now that I'm in the Hart building, I burst into Tessa's office.

"Why did you ask Dustin to work here?" I cut straight to the point.

My accusation escapes my lips as a question. Her head jerks back as if the question affronts her, but she's answering for the sake of our friendship.

"Because you needed some...help?"

"Okay. Okay. Did you hire him because I needed some help? Or because when this is over, I won't have a job?"

"Excuse me? What universe is this? Did I just step into the *Twilight Zone?* Of course, you're going to have a job when this is over. You helped me start Keep It Real. I don't care what happens; you will always have a place here, and unless I'm renting prime real estate in the looney bin, you will always have a position above Dustin. Period."

She means what she's saying, and I'm relieved, but I've only tipped the iceberg. I take a seat and look at her in a way that she knows I'm fully loaded and ready to fire.

"What's going on with you?" She rubs her nose. "Do I have a snigglet?"

I shake my head. "No, Tess. You don't have boogers. I came here to tell you something. You won't believe what happened."

I close the door behind me, more loudly than I mean to. I'm still in a state of disbelief.

"What's going on?" Tessa said. "You're clearly in the middle of a meltdown, and I just left you an hour ago."

"Dustin came into my office. One second we were talking about wrapping up the Christmas line because he finished up the art. And the next second, he was leaning in to kiss me."

She bolts straight and forward in her seat. "Stop!"

"At that exact moment, Nixon appeared in my doorway. Saw the whole thing."

"Noooooo!"

"Yesss! Then he stormed off, walked away. No sign of him since. Nothing. Not a word or a question. Not a 'what's going on?'. Not a 'how could you?'. Not a 'peace I'm out.' Nada. I'm jinxed—and you should apologize."

"Twilight Zone returned. How's it my fault? I didn't jinx you."

"Yes, you did, with your whole *'Nixon may be up to something'* talk," I say, questioning my own sanity. "Beware of Nixon. That's what you said. Now, look."

"First of all, I never told you to beware of Nixon. I told you to *be aware*."

"Same difference."

"No, no," she says. "No, no. Big difference. You just met him. No matter how much time you spent together *in the closet*, you don't really know him. I wanted you to stay on your guard, not dump the guy. God knows I didn't want you kissing Dustin. *Ew*."

"I didn't kiss Dustin."

"Then what's the problem?"

"The problem is—Nixon doesn't know that. He bolted out of there. I should've run after him, but I didn't."

"Okay. Then whose fault is that?"

I take a long deep breath when I realize my relationship with Nixon is complicated, not simple at all.

"But what if you're right about him...and what if I'm wrong?"

"Then we're back to square one, aren't we? Except you aren't jinxed. You're a big ole scaredy-cat."

Her words hit me like a right-cross from a heavyweight fighter. Maybe Tessa's right. Perhaps I am afraid. Dustin's presence at Hart is a physical reminder of how devastating heartbreak can be. And that only happens when you open your heart to someone new.

"How about this? Cody and I are going to MingMei's Christmas pageant this evening," she said, referring to Ming and Lee's darling daughter whose private school pageants border on Broadway production magnitude. MingMei is the product of a post-seven-minutes-in-the-closet union and SoBro's god-daughter, so they never miss an event. "Why don't you join us? It'll get your mind off things for a while, at least until you can figure out what you want to do."

I shrug.

"Come. It'll do you good. It's right down the street from our house at Georgetown Day. You'll have a ball."

"I guess. I'm short on options right now."

"Mia, if you take nothing else away from this conversation, take this: a choice is the one thing you will always have. Even when you do nothing, when you take no action, you're making a choice."

I hate her when she's like this. You know...right. But who'd ever think I'd be in this position. Stuck between a man who feels like Mr. Right and then Mr. Wright, a man I thought was "the one," but he turned out to be Mr. A.M Wong, also Mr. All Wrong.

One thing is certain—my choices are clear, but my ultimate decision is less so. Should I find Nixon and try to explain or let it go now before my heart truly gets broken?

"The pageant sounds perfect. This is exactly what the doctor ordered. I can gorge myself with cookies and something hot and chocolate."

"I thought you decided to stay away from Nixon," Tessa quips

"Ha. Ha. Ha. What's the pageant theme for this year?"

"T'was the night before Christmas. Not the Santa one, the Jesus one. MingMei scored a key supporting role. She's Angel Number One."

"Awww!" I shrug. "I suppose I'll be meeting you guys there. I'm going to drop off my briefcase at home. That'll give me time to clear my head."

WITH THOSE WORDS, I'M OUT OF HER OFFICE, INTO MY COAT, AND on the street.

One of the best things to result from Hart Enterprises' acquisition of Keep It Real Cards is the location. It's on K Street, which lies within a short distance of my two-story Victorian on U Street. After filling my lungs with some fresh cold air, I stop by my house to drop off my Christmas line; I'll finalize the files later when I return.

Then I beckon an Uber and head to Georgetown for Ming-Mei's big day.

By the time we get to Massachusetts Avenue, blocks from Georgetown Day, traffic's bumper to bumper, and we're not moving, so I ask the driver to let me out early.

I meander from Massachusetts to Davenport street, heading to the campus, collecting sporadic flakes falling from the sky on my hat and face. Some even greet my nose with an icy kiss.

Christmas is getting closer.

You can feel it and see it. People are kinder, more polite. The season breeds smiles like nurseries breed poinsettias. Lit trees sprout up in formerly darkened windows along the city streets, peeping through blinds and curtains signaling we're closer to the big day. We're ready for more snow, so it's quiet.

A hush falls over the city whenever a storm is imminent. Everyone hunkers down in fear of a frosty fall that will barely cover their ankles. The Snowmaggedon routine is a ridiculous and yet consistent DC tradition.

Along my trek, I begin to notice a disturbing pattern that makes me wish I'd driven the BMW that got me into this mess.

Every happy couple in the city has been drawn into my path. Lovey dovies holding hands or linked arm in arm, sharing the occasional sloppy snow-capped kiss. It's all so sweet. Gives me the urge to hurl myself in front of the oncoming 30-bus. Unfortunately, the strike wouldn't kill me because they stop too often to pick up speed.

Seems like only yesterday I was part of one of those annoying couples, and now I'm not. In fact, it was yesterday—life changes in an instant whether we like it or not.

On the one hand, I'm grateful to Dustin. While the thought pushes venomous bile from my gut to my mouth, I'm not certain I could've nailed down the art as quickly as he did. The task would've taken me a week or more. He achieved the feat in about a day, which means I can wrap up the files tonight and prepare them for submission to the printers tomorrow.

We're ahead of schedule, so changing the publishing line-up priority will require some renegotiating with Nixon, but that's the least of my worries.

If Cody and Tessa give final approval—which they will—not even Renee and Regina can stop that train. We'll finish way ahead of Christmas vacation so we can halfway "enjoy" the holiday season with the understanding that we've mailed in our effort.

So, I'm grateful, at least for my team. At least they'll get their bonuses, and we can take off as planned.

We'll recover our reputations someday. No, Valentine's Day. That's it.

I hope.

Dustin claims he's working on my behalf, but I happen to know Tessa's paying him a boat-load of cash. Who knows? He may end up with a new job to boot if I agree.

Honestly, I want to hire him as much as I want to hire the Grinch, but with us needing to fill the director slot and him being available, how can I refuse him a job, even if I refuse him my heart?

But Dustin and Nixon working for the same company at the same time...with me? Let's just call that three ways to hell. *Ugh.*

I've never known Dustin to do anything without getting something in return or at least wanting to get something.

Yet, here is Nixon, off to a running start. He's motivated by nothing else except being with me unless, of course, he's trying to steal the Christmas line. He gave me my first holiday date, not because he had to but because he wanted to.

Assuming he didn't accept the position at Hart to spark the downfall of Sweet-Hart cards, he had nothing to gain except putting a smile on my face and a kiss on my lips.

He gives me no reason to doubt him, but still, I do. The question I have to ask myself is whether I doubt him because of his history or mine.

Does his past make him a serious threat to hurt me—or do I fear giving in to him because I'm healing from a deep hurt?

Should I find him and tell him nothing is going on between Dustin and me? Or should I just let it lie and be thankful that Nixon's past didn't catch up with me?

No matter what Dustin does or says—and it all sounds right —something, I don't know, in my gut tells me I can't trust him. I can't explain beyond our history.

History matters.

A rush-hour driver lays on his horn in apparent frustration, and the blaring jars me out of my thoughts. I've arrived at the Georgetown Day entryway and ascend a short flight until I reach the hall foyer.

Cody and Tessa greet me with broad smiles, and I return the favor, even though I partly blame them for my angst. Had I not been persistently subjected to their bliss for the past year, I may have been content enough with my singleness and solitude to leave both Nixon and Dustin alone.

"Here, she is!" Tessa says as she waves me over. Halfcostumed munchkins pepper the lobby area, taking pictures with their proud families. Cody, in true gentleman fashion, steps over to help me off with my coat—old-school; they have a check-in. We used to hate him. He reminded me that men like him still existed; now Nixon confirms it.

"Ahhh, it's good to see you guys. It's been a while since we got to hang out like this," I say, scanning the nearby table and the vast cookie selection—lots of icing and punch. I smell Arabica beans; hot cocoa can't be far behind. Tessa holds a cup filled with red juice, but she looks happy as if she spiked it with something from her purse. All it needs is a swig of holly. "Yum! What are we drinking?"

"Punch...of course," Tessa says with a wink. "Christmassy, isn't it?"

"Sure is." I approach the table and ask for some iced cookies. Apparently, for me, sugar will have to be my drug of choice. "I'll have two, please. Thank you."

I return my gaze to them, and they're both giving me the eye.

"We'll be moving into the auditorium to our seats shortly," Cody says, trying to speak above the noisy minglers. "We're waiting on one more guest."

I've had the longest day in the history of long days. It's a miracle I didn't snatch Tessa's cup. "Wait, what did you just say? Who's coming?"

Before I can even give Cody the blues, he's saying, "Dustin!"

My backs turned, so I've not yet witnessed the horror with my own eyes.

"He's here," Cody says, cutting me off before I can blurt out his real name. He gestures his hand against his neck as he peers behind me. "We didn't think you'd make it. You said you had to work late."

His eyes bulge as if Dustin's somehow arrived by surprise, and it's no surprise to anyone except me.

"I couldn't miss an opportunity to hang out with my new

boss, could I?" he says and laughs like an old uncle who's had too much brown liquor.

I contort my body until I can see above and behind me, and sure enough, he's here, with his ego, depleting all the good oxygen from the room.

"Dustin," I say flatly. Honestly, I tried to force nice, Christmassy words from my mouth, but the only thing that emerges is, "Speak of the devil, and he shall appear."

"The devil," he says, "Well, at least you're back to calling me names that won't get you fined by the FCC."

I chuckle. He's funny. Factual, but funny. "What are you doing here?"

"Cody invited me. I came to see Mei Ling." To be fair, I broke up with Dustin; Cody never did. They've known each other from industry circles for years.

"MingMei," I say. At least Tessa's not responsible for this travesty.

"Care to share?" He asks nicely, eyeing my cookies before reaching to grab one as if he and I are together. Please. I'm saving all of my cookies for Nixon—or someone like him.

"Touch them and die," I bark with a wide smile while shielding my treats from his grubby little paws. "We both know I'd have killed you long ago for lesser reasons."

In what can only be described as perfect time, Tessa reappears. "Dustin?"

She's not smiling. At all. Her expression is as tight as mine.

"Imagine that, Tess. It appears as if Satan's gatekeeper got a night off. He should enjoy the pageant. Lord knows, he needs Jesus. Maybe Dustin can meet him during the play."

Everyone laughs, even Dustin, even though I was laying out the facts like the Notorious RBG. He slides into the spot like old bacon grease and makes himself comfortable as if he's one of the crew.

"I just wanted to come out and support my old friends. I

can't wait for the show. Ling Ming should make a wonderful shepherd."

"MingMei," I say. "And she's Angel Number One." Turd.

Trying to make the best of what is, at best, an awkward situation, Tessa beings to make what should be small talk, leaving me some mental space to conjure up a plan for my escape.

"So, Dustin," Tessa begins. "How have your first days at Hart been? I imagine things have changed quite a bit since your last stint here."

As a sign of sheer desperation, I consider the ramifications of playing dead and decide embarrassment outweighs the effectiveness because I will not , in fact, be dead.

"You know me," he begins. "I'm always up for a challenge. It's like I never left. I picked up right where I left off. I'm just glad I could come to rescue Mia when she needed me."

Rescue Mia? Somehow, by what only can be described as the grace of heaven and holy Mother Earth, I hold my tongue. But my face must shift into deliverance mode because Tessa reaches over and grabs my arm. I look down, and my fist is rolled into a tight ball. I didn't even feel it happen. Her touch looks gentle and friendly, but it feels as if I've been locked down with a vice grip.

"Ahem," is the only sound I manage to squeak out before I chuck down my cookies. Dustin's so focused on deepening the shade of his already brown nose; he's oblivious to the fact that he's literally inches from death.

The more he changes, the more he stays the same.

"Don't get me wrong. Mia's team is great. She's done a phenomenal job. But nothing can substitute for my level of experience."

Now I'm contemplating murder and calculating the time I'd be forced to serve if I choked him with his own ego.

"You forgot the depth of your—"

"Mia," Tessa barks.

"Generosity. I was going to say the depth of your generosity."

I meant bull crap.

"When it comes to Dustin, there are no substitutes. Thank heavens!" I say, taking another big bite of my cookie. Everyone's giving me the side-eye when I realize what I've said. I hurry to chew and swallow.

"I mean, thank the mighty heavens for you and your experience," I'm looking him dead in the eye now. "You used your powers for good...and came to my rescue. What can I say?"

"I'll always be Superman for you," he replies. I know what he said and what he was trying to say. If those words emerged from another man's lips, like Nixon's, they'd sound a lot less pretentious and boobish.

"Just call me, Lois," I say and then mutter to myself, *and an Uber so I can get the heck out of here.*

Dustin launches into some smaller talk about himself and how he was killing "it" as his last job. I suspect "it" is brain cells. According to him, he was so good and so intimidating; in fact, they finally let him go. He's selling a truckload of buffalo puckey, and I don't know if anyone else is buying, but I'm not.

In a most fortunate happenstance, my stomach bubbles audibly. Faking death may be out of the picture, but a stomachache may be my ticket to Sayonara-Ville.

I grip my stomach and wince. "You know. I think I'm going to cut my evening short. Those cookies are messing with my stomach. Maybe not enough gluten."

My stomach bubbles again in perfect timing. It sounds terrible, but I feel perfectly fine, except I'm percolating as if I'm gonna blow any second. Hopefully, not out of my rear end.

"Here, let me see you home," Dustin motions as if he's about to help me. Tessa and Cody co-sign.

"Absolutely not. Ruining the pageant will only make me feel worse. And I don't want MingMei to miss her cheerleading section. This is such a big deal for her. Please, everyone stay. Don't worry about me."

I zip to the check to retrieve my coat as fast as possible

without breaking into a full-out sprint. "I promise I'm fine. I'll see you all at the office tomorrow. It's the big day. We submit Dustin's awesome files."

They say their goodbyes, and I make my escape with as little disruption (and as much expediency) as possible.

In no time, I'm home when I find a welcome surprise sitting on my snowy front stoop.

"Nixon?"

CHAPTER 19

ixon

I'M DUE TO DELIVER THE COLLECTION TO RENEE AND REGINA tomorrow, and I've got nothing—no idea, no collection, and worst of all, no Mia. Instead, I'm on the phone with Brooks, hoping he'll talk me into leaving Mia's front porch with some semblance of my dignity. He's not having any more luck with me than I am with myself.

"I've tried to get her off of my mind, but I can't. There's nothing out here except me and frostbite, but I'm still outside her door like she's got the cure to stupidity, and I'm in Stage Four. What the heck is wrong with me?"

"Sounds to me like you know what you need to do then."

"Unfortunately."

We hang up.

The snow's coming down, and I've lost all feeling in the tips of my fingers. The neighborhood is gentrified just enough that I'll get arrested if I sit here much longer. I've already been here five minutes too long. Just when I concede to give up and decide to leave, an angel calls to me.

"Nixon?"

It's Mia. My heart bursts and shudders at once. Now I feel like a stalker with a side of ridiculous. How did I get here?

"I'm sorry to invade your space. I was just leaving."

"Don't. Please. Listen, what happened today...I'm sorry, it's —" she begins. Then she pauses for a moment that seems like an hour.

"So? You gonna leave me in suspense?" I ask. There's not an ounce of tension or bite in my voice. She probably can't say the same would be true if she were in my position.

"Nixon, honestly. It's not what you think." She's nervous and apologetic. Her shiver reflects more than the cold, and her eyes seem to ask for forgiveness. I hope my eyes say I do. Maybe she cares more than I've allowed myself to believe.

"Yes, you said that already," I reply, "but I'm curious. What do you think, I think?"

"I think you're questioning how we went from committing to dating each other one day, and the next, you find a man in my office getting ready to kiss me?"

"Mmmm...pretty close," I say. "Some might say you pinned the nose on Rudolph. So, uh, what's happening there?"

"Nothing...and when I say nothing, I mean absolutely nothing. The man you saw, Dustin, he's my ex, the one you probably would've seen last night at the restaurant had I not been so busy—"

"Kissing me to make him jealous?" I reply. "I've got to say; I'm not disappointed that I didn't get the opportunity to check him out if that's the case. I'll take that trade-off any day."

She smiles, and my lungs have emptied and refilled. The sight of her relief calms me, something I don't realize until the tension releases from my shoulder.

"Tessa hired him. It's partly my fault. If I hadn't fumbled the

Christmas line, she wouldn't have needed to find a creative director to help us."

A creative director. I should be working for Sweet-Hart cards, not working on some fool's errand for Renee and Regina. Now I'll never get the opportunity to show Tessa and Cody what I can do.

"I'm sure you feel worse than the situation is."

She shrugs as if she doesn't want to speak her mind. She doesn't trust me enough to confide her secrets. Look who I work for—I wouldn't trust me too much. However, I'm not quite there with her, either.

"Regardless. He came in my office uninvited, for business, and I told him under no uncertain terms to keep our relationship strictly professional or pound sand. I thought he and I agreed until he tried to kiss me. Can you believe it?"

"Of course I can...but, uh, you said '*tried to*'?"

"Oh, he failed on every count. He's lucky he left without my palm print on his face, and by some miracle, all of his teeth stayed in his mouth. I was the girl's boxing MVP at my dad's old gym for two years in a row." She blows on her knuckles.

I chuckle, and so does she, but her gesture is more uncomfortable than mine.

"So, he's leaving?"

"His employment at Hart is temporary—until we get the line out. Then we'll see how it goes. He'll work with Zeke ninety-five percent of the time."

"Okay, then," I say. "To be honest, you didn't need to explain. I believed you before you spoke a word. The woman who found and bought me that beautiful tree, the one who presented me with the gift of Christmas by returning the joy of the season to my life, she wouldn't kiss another man the next day, not willingly."

Her relief is revealed in her smile. "Certainly not after that beautiful serenade."

"I figured he blindsided you."

"Really?" She jerks her head. "So, that's it?"

"Unless you'd like to endure the McCloud inquisition," I reply.

Her laugh drains all the tension from the air.

"But...I have one more thing to add. So, not quite." I walk over to her and press my lips against the curve of her cheek, my favorite part of her smile. In one gesture, we make the end the beginning.

She escorts me inside her place. We kick off our outdoor gear in a tray set out for our boots and a coat rack. Then she lights the fireplace, setting the mood. I'm a sponge soaking it all in.

"Do you mind if I slip into some jammies? Full disclosure, they're not sexy. At all. They've got feet. But I'm cold through the bone. I'm questioning if I'll ever warm up again."

"Please. You're home. Make yourself comfortable. You could wear a box, and you'd still be beautiful to me. As long as I could be here with you—and I promise, I'll do my best to help you warm up."

Her lips part and reveal all of her teeth and some of mine.

"You mind if I use your restroom?" I ask.

"Please, go ahead."

A few steps into my journey, I trip over something hard and hear a thunk on the floor. I glance down—it's not just a briefcase, it's "the" briefcase, the same one I've seen attached to Mia's hand at meetings or stashed nearby her beneath tables and desks.

"Ooh, careful," she calls out. She's near or inside her bedroom now. Then I hear the door shut, and her voice is muffled by it. "That's my Christmas campaign. I promised Tessa I'd deliver it tomorrow at nine a.m. I'm going in early. If anything happens to that briefcase before I get the files to the printers tomorrow, please hand me a cyanide capsule."

"What a coincidence. I've got a deadline tomorrow, too." My eyes clench shut and then open—not only because of what I'm thinking but for what I need to do.

This is it, I tell myself, *this is the reason I was hired to work at Hart.* I'm holding the briefcase containing the contents that will allow me to replenish all the money I gave to my mother and set me up financially for a long time. I pick it up and examine the top and sides—the supple brown leather, the combination lock. I press my hand against the lock to muffle the popping sound and peer inside before closing it—a surface pro. Of course.

"I'm going to sit this out of the way. We definitely wouldn't want anything to happen to it," I say before heading to the restroom.

After washing my hands, I'm ready to leave, but stop and stare at my expressionless self in the mirror. I'm not sure whether to feel disgusted or ashamed. Either way, Mia doesn't deserve the result of my mission, but I can't think of any other way out.

I return to the couch, where she joins me. Now she's wearing Mickey Mouse pajamas with the feet in them, a far cry from Tami's never-ending collection of secrets from Victoria. But Mia's cute is sexy on a whole different level. I'm sure there'll be time for Victoria in the future; the happy rat's here now. The moment is perfect...except for the task I'm forced to complete.

"I'm so glad you're here." She snuggles close to me, wraps her arms around my waist, and lays her head on my chest. "Maybe it's just me, but I feel like we got a second chance today."

"Me too."

"We've laid everything out on the table and still choose to try."

"I've given some thought to what you said the other night. You know, maybe we shouldn't keep our relationship a secret."

"Oh?" I reply. I don't know how to respond. She's about to give me exactly what I wanted, what I asked for, and now I stand to lose everything I hoped to gain.

"I can't help but think that Dustin's lean-in never would've happened if I had been more open and honest about what's going on between us. About how we met and the fact that we're trying, even though what we have is new."

"You. Maybe I was too hasty. I shouldn't have pressured you."

"Maybe I wasn't hasty enough. I mean, it's not like you're proposing marriage, but we should be honest with ourselves and others about where we are, even if we're not sure where this is going."

"That's true....but—"

"You weren't suggesting we make a full-out commitment, only that we'd like to explore the possibility of it. That's fair."

She's right. It's the level where we should be, where we could be if this Renee and Regina cloud weren't hovering over my head. They'd used my history to get me into this trouble, and it worked without the slightest—

Wait a minute. My past. My history. It may have gotten me into this mess, but it also holds the answer to all of my problems. The only real way out of this predicament is to give Renee and Regina exactly what they've demanded I deliver tomorrow—the Christmas collection, copy, art, and illustrations. I'll provide them with everything they want and then some.

"You know what? I'm all in," I say. "One-hundred percent. I mean, we don't have to make any big announcement."

"Exactly. We're simply not hiding any longer. And we're still going to the Christmas Card-Fest Party together, as a couple, right?"

"You asked me out on a date. Of course, we are." I lean in to kiss her but stop short. "Tonight's a school night. I should be going, but how about we go out tomorrow. I think a trip to the Jolly Jumper would be perfect to celebrate our new beginning."

"Ooh, joint shopping for ugly Christmas sweaters. This is all so...sudden," she says with a little chuckle. "But since we'll be out, how about we grab chili dogs and French fries?"

"And beer. Don't forget the Mad Elf Holiday Ales in frosted glasses," I continue. "I hate to leave, but I've got a lot of work if

I'm going to finish my first assignment for Renee and Regina by tomorrow. I'll wrap it up so you and I can indulge in holiday fun."

THE COLD NIGHT TURNED INTO A FROSTY MORNING, AND I'M SHORT on sleep. I've been working all night to right a wrong. The stores open early for holiday hours, so thankfully, I'm able to pick up all the supplies I need. The deed is almost done.

Now, I'm at the office, and it's time to deliver the goods to Renee and Regina once and for all. I did what I had to do. I'll give them exactly what they paid for. It's almost noon, and I'm fifteen minutes late for my 11:30 meeting with the twins. I unload my coat and things in my office and then prepare to say what they want to hear.

I take quick paces to their door. When I'm a couple of feet from the threshold, I slow my gait, wondering if I've made the right decision. I try to play it cool, but cool has exited the building leaving a knot of nerves behind.

I approach the threshold, tap on the frame, and peer inside. "Sorry I'm late."

Renee waves me inside. She's sitting beside Regina and is the first to catch a glimpse of me. Soon Regina looks up and leans back in her seat.

"Well, well, well. We'd begun to wonder if you'd given up," she says.

"Give up?" I reply. "Those are two words that have no place in my vocabulary."

"That's why we hired you. So, what's going on?"

I walk inside and close the door behind me, then cop a seat in the guest chair. "I've been working on our little project."

"Any progress?"

"I wouldn't be here if the answer was no."

Their heads lean toward the side. I'm empty-handed.

"Yet. I just need a little more time, and I'll have everything you need."

"What's a little more time?"

"Close of business. The files are complete. By the day's end, you'll have your Christmas collection. The question is—will you keep your end of the bargain."

"When you say you have everything..."

"Copy images. The entire line."

"If you have it, you will receive everything we promised, including a creative director position, that is if you still want it."

I offer the smile they expect and head for the door. The gaze at me as if they were waiting for me to fall on my knees and bow down to them in gratitude.

I'm not grateful. As a matter of fact, part of me is downright resentful. I've been reduced to underhandedness. The only way I can take care of my mother is by executing a shady plan, one that crosses the woman I've grown to care for. All I want to do is put an end to this entire scheme so I can get what's coming to me. I can only hope the ending will leave room to salvage some semblance of my relationship with Mia when it's all over.

Back in my office, I take a seat at my desk and retrieve the briefcase from underneath. I pop the dual locks and leave the combination unset so Renee and Regina can open the case with ease when I hand it over. I brush my hand against the soft brown supple leather containing the Surface Pro and rest it on the floor beside my feet. *The deed is almost done*, I mutter. *The deed is almost done.*

 ia

It should be illegal to feel this intoxicated and high without intaking an ounce of manufactured chemicals. Nixon just left my place on this glorious night, and I'm floating above the air, in the atmosphere, among the stars, and I don't ever want to come down. We're on a new trajectory, one with an undefined destination. Where will we end up? I'm less confident, but with him at my side, I'm going to revel in the journey.

No music is playing, but I'm dancing and swaying to a Christmas tune in my mind. I hear melodious bells ring and horns blow. Then the bass kicks in, and the drums *ba-dum-bum*. It's jazz. It's not audible to anyone else, but I hear it in my bones, in my spirit. Nixon's left me with this sound that's filled with blissful shades of reds and blues. I'm lost in it when a knocking sound startles me out of my thoughts.

For a second, I freeze in silence, unsure whether or not I've imagined it until the noise repeats.

I scan my Mickey Mouse pajamas, wondering if I'm decent

enough to answer before peering out of the door. It's...Dustin? What the heck is he doing at my house, at this hour? I ditched him at the Christmas pageant, and I thought successfully. Suddenly, I'm uncomfortable in my pajamas, in my skin. But his smile is visible through the peephole, so I open the door. Here we go!

"There she is!" He almost sings the words as if he's meant to be here. Still delusional.

"What are you doing here?"

"Is that any way to treat your Superman?" he says with a straight face. I'm barely able to maintain decency in mine. He holds up a paper bag. "You said you weren't feeling well, so I brought you some soup. Can I come inside?"

I want to say no, begone you little peon, but I step aside and allow him to invade my space. After all, Superman did save Lois, didn't he? Or was it the other way around?

He sits the soup on the kitchen counter. I gesture him to take a seat at the couch, and he obliges.

"I was worried about you after you left the restaurant, but I guess you're feeling okay now. I saw your little company leave just as I arrived. The man?"

First of all, there's nothing little about Nixon. When using that word, Dustin must be referring to his own brain, his sense of decency, his cold black, dead-heart, his chances of getting back together with me.

"For the record, I had no idea Nixon would show up on my doorstep tonight. He came uninvited—like you. With that said, I do have a nine-thirty deadline. I've got to be in the office early, and it's late...as you were aware of when you popped up here."

"Invested? He was waiting for you in this weather? Hmm— must've been desperate to see you," he says, sounding all suspicious for someone who has zero stakes in this game. I can see the hamster wheel turning in his brain. "It's funny he thought it was okay to come. I mean, you two are closer than I realized."

I shrug. "And?"

"And I just hope you know what you're doing."

"What's that supposed to mean?"

"It means, I hope you know what you're getting into with him," he says. "Let's face it, he's got a couple of reputations and not only as a shrewd, ruthless, businessman."

"We all have a history, don't we, *Dustin*? I mean, we can only hope that we won't be judged by the way we've treated people in the past. When I say past, I mean our ruthlessness in our dealings with others." I stared him down until he caved.

"Touché," he replies. "I see what you did there."

"Good. I was aiming for obvious and in your face. Now, Superman, can we wrap this up?"

"I've apologized for my behavior toward you in the past."

"Yes, you have." I restrict my shrug to the confines of my mind.

"That doesn't dismiss the fact that it only takes a Google search to see his history with the high-profile ladies."

"You searched him?"

"I like to know who I'm working with. You should, too. His history is all over the Internet. One model chick after another. I don't mean any harm, but you're not his type."

"Thank you?" I reply. "Also, based on the breakup between you and me, then Penelope Paul, I'm not your type, either...and yet both of you showed up on my doorstep tonight. Funny how 'types' work, isn't it?"

He huffs. His ploy isn't working, and he's frustrated. I can tell. Sweat beads are forming around his hairline.

"Listen, I'm not trying to upset you, okay? The fact is, I don't trust that guy, and I need you to be careful." He stands to his feet. "I should let you get some rest. I just wanted to make sure you're okay."

"Well, thank you for the soup. That was considerate and surprisingly kind of you." My voice softens. I'm not lying. The soup was the only part of his visit that I appreciated, although I really didn't need it. What if Nixon had been here? That could've been disastrous given our agreement tonight. I needed to tell him the truth to eliminate the remote possibility of another lean-in situation. "Before you leave, you should know that he and I have started seeing one another. I'm going into this with my eyes wide open, too."

"And I'm looking straight at you, Mia. Nowhere else. At no one else. I realize I've made mistakes in the past. I've looked through you, past you, but now my eyes are on you, my heart is with you."

They are words I longed to hear...a year ago. Not now. Why now?

"I dated you for a long time. We'd planned to get married. Why are you telling me this? What do you want from me, Dustin?"

"I want to start over again, and I want to be a better man for you this time around. I want you back, what we shared, the way you made me feel. I'm going to do whatever it takes to convince you there's nowhere else in the world I'd rather be, and no one else I want to be with."

I'm paralyzed. I don't know what to say or do, but I back away when he leans into me. He's been successful in one task—infusing doubt where none existed. I'm confused because I wanted him for so long, I wanted to marry this man, and he refused me in front of 20,000 Wizards fans a year ago.

On the other hand, he's here now, and he's helped me complete a daunting task that I had hoped I had enough skill and experience to do without anyone—especially him. Despite doing what he does best, offering backhanded claims to be saving me, what he says now is sweet. But lest I forget the routine—saying I'm doing a great job but...there's always a 'but' with him, always some exception. His 'but' always proves costly to my heart, more than I should ever have to pay.

A quick escort to my door rids me of the unexpected and uninvited source of puzzlement. I don't need this kind of confusion in my life.

"You should go." When the door opens, a burst of cold air rushes in. He puts on his coat, stops in front of me, and caresses my cheek.

"Thank you for the soup."

"Mia, I meant every word I said."

After I cover his hand with mine to free my face from his touch, I gently nudge him all the way out the door and send him off with a wave goodbye. I take a moment to breathe and re-center before wrapping up some final work details.

After making my final edits, prepping the submission files, and getting into bed, I stew in my thoughts. I regret that my position on Nixon may have sounded weak to Dustin. I should've resolutely given Dustin the boot. The last thing I want him to do is to leave my house with some vague hope that he and I could ever be together again.

Rather than leave the situation alone, I shoot him a late-night text, about as far from *"What You Doin"* as possible. I send "We need to talk"—the definitive sign of a breakup. He spoke those exact words to me in the Verizon Center, right before he kicked me to the curb on the Kiss-Cam. He'd take my text in the spirit I sent it; I basically told him to kick rocks in private, a mercy he didn't offer to me.

Regret overwhelmed me the minute I put my phone down. Dustin had just enough ego and pride to respond in kind, but I receive no immediate reply, which makes my stomach sink. After pacing the floor, I execute the mental contortions necessary to make myself believe he's swallowed the news, and I'd suffer no repercussions. Still, my better judgment tells me I'm more delusional than accurate. The only good thing about tonight is that the line is finished. Tomorrow, I only have to submit it to the printer, and I'm free to focus on the Card-Fest submission and the Winner's ball, where we will undoubtedly lose, but we'll win next year.

My stomach flips again.

I'll apologize to Dustin for texting him instead of telling him face to face. That's my only regret.

THE MORNING ARRIVES LIKE THE FLU—FAST, OVERWHELMING, AND all at once. I chuck down a green smoothie to fortify my body and energize me enough to get through this day. I'm dressed and inside the Hart offices before the streetlights shut off. The sound of roaring metro busses fills the pre-rush morning silence and kicks off the first minutes of the day. I bubble into the office, sucking down my smoothie and toting my briefcase, swinging it like a little girl with a new purse. It may not contain the collection I promised, but I'm happy the ordeal will reach its end when I turn in the files. Then I can look forward to the days ahead when Nixon and I make our first appearance together as a couple at the industry shindigs.

My morning drink returns to haunt me before I drop off my files. The ladies' room calls, and I'm about to burst. I tuck the briefcase beneath my desk and close my door behind me before heading off. Not even five minutes later, I'm back at my desk—and something is missing.

"What in the world is going on here?!" I mutter.

No one can hear me. I'm alone and the only one in the building, or so it seems.

Yet, the briefcase is gone—nowhere to be found.

My head spins as if it's on a Tilt-a-Whirl. I'm getting motion sickness standing still. After seconds that feel like hours of paralysis, I go into action, retracing my steps, running up and down the hall. At my desk, I kneel and pat down the floor as if I'm arresting it. I try to lift the carpet; maybe there's a trap door.

I'm wrong. It's glued; there's nothing.

Then I go into CSI mode, searching for footstep imprints. Indeed there's no evidence of the person who stole it. It's the mole. It must be the mole. Not a footprint to be found in the ugly, industrial Berber. I've got no evidence of anything. I check the closet and the drawers. Why? I know it's not there. It won't even fit, but I'm in utter disbelief that this could be happening to me.

How could someone creep in and steal it?

I check around my desk again. Nothing.

By now, my heartbeat's drumming like a bass—a whole marching band percussion section. I fold over and grasp my knees. I'm having a heart attack. My brain disappears in a fog but, somehow, I find enough presence of mind to dart into the hall and launch panicked glares up and down, looking for signs of movement, of anything, of anyone, who could've stolen my work and, with it, my entire professional life. I spot house-keeping trash carts in the distance and wonder if they picked it up to turn it into lost-and-found or something. Long shot, but it can't hurt to ask.

A glance at the wall clock confirms nine am is approaching, and my deadline is on my butt like Fruit of the Loom. Out of breath and almost out of time, I dial their number and, at the sound of a friendly voice, says, "Good morning! Sorry to bother you, but I was wondering if anyone's been into clean suite C270. I'm missing a briefcase. I'm not accusing anyone of stealing it, of course. I'm only checking to see if someone accidentally set it aside or on their cleaning cart by mistake while they were vacu-uming or something."

"Ma'am, I don't think so, but let me check with the staff." She speaks with a heavy West Indian accent and offers me no comfort. My stomach binds in knots waiting for her to return with an answer. I'm not aware that I've been holding my breath until, at the sound of her return, I release it.

"I'm sorry, ma'am. They started cleaning on the C-level about fifteen minutes ago and haven't reached your suite yet."

"Okay, thank you," I respond. I want to curse everyone out, but it's not anyone's fault.

What am I gonna do?

I called to set up an emergency meeting with my creative team, now only minutes away.

How can I tell them all their hard work disappeared? Vanished into thin air? I swing by Nixon's and Dustin's offices immediately after, no sign of either one. My mistrust of both hits a fever pitch.

Neither one has arrived, which I find peculiar. They're both early risers.

I shrug off the thoughts and head to the dreaded meeting. I have to break the news.

After we exchange some tense morning greetings, I rip off the Band-aid.

"All of the work we've done over the past few weeks is gone. The briefcase. The files, all my edits, and revisions. Everything's gone," I begin. Jaws begin to drop. Everyone is rightly stunned. "Someone took it all from my office this morning. Right now, we've got nothing to submit. The bad news is we've only got three days. The good news is we've still got three days."

I've heard of conniptions, but I've never seen so many in one place at the same time. Some team members' hands thrust in the air out of pure frustration, some faces phase from colorful to pale, some fists pound on desks.

"Need we ask who is responsible?" Zeke scans the room and seemingly takes note. "I think we can all see who's missing. We've suspected a mole at work for a while now, but I'd be remiss if I didn't mention the noticeable absence."

Yes, Dustin's missing. The thought had crossed my mind.

He'd be the first suspect on my list if I didn't see him last night. If he hadn't brought me soup. Even he's not crappy enough to profess his undying love for me last night and destroy my entire career, and by default, my life the next morning.

No, he'd wait a day or two, lull me into a false sense of security, then *Wham!*

"What are we going to do?" Zeke asks.

Why won't the floor beneath me swallow me whole?

"I'm going to wait a couple of hours to see if it shows up. In the meantime, I'll work on Plan B and break the news to Tessa and Cody. I'll probably run out to pick up The Post. They're supposed to have an extra jobs section. Maybe I can get a lead on some new employment before they fire me," I say, trying to lighten the room's heaviness. "In the meantime, go grab a coffee and muffin or something, stand down until I tell you the next steps."

Despondent is not even the word. How could I let this happen? I had one job, only one job, to protect the line. I've now failed miserably on too many counts to number. All I want to do is hide in a corner and curl up in the fetal position.

Where's my shoulder to lean on? Dustin and Nixon have ghosted me today. The question is why Nixon's absence is the real mystery. No text from him, no sign of him. This is when a paralyzing thought jolts me—Nixon tripped over my briefcase. He knew the full contents, my deadline, and my plan to be in the office early. I trusted him. He wouldn't...would he?

A Google search later, and I'm no longer paralyzed—I'm a dead woman walking. Article after article in The Washington Business Journal details Nixon's antics. He's much more than an aggressive businessman. He's a hatchet man. A paid corporate mercenary. As someone who's just been "hatcheted," I've got to go talk to him. I need to find out who he really is.

CHAPTER 21

ia

PICTURE THIS: THE YEAR IS TWO THOUSAND SOMETHING, AND IT'S high school prom. I'm in love with the track star. Not only a track star, though. He's an all-around athlete—track, wrestling, football, and basketball. Relationships were new for me because I was shy, and my love was unrequited and quiet. No man had loved me, really cared about me, except my dad. But Derek, he loved me, and I believed him over my gut, which warned me not to trust him on more occasions than I care to remember.

He met me every day after all of my classes, and after school, we hung out at the local pizza joint. I fell in love with him because when no one else treated me as if I was attractive, he saw into me, not past me, not even when I had more pizza sauce on my face than makeup.

We laughed together at the same silly inside jokes. We played old Galaga and pinball machines. We shared the secrets of our childhood. We caught fireflies and set them free. We took long walks on Haines Point along the Potomac River Park...when his dad loaned us his car.

I was in love. He was, too. At least that's what he said and what I believed. I knew we're destined to marry, at least I hoped so...and I convinced myself that our lifelong commitment to one another would begin with prom.

He graced me with an invite. No promposal back in the day, only a simple question met with a yes. The theme couldn't be more perfect: The Prince's Ball.

I'd signed up to be Derek's real-life Cinderella.

Drab to fab.

It was the perfect set up.

Set up.

After preparing to enjoy the night of my life, nightfall turns out to be everything I never imagined.

In my living room, I waited for Derek, wearing the dress, an off-the-shoulder number with a taffeta skirt; I added kitten heels because my other name was Awkward McClumsyPants. Mom sprung for a trip to the hairdresser—rows and rows of coiled curls in a ball bun. The day before, Derek announced he'd arrive at five pm. We'd begin the evening with dinner, and, in a sweet secret between us, we'd end the prom with "dessert." See, we'd never *done the do.* I'd saved myself for the man I planned to marry. I'd never told him he was the man, which may, in part, explain what happened next.

At last, the time was upon us. Five pm came. Five pm went.

Six pm came. Six pm went.

At 6:37, exactly, my best friend Angie called to ask if I was okay. I found the pre-prom check-in odd until she explained why.

"Derek just showed up at the school gym with Charlene."

"Wait. What?"

"He's wearing his tux, and she's in a gown that matches his bow-tie and cummerbund."

All the air left my lungs. I struggled to catch my breath. But the humiliation wasn't complete until I confirmed one final detail. "When you say, Charlene...you don't mean my cousin, Charlene, do you?"

"Ummm...she's the only one I know."

See, Charlene had a reputation that stretched the entire DC-Maryland-Virginia area. She was easier than a Commodore Sunday morning. I'd held out on him for months; she, on the other hand, was a sure thing. Although I'd guessed his rationale, my suspicions were later confirmed by what he told himself— and at least ten of our mutual friends. By what can only be described as Karma, they both contracted gonorrhea, and the rumors spread as fast as their STDs. Even though I hadn't listened to my gut, the universe found a way to expose the truth in a way neither they nor I could deny.

Quick-stepping to Nixon's house, I relive the moment I sat in my prom dress, waiting for that humiliation. My nerves teeter on edge, and I could crumble at any moment. I want to be wrong about him and almost manage to convince myself I am...that is until I round the corner to his house.

As I approach Nixon's place, the prom night memory fades, but one feeling intensifies: 6:37. The anger, the betrayal, the sadness I felt at that precise moment is what overcomes me as I approach Nixon's house, and the universe reveals the truth.

I see him.

He's flouncing past his doorman, dressed for success, with what looks to be my briefcase in his hand. I erase half a block of the distance between him and me in a matter of seconds. Did I fly? I don't know. But by the time he descends the steps, I'm standing beside him. He's stunned to see me, at least that's what his wide eyes say. My narrow eyes scream at him, tell him I'm exponentially ticked off. Soon my mouth follows suit.

"Nixon? What are you doing with my Christmas campaign? How'd you get it?"

He clenches those sweet baby browns shut and his broad

shoulders slump. "Mia, I know how this must appear, but it's not what you think."

"Not what I think? Come on, Nixon. Keene, Blanchard, and Livingston? Bartholomew and Fink? I've been working with the hatchet king himself. Surely, you can think of a reply better than that."

"You Googled me. And you only read the headlines."

"I tried to trust my gut, but when my briefcase disappeared this morning..."

"Wait...your briefcase disappeared?"

"It's in your hand!"

"After spending time with me and getting to know me for yourself, you honestly think I'm the kind of man who would steal from you?"

"The eyes don't lie."

"They also don't tell the whole truth."

"You're really going to stand here and try to turn the tables on me? Even as I look at my Christmas campaign in your hands, and my back is bloodied from your stab wounds? I'm just another casualty, collateral damage to a man who creates nothing, who only spends his energy breaking apart what other people spend lifetimes building. That's all I am to you—a target. You've been using me the entire time. Well, congratulations. Bull's eye."

"Mia, I don't know everything that's going on right now, but what I do know is that I don't have time to explain. Not this minute. I need you to trust me. Just for a few more hours. I know this looks horrible given what's going on, but—"

"I shouldn't believe what I see? Yeah, I heard you the first time, except I'm not listening anymore. Not only will I never trust you again. I'll never trust anyone." I turn and walk away.

"Not even yourself?" Nixon asks as his voice crawls into me like an earwig.

I stop abruptly and fire back a glare lethal enough to take him down at the knees. "Especially not myself. You and me. Here and now. This is what trusting my instinct gets me every time. I don't know why I thought this time would be different."

My heart disappeared from him, and my feet followed. In my huff, circled by a cloud of anger and doubt, I realize I'm not going to recover the briefcase or its contents. Nixon should've given it back to me, and he didn't. If he's serving at Renee's and Regina's beck and call, there's no way I'll ever get it back, which means I'm screwed. Sweet-Hart Cards is screwed. Holiday profits are screwed. Tessa and Cody—totally screwed.

His betrayal has put to rest one mystery, though—the mole, the compromised campaigns. Nixon may be a branch of the tree, but it's clear now that Renee and Regina form the very rotten root. The only question lingering in my mind is, what do they have to gain? They're corporate officers of Hart Publishing. How can they use the information? That is the part of this messed up equation I don't understand.

Why would they be so blatant as to hire someone, a high-profile hatchet, no less, to do their dirty work? And what did they stand to gain by taking down their own company? Their father's legacy, pride, and joy? I don't understand, but what I do know is I have to tell Cody and Tessa what happened.

I'll shoulder the blame because it's my responsibility, and I'll pray they don't fire me on the spot.

Jittery doesn't describe my mental and physical state when I walk into Hart Enterprises and catch the elevator upstairs. My heartbeat pounds through my chest with every step. I'm taking the employment green mile on my way to a pink slip. It's time to face the music, and it's out of tune and offbeat.

I knock on Tessa's door. She waves me in. Just my luck, Cody's already inside.

"Mia, you okay?"

I clearly look the way I feel. That's how well she knows me. I expend a great deal of energy, trying to suppress my panic to no avail. She's sniffed it out like a best-in-show hound on a fox.

"I wish I could say so."

"What's going on?" Cody responds. He's giving me this brotherly vibe as if he's ready to kick some butt over what's hurt me.

"The Christmas line. It's gone."

They both fall forward in their seats, and now their eyes burn on me.

"When you say gone..." Cody manages to squeak out.

"I mean, vanished. Poof. Someone took the briefcase containing the images, copy, files for the printers, everything. I thought I locked the briefcase, and everything would be safe. Not so much."

"What do you mean somebody *took them*?"

"I mean I sat them down in my office for five minutes while I ran to the bathroom. Green smoothie this morning—"

"TMI," Tessa interrupts.

"When I returned, it was gone."

Together, they blow out frustrated breaths and wince. Their eyebrows are tighter than a hummingbird's butt. That's when I deliver the crushing blow...to me and them.

"It gets worse. I know who's responsible. At least I think I do," I begin.

"Who? Who is it?" Cody replies.

"Nixon."

"Stop!" Tessa exclaims. She's in total disbelief; Cody's less so.

"He insisted I'd been mistaken, but I saw it. The briefcase was in his hand. He didn't even offer to give it back, and it's not like I could wrestle him for it. I mean, he's rather large; I want to live, despite appearances."

Cody pinches his lips. "Nixon, huh? I'd had my suspicions about him from the moment the Devilment Twins hired him. Now they leave no doubt...about a few things."

He and Tessa exchange tense glances.

"No doubt whatsoever," she parrots.

They turn back to me, and Tessa slips into BFF mode. "Are you okay?"

"You mean, besides the fact you trusted me, put your faith in me as the VP of Sweet-Hart Cards, and I failed *worse than* miserably?"

Tessa walks around to the front of the desk. "Mia, this is not your fault. Nobody blames you. I certainly don't. Cody doesn't." She glances back at him over her shoulder. "You don't blame her, do you?"

"Of course not. You didn't hire Nixon; Renee and Regina did. It's clear they did so intending to undermine Hart Cards, which means they meant to hurt Hart Enterprises. You should be able to walk away from your office for five minutes in this building without fear that someone's going to steal your property. No, it's not your fault."

I breathe a little easier, but I can't help but believe if I hadn't trusted the wrong person, if I would've been more cautious, I'd have my briefcase. Maybe I wouldn't have revealed the contents.

I trusted my gut, and it led me down the wrong path.

"I can't help but feel like I let you down."

"The thing is," Cody says. "I've been wondering if this VP position isn't a bit...*over your head.*"

Tessa snatches her head to face him and then back at me. The bomb he's dropped appears to surprise both of us.

"Maybe you're better suited to the Creative Director position. It's less pressure, and it'll allow you to focus on the part of the business you're really good at."

"Excuse me?" Tessa says, offended on my behalf. "Cody, let's discuss this offline, please." She says that with her back to him. She's not happy.

"No, Tessa, I pipe in. It's fair. Maybe Cody's right. Perhaps I'm not suited for the VP position. Maybe you'd both be better off with someone like...Dustin." The words taste like baby upchuck.

"He didn't even show up to work today." Tessa pinches her lips together. "He called in sick. Mabel gave me the message."

Now *my* eyebrows tighten. I understand my text to him last

night might've been a little upsetting, but that's no reason to take the day off, especially in this critical period. I came in early to get the business done. That's what you do in crunch time, not take a breather. It's odd, to say the least. He must be off somewhere licking his wounds. His recovery will no doubt be swift when he learns Cody's considering him for my job.

My heart breaks a little. "I should leave. I'm sure you two have a lot to discuss. I'm going to figure out where we go from here."

"Mia, I know this is a difficult situation, but we've faced them before. There's one thing we never do."

"Quit," I reply. "We don't quit."

I leave Tessa's office as deflated as ever. This day has gone on one hour too long. I'm going home.

Dustin was right about one thing: I didn't do my research. I had no idea about who I'd gotten involved with, and my mistake's costing me everything I've worked for, everything I wanted.

ixon

THE OPTICALS ON THIS ONE LOOK BAD FOR ME. REALLY BAD. MIA figured out what was going on faster than I expected. I thought I'd have time to deliver this package to Regina and Renee and explain what I've done, so she understands.

I've got to make this delivery for all of us—her, me, and my mother.

What I've done will impact everyone I care about.

So I did what needed to be done.

Gripping the briefcase, I enter Hart Enterprises ready to do the deed, but everyone seems to eye me suspiciously as if they know I'm up to no good. Judgmental glares stalk me all the way to Regina's office, my first stop. I tap on the closed door and wait for the invitation. It comes from Renee's suite, one door over; it's open, and they're both inside. From the threshold, their eyes zero in on the briefcase, and insidious smiles seize their lips. I hold it up and pat the side with my palm.

"Well, you did it," Renee says. "Come in and close the door."

Not even a second later, I'm in the chair. All I want to do is get this over with.

"You sound as if you doubted me." I play along

"I don't know about Regina, but I certainly did," Renee begins. "You've been awfully cozy with Mia. I'd begun to question your loyalties."

"Appearances are funny that way; nothing's ever what it seems. My loyalties remain one hundred percent intact. I've never wavered. Never will."

"We hoped that would be the case. I'll admit I had all the questions, that is, until you walked in the door with that briefcase. Congratulations."

Congratulations. Funny, her choice of words. A nod is about all I can manage.

"Yeah, the briefcase did it for me, too. Mia's had it attached to her hand for the past few weeks."

"You've managed to become quite the distraction, left Mia completely off of her guard," Regina says. "For that alone, you deserve what you're getting. You'll receive your payment after the delivery is complete."

I'm almost afraid to ask.

Renee goes to her file cabinet and retrieves a check. She sashays over and hands it to me. It's twice what we agreed.

"Thank you, but why so much?"

"We appreciate what you've done. Now that we've kept our promise to you..."

"Oh, sorry." I reach out my arm with the briefcase dangling in the curve of my knuckles. But, to my surprise, Renee shakes her head. "No, we don't want the briefcase, but you can provide us a flash drive with the files."

They don't want the briefcase? Why? That was the whole point of hiring me. Or was it?

"Yes, you keep the briefcase," Regina says. "Let it be a souvenir of your employment here."

I've already created the flash drive, so I retrieve it and hand it to them. "Everything you need is here."

"I think this concludes our business," Regina says. They don't even shake my hand and wish me well. They just show me the door and send me on my way.

Outside, my first thought is to hide the briefcase, get it out of sight. Everyone knows Mia walks around with it. Spotting me holding it will only compound the I'm already in today, of all days. I stash it in my office and head directly to Dustin's squatting spot. He's got a lot to answer for what he's done.

After offering tense hellos to passersby in the hall, I bumrush Dustin's office, ready to give him a four-knuckle greeting.

He's not there. Of course.

"You looking for Dustin?"

It's Mabel. As Tessa's Executive Assistant, she knows all, sees all. "Yes, have you seen him? I need to speak to him about Mia. Clear the air. There's been some confusion."

He's got me all mixed up. I'm going to bring much-needed clarity.

"*Humph.* You can say that again."

With a flick of her index finger, she gestures me to follow her out of range of prying ears.

"Oh, I've seen him all right. He called in to tell me he wasn't coming in today. Claimed to be sick."

"Claimed? You think he wasn't?"

"Oh, I'm pretty sure he wasn't. If I were to offer a percentage for my accuracy, I'd land somewhere around 99.9 percent."

I jerked my head back. "much closer to one hundred than I thought. How?"

"See what had happened was, my daughter needed my help this morning. She had a big interview for a new job. I won't name the company, but they compete with Hart and sell a lot of books," she says with a wink.

I'm just left of exasperated and in no mood for in the weeds details. I suppress my urge to huff out loud as I'd like to and offer a smile and patience I don't have.

"Anyway, I dropped off my granddaughter at the daycare, and I arrived here...oh, sometime between 7:30 and eight. Most folks don't roll in here until 9:30."

"Yes, that's exactly correct from what I've observed. I'm usually in pretty early."

"I've noticed," she replied.

"So, Dustin?"

"I'm getting to him. When I pulled into the parking lot, there were only four other cars here. Renee and Regina's cars. They drive the matching Benzes. Mia was here. She drives the black Bimmer. And Dustin, well, I don't know his car, but I know his face. Apparently, he didn't see me. I was parked right in back of him...when my phone rang."

"He called you?"

"See, he doesn't know that my desk phone rolls over to my personal cell phone. I set it up that way in case I'm running behind with my grandbaby or something. God forbid the front desk phone ring, and I'm not there to pick up. Tessa can't stand the sound. So, when he called me this morning, he didn't have any idea that when I answered, I was right behind him."

My eyes widen. "So, wait...he was here? This morning?"

"Renee and Regina, too. I don't spend much time on that side of the building, but I didn't see any of them on the Sweet-Hart side when I got upstairs."

Before I had my suspicions, now I'm almost positive that Dustin's conspiring against Mia and the company. "Mia. I need to find her. Do you, by any chance, know where she is?"

"She left after meeting with Cody and Tessa. I got the distinct feeling she'd landed herself in some hot water. Let's put it this way; if she's not putting one on, she should be. I'd be chugging a few if I were her, and I don't even drink...before six p.m."

I chuckle, but it doesn't last long. Not nearly long enough. "I need to go. Thank you for the enlightening discussion."

"Nothing to it but to do it," she says. "Make sure you look out for Mia. She's a golden lady...no, platinum."

"I promise you, I'm going to make sure that she's fine."

She looks at me with the warmth of a hot breakfast biscuit. "I believe you will." She taps me on the shoulder. "I believe you will."

After talking to Mabel, my new mission is clear.

BY THE TIME I REACH MIA'S HOUSE, MY HEAD SWIMS AND I HAVE SO much I need to say. I bang on the door not knowing if I'll find the words if she answers. So many thoughts flood my mind. I tighten my hands around the briefcase handle, ready to give it over to her so she can look inside. She will find the truth there—nothing is what it seems.

She believed Dustin to be an ally, and he was an enemy. She believes me to be an enemy, yet I'm an ally. Maybe she's not home. My first instinct tells me to sit down on the stoop and wait for her. The second tells me to walk away but leave the briefcase. Once she looks inside, she will understand.

I sit it by the door, near the bush so she can't miss it, but passersby will. Then I go home, strip off my outside clothes (as my mother would say) and collapse in front of the tree. Funny how time changes things so quickly.

The Douglass Fir I once treasured for helping me revive the joy of Christmases past, now serves as a painful reminder of what I've lost in Christmas present. Mia came to me as a gift, and now she's gone.

One good thing has come out of this mess. Maybe Christmas wasn't about me or the tree. Maybe it's all about one courageous, loving woman. So I call.

'Mom, hey! How are you?" I try to conceal my disappointment and frustration.

"There's my baby. Now, what's wrong?"

"Wrong? What makes you think something is wrong?"

"Baby, I gave birth to you..."

"On the coldest day in DC in 1990. I know. I know."

"I changed almost all of your diapers. Your dad wasn't really into potty issues. He was the play pal," she says. "I put the Band-aids on all of your boo boos and wiped your tears from—"

"From the crib to college and beyond. I know."

"If you know, then you understand why I can tell when something is wrong."

I'm not used to discussing my women troubles with my mother, but I need an ear.

"It's Mia," I begin and then explain the events of the past couple of days. The positive and the negative of it. "I guess the good news is I've got the money. You won't have to worry about the mortgage again. Ever."

"Yeah, but at what cost? Your soul? Your heart? Don't get me wrong, I'm grateful and I love this house. Every good memory of my life is centered here. But nothing means more to me than you."

"That's the trick about doing the honorable thing. It's only viewed that way if everyone's looking through the same lens."

"Yes, I always wondered why men love playing Superman. Even those people he saves remember the collateral damage more than the good."

"Tell me something I don't know. I can't win. Even when I'm trying to use my powers for good."

"She'll come around, baby. It's Christmastime. Get ready for your miracle."

"She's my miracle."

"Then get ready. Everything's gonna be all right."

ia

Yeah, I heard he-who-shall-not-be-named knocking on the door and ignored him.

I've had it with the Nixon's of the world, seeming all perfect and beautiful, then they con you to put your trust in them, and you end up groaning as they stab you in the back. They're like serial killers, except they murder your dreams, hopes, and wishes instead of taking your life.

They force upon you cold hard facts that this Christmas will be exactly like the last. Crappy and lonely.

I'm knee-deep in a tub of Moose Tracks, sucking on ice cream-drenched fudge and peanut butter cups, and an arm's length away from me sits a Christmas-red cocktail so large I could drown in it, if my head fit into the glass. My phone rings incessantly, first Tessa, then Tessa using Cody's phone. Then Nixon, Nixon, Nixon, Nixon, and Nixon. Then nothing.

People don't seem to get it. I'm in no mood to talk about anything. I'm in no disposition to do anything except eat, growl, and drink. In my drain circling, a text buzzes my phone, and the vibration startles me. A glance reveals its SoBro. Probably more *So* than *Bro*.

SoBro: Answer your phone. We promise no talking. No questions.

Now I'm intrigued. Why would they need to call me, especially if chatting isn't on the menu? I'm not intrigued enough and ignore the text until...

SoBro: Answer my call now, or I'll email blast everyone we know about the college incident.

Me: That's Blackmail, and it's not very attractive.

SoBro: Perhaps, but it is effective. Pick up.

And I pick up when it rings. She's correct.

Blackmail's quite useful. I offer only a "hello."

"We know you're not in the mood to talk, so please just listen. Also, feel free to join in if the feeling hits you." This is the part at which they begin to sing Grandma Got Run Over by a Reindeer.

They sound country, absurd, ridiculous, and glorious all at once. Eventually, my sides ache from the laughter. I'm strengthening a whole abdominal muscle.

They go straight for the funny bone, my emotional jugular, because they know I can't resist a chuckle. And they both know this, especially Sophie.

"Fine! You win," I say before my joy fades.

"We just wanted to make sure you're doing okay. Tessa told us your day was pretty rough, although she didn't give details."

My eyes roll. "Really? If she hadn't given you all the details, you wouldn't have called me with that song."

"The point is not the details," she says. "The point is, are you doing okay?"

"I've been better." They lift me, but I feel myself sinking again. "I'm not okay right now, but I will be. Honestly, I'd like to hang up the phone so that I can follow the Moose Tracks."

"Excuse me?" Sophie says.

She doesn't know I'm referring to ice cream.

"I'll check in with you tomorrow."

We end our call, and the day has dragged on for so long it feels like midnight, but it's only 6 pm. I'm too wired to sleep, too amped for the cocktail to slow down my mind. My thoughts race so fast I can't keep up, let alone make sense of my emotions. The person I'd want to confide in is Nixon, but he is the enemy.

Strangely, I've not heard a word from Dustin, who only a day ago had half-convinced me that he gave two cents about my life.

Today, he's nowhere to be found. I decide to spend my evening watching the Wizard's game, not because I have any particular interest in the game. I've lost my taste for basketball since humiliation day, but they play the best commercials, which I hope inspires an idea. That's when I hear a knock at my door.

At first, I'm thankful for my closed blinds and don't budge. Probably Nixon again, and I've got no desire to speak to him whatsoever. The deed is done. My verdict of him is written in stone. I squiggle further down into the cushion and under my blanket when I hear the sound.

"Mia, open up. It's me."

What do you know? Sometimes, you don't even have to speak of the devil, and he'll appear.

I drag my feet across the floor and twist the knob; there he stands looking even finer than usual. I sure could pick them. That thought cuts two ways.

"Dustin?" I say and quickly step aside. He's brought a brisk winter wind with him, and even a brief puff gives me chills.

He comes in stuffed full of himself, but his presence isn't entirely unwelcome given I'm in the dumps and misery loves company.

"Superman has arrived to save the day, Lois."

"Oh, you heard?"

"Heard what?" he says, genuinely clueless—I can tell. There's a smugness missing from his expression that's usually there when he's ahead of the curve.

"About me? Work?"

"Oh, that. Yeah, I spoke with Mabel earlier. She told me everything."

I exhale or deflate, whatever you want to call it. Then I return to my spot on the couch.

"Oh, no, no, no, no. You're going with me." He tugs my arms, trying to pull me off the couch. I resist like a toddler mid-tantrum on the grocery store floor. I'm not leaving my house...again...ever, but he's piqued my curiosity. "Where do you think you're taking me?"

He whips out two tickets from his back pocket. "Wizards. Floor seats and I've got a car waiting outside. All you have to do is throw on some clothes; do, you know, something with your hair; and we're out."

"You sure you want to do this?" I say. "Return to the scene of the crime?"

He kneels beside me and cups my hand in his. "I told you I'm sorry about that, and I'm going to make it right. Today is the beginning of something new for us. I promise. But, first, you've got to get dressed and come with me."

Either he's crazy or sincere. I'm not quite sure which is the case, but he'd have to be one or the other to invite me back to the place where he'd crushed my soul and dumped me.

As resistant as I am, I have to admit, floor seats are an excellent way to watch the game. He's got season tickets but not on the floor. In my mind, I question how much butt he's had to kiss to get these tickets. Then I capitulate.

"Fine, I'll get dressed. But I think it's fair of me to request— no surprises. They don't work for us. We're just two friends watching the game."

"I can't promise no surprises, but I can promise there won't be any bad ones, cross my heart." I'm surprised to learn he has a heart.

In the back of the Town-car, he's blathering about himself all the way. Except for complimenting me on my chic outfit and knee-high boots, he catches me up on every professional win he's had since Jesus was a carpenter.

I want to ask him if he's auditioning for a role—king of the world, or perhaps just king of my world. He's yapping as if he's impressing me with his resume, reminding me of what a great package he is, and how I should dote on him as much as he does himself.

If he hoped for any semblance of success, he's failed miserably. An hour of incessant jabbering, and he's only managed to convince me of how great and perfect I once had it with Nixon. Sadly he didn't realize in a year what Nixon understood in one day. Bragging or unloading on me his encyclopedic-length references to his career success was unnecessary. He only needed to *share* the moments we shared rather than always trying to be the moments we shared.

In the Verizon Center, he doesn't take my hand to hold it. I'm walking two steps behind him to steps like a Dubai bride as he high-fives and greets everyone and their mother on the way inside, which allows me time to sneak away and grab my John Wall Christmas ornament.

He knows a lot of people, and he wants to make sure a lot of people know that he knows a lot of people who recognize and acknowledge him.

That matters more to him than anything, including me. It's always been that way. I used to hope he'd someday change; I know he never will.

Ever.

Thankfully, I'm just here for the game.

We take our seats, the third row off the court, and as close as we can get to center court without sitting at the announcers' table. These seats rock even if he doesn't.

As I look around, I'm awestruck, not by the Verizon Center's grandness, nor by the number of people, nor the two men sitting to the left of me wearing enough gold to cash n and buy Hawaii. No, what's strikes me is I've walked about the length of a football field in new boots, and my feet don't hurt.

I'm winning.

"How are the seats?" he asks, knowing what the answer is.

I smile and nod, smile, and nod.

"I know how much you love basketball," he says.

When we were together, I loved basketball because he loved basketball. For me, it was a concession; for him, it was an obsession. Now I love the commercials, and I'm just bougie enough to appreciate premium seats.

I "ugh" inside. A can of paint could be sitting beside him, and he wouldn't know the difference as long as I speak when spoken to and wear skirts with knee-high boots. This man doesn't know me at all. Good thing a basketball game is only four quarters.

The cheerleaders take the court, and I'm expecting his eyes to be glazed over in butts and boobs when I glance over at him; instead, he's looking at me.

What's wrong? I immediately starting wiping my nose with my sleeve. I must have a snigglet.

Then I realize something is wrong, very wrong.

Dustin's eyes shift from me to the Kiss-Cam, which begins to spin toward us, and way too early, I might add. This event is usually reserved for half-time; I know from experience. Before I can ask what's going on, I shift my eyes back to Dustin, and now he's on his knees. The once-boisterous crowd around us is now hushed.

"Dustin, what's going on?" I ask, genuinely confused.

This turns out to be a lesson, a cautionary tale, never to ask a question you don't want the answer to. This advice is even more appropriate when you've already got the answer you wanted.

My mind is telling me no, stop him. This is a mistake. But my body is shocked, paralyzed, and my mouth is frozen shut. I can't even push my lips to form words. He's still smiling at me as if this'll get better, and I'm here to tell Superman, the best is not yet to come. Maybe in another year or so, with a different woman, preferably someone who knows better, but here and now?

"Mia, I've got something to ask you."

No, you don't, I say in my head. Again nothing's coming out of my mouth except a gasp. He's not gonna do it. He'd better not.

"Mia, I truly believe that you and I have a second chance. Leaving you was the biggest mistake of my life. The most important thing I learned after letting you go was realizing that I cannot live without you."

"Dustin," I finally manage to squeak out, but he gives me the hand so he can keep talking.

This is when the bad part begins.

I mean, it's all bad, but now the optics match. We're on the kiss cam.

What are the chances?

"Did you set this up?" I ask.

He nods. "I have a friend. He's been running the camera for years. He did me another favor. Now, if you'll please let me finish."

As he reaches into his pocket, my mind churns.

Another favor.

Another?

His friend runs the camera. That means Dustin knew we'd be on the Kiss-Cam when he broke it off with me, and my humiliation was no accident. He chose to break up with me in front of 20,000 people; it was no accident.

Now the ring's shining in my face. It's a beaut! At least two carats. Princess cut.

My smile's as fake as a PETA mink, and a burst of anger surges through me so fast, and hard it unsteadies me.

"Mia, make me the happiest man alive and consent to be my wife."

My lips stretch into a wide smile, not because of what he's done, but for what the universe is calling me to do.

I reach down, caress his cheek, and say, *"We really need to talk."*

"Excuse me?" he says in perfect time.

"No, I won't marry you. Not today. Not tomorrow. Not if Moses descends from heaven, and your proposal is engraved in a tablet. No."

Then I grab the ring from his hand, crane my arm back, and hurl it across the stadium.

"Mia!" he screams. "Why?"

He doesn't want me to answer that question.

He runs off trying to find his investment, which allows me to make my escape in the opposite direction.

It's the longest walk of my life. I'm Bridget Jones in the bunny suit at the Tart's and Vicar's party. Everybody's staring at me, and I think I've been booed more times than the Pacers. In all of this confusion, only one thought goes through my mind. *Please don't trip and fall. I don't want to go viral because I faceplanted after rejecting a proposal.*

Outside the Verizon Center, I finally open my hand and glance down at the ring box. Of course, I didn't throw it. I needed him to believe I did to create a distraction to make a clean getaway. I'll drop it by his office, or better still, I'll ask Mabel to deliver it on my behalf.

Tomorrow.

Dustin's human scourge. Super scourge. And I'm rid of him and his semi-truck-sized ego once and for all.

At home, before I snuggle under my covers, I glance out of my bedroom window and see a Christmas star that seems to twinkle just for me. It gives me hope for a better tomorrow.

The next morning, the sound of my phone vibrating snatches me out of the best sleep I've had in years. In a fog, I glance at the screen.

Zeke?

I barely press the button before I hear Zeke's breathless and panicked voice.

"What's going on?"

"Go to your computer and jump onto Instagram. Love & Kisses is live and announcing their new Christmas line."

"Why do we care?"

"Trust me, we care."

With my phone pinned between my ear and shoulder, I dash to my MacBook and flip it open. My fingers sprint across the keys until I'm in the Love & Kisses IG live. My jaw hits the ground with a thud that could shake the city.

"It's Dustin." He's standing there representing Love & Kisses, making a startling announcement—he's the company's new vice president.

"I'm watching," I say to Zeke. By now, I'm almost ready to join my bottom jaw on the floor.

"Their Christmas line is our Christmas line, as you can see," Zeke replies.

As I stare in total disbelief, this scene is playing out like a corporate soap opera.

He's announcing his position as Vice President and shows a tweaked version of our line. He's made just enough changes but not too many. If we use our own concepts, as is, Hart will appear to be copying Love & Kisses.

"This is a disaster," he says. "There goes our line. Our bonuses. Our jobs."

"Not your jobs, Zeke. My job. This one is on me. I've got to go. I need to talk to Tessa."

"What are we going to do?" he asks.

I've got no answers.

"I'll talk to you later. I need some time."

That's it. I've failed. It's over. I drag myself to my desk and pull out sheet of paper to draft my resignation letter. I'll never recover from this—Cody's right. I'm over my head, out of my depth. It's time for me to leave the company.

CHAPTER 24

ixon

I CAN'T BELIEVE WHAT I'M SEEING AND DEFINITELY NOT WHAT I'M hearing.

"Pick up a card from the new Love & Kisses Christmas collection today!" Dustin says, looking as slick as a used car salesman.

He's on Instagram live promoting their new Christmas line, and when I say "their," I use the term loosely. I'm only signed in to listen to a morning Magnificent House Party set from DJ Jazzy Jeff on Instagram, and Dustin's duplicitous mug greets me.

"What the hell's going on?" I yell to no one.

Yesterday, Dustin was employed by Hart Enterprises, as he was specifically brought in to work on the Sweet-Hart Christmas line. The next day he's on a rival card company's IG live pimping a card collection that I'm almost sure is derived from Mia's team's collection. It has to be. And if he's stolen her collection in any part for Love & Kisses, then I know she's stuck. Any legal remedy might take years, and that wouldn't help her now.

This year she'll end up with nothing. She'll have no Christmas collection and end up costing Hart an untold number of sales that would've boosted its flagging profits. For a company already struggling to get out of the red, this could be the death knell, if not for the Sweet-Hart line, then maybe for Mia's term as Vice President. It's not her fault, but they'll blame her.

No, I heavily suspect the fault lies with Renee and Regina. I've no doubt they are the moles and have been stealing the Sweet-Hart card lines. The only question I have is why? Why would they go through such extremes to undermine their own company?

Dustin. Love & Kisses. Renee and Regina.

The answer comes to me in a flash. And my stomach turns.

I've got to do something, but I'm not sure what's the next best move. I've got no idea what my strategy should be. Mia won't even speak to me, and this isn't news I can communicate to her over a text. Going to Cody and Tessa may cause her more trouble than I intend.

What I really want to do is find Dustin and punish him. Maybe another opportunity will present itself.

Right now, I have other business to take care of.

My morning routine is out the window. I suit up, take a melancholy glance at my Christmas tree and its sole ornament, and head into the office to confront my bosses, not only about what they've done, but what I suspect they're about to do. As usual, I find them both in Renee's office. Before I can barge in, Regina glimpses my approach and sits back in her chair, awaiting me to enter the lair.

"We figured you'd show up sooner than later."

"Dustin? Why?"

"I'm sorry. You've must've mistaken this for the final minutes of a Law & Order episode. But I personally think *you've* got some explaining to do."

"I'm not sure what you mean."

"Oh, you know exactly what we mean," Renee says.

"We hired you to do a job," Regina follows

"And I did the job. You wanted a Christmas line, so I gave you exactly what you asked for," I reply.

"You gave us a Christmas line, not the Christmas line. It's fortunate for us that we had the foresight to put two men on the job and not one."

"Dustin."

Renee just smiled. "I'll admit. What you provided us with is borderline fantastic. It's clear you're very talented and creative."

"Yes," Regina says. "You would've made an excellent creative director, but it's clear to us your loyalties...well, they lie elsewhere."

"I see."

"Don't get me wrong, though. We will be keeping the line you provided and make good use of it in the near future. That's why we won't require you to return the bonus money we paid you. After all, fair exchange is no robbery."

"Nothing about what you've done, nor what you're about to do is fair to Mia, to me, or Hart Enterprises—your own company."

They both sigh, and then they snap, one after another.

"See, what you're not going to do is come in here and judge us when you have no clue about what you're talking about," Regina says.

"What's not fair is when your father crowns you little brother as CEO when he's got two older daughters from his first marriage who perfectly capable of serving in that role," Renee barks.

"I thought I read it somewhere in an article that he's the only one of all the Hart children that had worked at the company since he was a kid."

"That's beside the point," Renee says. "We were passed over because we don't have what Cody has..."

"What's that? Work ethic? Integrity? Honorability? Because if that's what you're talking about, then you're right. You don't have what Cody has, and you never will."

I've set the devils on fire, and they like to burn. They're appalled that I've got the nerve to speak the truth.

"It's easy to judge us from the cheap seats. We've never been allowed to demonstrate our capability because Cody shoots down every idea we've had to change the company, to progress from the dark ages. As long as he can keep us contained in his own little box, he feigns fairness and pretends that he's looking out for his family's best interest. But we're about to destroy the illusion of the happy Hart family."

"I think the illusion was destroyed on the front pages of every national newspaper across the country with all the court fights," he says. "He won those fights, by the way."

"Did he? Or did he win the battle and lose the war?"

"No one ever wins when you go to war with family," I reply. "But I can tell you, there's no question in my mind what team I want to fight for."

"Good to know," Renee says, heading toward the door. "Now, you're fired. You know the way out."

"And take your principles with you," Regina says. "I hope they keep your bills paid."

Her words sting because it's barely been a week. I'm jobless again. And the money that I've earned replenishes the black hole left from paying Mom's debt. So while she's squared away and no longer under threat to lose her home for a long, long time, I'm back where I started. Except now I'm unemployed *again*, and I'm certain not to get a Hart Enterprises reference.

Good thing I've saved my mother's home because I may need to move into it. This is new to me. I usually don't get fired; I quit.

I head back to my office to clean out my desk, and, while packing, I feel a presence in the doorway.

"Well, this is disappointing," Mable says. "I thought you'd survive."

"Somehow, I knew I wouldn't, but I took care of what was most important to me—my mother. I tried to take good care of Mia."

"You're a good son. And a good man, if I do say so myself."

"A good man?" I ask. "How do you know? You heard?"

"I might've been passing by Renee's office at an opportune moment to press my ear against the door," she says. "I mean, I'm not saying that did happen. I'm just saying that it could've."

"Mmm-hmm," I reply. She somehow manages to eek a smile out of me. "What purpose is being a good man if you can't help the people you—"

"Love?"

I clear my throat. "Care about."

"Did you know I use to work for Hart Publishing?"

I shake my head.

Of course, I didn't know, but I'm trying to figure out why I should care right now. I don't, but I'm not going to tell her both out of respect...and fear.

"Yes, I used to be a reader for the editorial department. I decided I had a better personality for the phones, for connecting with people doing business with Hart."

"Okay?"

"I do have a point. I'm coming to it."

"I trust you."

"The thing is, I read all kinds of stories, short, long, snoozers, page-turners. And everything in between. And I made two key observations about why they failed to resonate with the editors."

"What's that?" I ask.

"Most authors didn't know where the story began, but there were a few who didn't know where the story was supposed to end. A good author knows not to let a novel go on for too long, but they also know how to let the plot play out long enough to satisfy the reader. You're grown, and you don't need advice from an old woman like me, but if I could offer a word on your behalf, I'd tell you—don't end the story too soon. Sometimes, if you want the happy ending, you have to let things play out."

I smile on the inside if not out. She doesn't know what the future holds. Neither do I. All I do know is I want Mia, and I want to feel whole professionally like I'm using my powers for good. And for me, that means not being shady. I'm not about that life anymore. There must be a better way, and I plan to find it.

"Thank you, Mabel," I say. "Your words have a way of putting my situation into better perspective."

"Is that right?" She says. "So, what are you going to do next?"

"I'm going to take a piece of sage advice I heard once from a wise, wise woman...let things play out."

LATER ON, I'M HOME AGAIN, THINKING ABOUT MIA, WONDERING IF she's lost her job, her mind? Wondering if she needs bail following an assault on Dustin? I pour myself a highball glass of whiskey and plant myself in front of my dark tree, vowing to buy myself some lights when a knock comes at the door. Brooks knows I've been fired and why. Maybe he's come to cheer up his unemployed friend.

I open the door, and my mouth hangs open.

Here stands the last person I expect to see.

CHAPTER 25

ia

IT'S OVER. I'M DONE. THE MERE THOUGHT WEIGHS ME DOWN. I don't know what I'm going to do next. There's no light at the end of the tunnel. For the first time in my life, I have no way forward except to deliver this resignation. Even though I'm giving my notice, I'm not quitting. I'm trying to do the best for everyone and minimize collateral damage to my best friend's company. The best way I can do that is to remove the weakest link. Me.

Funny, I never made an alternate plan. As far as I knew, I'd end my career at Hart Enterprises. I invested all my dreams in Keep It Real, Tessa's dream, which became mine. I never imagined Hart would acquire her company, or I would become the Vice President. Like a good soldier, I marched forward. I never envisioned what would come next if I left. There was no leaving, no next. I'd only grow in my current role.

Now, I needed a "next," and I had no idea what to do. The moment this realization stings me, I grow angry with myself.

I scanned the room, looking at the boxes of ornaments strewn about.

Maybe now the time had come to investigate my ornament business—a holiday pop-up, and then I'd grow from there. But what good would that do Hart Enterprises where I left an enormous mess for Tessa and Cody to clean up?

How could I allow my career to disintegrate like this?

How could I not have a Plan B? Then I answered myself—because I hadn't achieved my Plan A.

I didn't want to drop off this resignation letter.

I wanted to fight, but how? I had nothing.

I stopped at my bedroom mirror in the midst of my furry and looked at myself. On top hung the reindeer antlers Sophie gifted everyone at the party, and I put them on my head.

Thinking of Nixon, I lit up, inside and out. We had so much fun playing Taboo.

Taboo?

Yes, Taboo!

"That's it!" I yell, almost startling myself. In a flash, I've got the concept and idea for a new, innovative, and cost-effective Christmas line that I promised Tessa when I accepted the VP position.

It's been here, sitting front and center of my brain since Friday, and I missed what I had all along.

I sit down at my home computer and remember all of my systems back up to the Cloud. With Zeke's help, I can tweak the existing images. A little blur here, change a background there. He and Photoshop will save the day.

I wrap my fingers around my favorite pen and the copy just pours onto the page; laughter erupts from my gut with every word. The copy is truly inspired.

When I'm done, I collapse back in my chair and breathe for the first time in a couple of days. My mind churns over the upcoming schedule. I've no doubt that with Zeke on the mission, we can get the campaign to the printer on time, and we'll beat Dustin and Love & Kisses at Christmas Card-Fest by a landslide.

And I couldn't' have done it without my one and only —Nixon.

I glance over at the Christmas tree and beside it I see my briefcase, the one Nixon stole and returned. I suppose I should be grateful that Nixon bothered to return it at all. I grab it so that I can capture my ideas on the laptop I'll hand over to Zeke and pop the locks. I retrieve and turn it on.

One glance at the home screen, and I'm instantly deflated. "Oh, no."

What have I done?

I've made many mistakes in my life, but none has cost me as much as my failure to trust my gut.

A glance back at the clock reveals it's almost noon. I call Zeke to set up a meeting with the team, which we'll begin when I arrive, and I get there with no time to lose.

With not a single breath to spare, I barrel through the office and into the conference room to pitch the new idea to the team— and to my surprise, Tessa and Cody are present, too. I don't mince words. Instead, I launch into my spiel and speak from the heart.

"Thanks everyone for being here today," I say, scrambling around to hook up my laptop to the screen projector. By the time I'm done, everyone's looking at me, ready to get this over with.

"I think we can safely say last night was a disaster. A wise leader taught me that when the going gets rough, you can't quit. You've got to step up and figure out how to get the job done. Not just for your team, and not just for your company, but for yourself. Hart Enterprises is family to me, and I couldn't stand by and allow Love & Kisses to destroy everything Cody, Tessa, and the rest of our family has built here. We will not struggle for survival against that shady operation, not today.

"So I've come up with a new idea, something I believe we can customize for consumers that love both companies. The thing is, I never thought two opposites—like Hart Cards and Keep It Real—could complement each other well. But the truth is when you examine more deeply beneath the surface, you find that they are a perfect match."

They're all hanging on my every word. I've never held such a captive audience. Smiles and nods surround me. The team is on board so far. I hope they stay that way after they hear what's next. This is either a new beginning—or my end.

"Okay. Picture this: an image of a roaring fireplace. Stockings are hung by the chimney with care. Twinkly lights are draped along the lip of the fireplace." An image on the screen focuses on Santa from the black belt to his boots and facing the chimney. At the top of the card are a starry sky, a sleigh, and reindeer waiting on a roof. He's standing next to a tree with a bag half-filled with gifts. "As he prepares to ascend the chimney and—are you with me?"

Everyone nods. Their eyes are wide and curious as they await the big finale.

"The cover copy next to the chimney reads, simply: Up Yours," I say. "Then the inside copy reads: May this card lift your holiday spirits to the stars and beyond—Merry Christmas to you and yours."

There's a moment of silence during which I can see the team mentally process what I've said. Then there's a chuckle. Then a wave of laughs. Then howling erupts around the entire table. I breathe a sigh of relief.

"And that is the concept for our new Christmas line. It's Hart Cards and Keep It Real in a single card, but we can also use the same exact images for more a traditional Hart line—kinder, gentler messaging."

"Short. Funny. But poignant. Certainly, unforgettable," Zeke says. "What you've got here is the perfect recipe for a successful, viral Christmas collection. I'm going to have fun with the social media campaign."

"You think so?" I ask.

"I've been doing this a long time. I'm sure of it," he replies, wearing the cheesiest of grins. "The double entendres. You could give the card to someone you love...or not."

"What I love," Cody begins, "is we can use the images for Hart and Keep It Real cards – Sweet-Hart. We could change 'up yours' to something like, 'Wishing you Magic and all the joy of the season'. Syrup with a side of toothache. It's perfect for Sweet-Hart."

"It could be a good Christmas combination," Tessa says. She's not cracked a smile yet. I'm worried. "But do we have enough for an entire collection?"

"I've got enough, I think. For example, a plate of cookies sits on a table next to a Christmas tree. Santa's cookies, you know. Fresh out of the oven. Steam rises from the top. Of course, we can't forget the glass of cold milk. The glass is sweating."

"Nice. Very nice," Zeke says. "Good detail."

"For Keep It Real customers, the copy reads: Bite Me."

A wave of chuckles fills the room. Zeke laughs harder this time. "I've got a few names on my list for that one."

"For Sweet-Hart Cards, maybe the copy reads: Something hot and chocolate for Santa."

Laughter erupts again.

"That borderline sounds like Keep It Real," Tessa says. She still doesn't break. Even Cody's leering at her as if she's lost the last piece of mind she had left. "Is that it?"

Any confidence I had has vanished out the window and into the wind. I glance at my watch and say. "If we decide to move forward, Zeke and I will work the copy after this meeting. We can tweak the existing images. Those are done. We're going to have a couple of really long days, but we can still submit on time; I mean, in time to be late."

Now Cody and Tessa both look expressionless.

"I know I've made some mistakes, but I believe this line embodies the best of Sweet-Hart. If you want to fire me after I finish this, then I'll hand in my resignation. But I stand behind this concept. It's fresh. It's funny, original, economical—two lines, one set of images. It's a thousand times better than what Dustin stole, and most importantly, it'll generate the buzz necessary to carry us into Card-Fest and we'll reign victorious at the Winner's Ball."

I'm panicked. The rest of the team loves it, but, clearly, we're alone. I'm done. My proverbial Christmas goose is pan-seared and cooked way past perfection. Burnt to a crisp. That's it. Hey, I gave it my best. Nothing beats a failure but a try. I tried and failed. "Okay, then. I guess you don't like it. I'll leave the computer with the concept in my office." I move to grab my purse and head out the door when, finally, their silence is broken.

"You're not going anywhere," Cody says. "This is nothing short of brilliant."

"I agree," Tessa says. "Let's do it. Shoot the copy to Cody and me, and we'll conduct iterative reviews to keep production rolling quickly. We'll get this rolled out the door in time. We're off schedule, but if the extra time allowed you to come up with this concept, then I say we're not late, we're right on time. Amazing work! Congratulations on a collection that I think has the ear-markings of a big hit."

As Tessa and Cody leave, I trot out to catch them. Sure, the Taboo idea originated with me, but I never could've dreamed this concept had I not been so inspired by my contempt for Nixon. Well, perhaps it wasn't contempt so much as it was intense feelings of simultaneous lust, disdain, and admiration—and a lot of "like."

"Tessa? Cody? May I speak with you for a second?"

They both spin around and say, "Sure."

I launch into an explanation of the betrayal that never was—Nixon never turned on us even though all appearances seemed to the contrary. I detail the actual contents of the briefcase he delivered to Renee and Regina. Although Taboo was my idea, what inspired me was, well, the pressure, plus he and I working together toward the same goal.

"So," Tessa says. "What's your bottom line?"

"My bottom line is this. When Renee and Regina find out what's in the briefcase, he's going to be a darn good Creative Director without a job, and we need one."

Tessa smiles. "Well, you're the Vice President of Sweet-Hart Cards, so what are you going to do about it?"

I smile, press my hands together, and mouth the words, "Thank you."

She tells me to send him in for a discussion.

We've got a card line now—and a Creative Director, if he accepts the job. The question is whether I'll have someone, "the one," to spend Christmas with. We missed our date to the Jolly Jumper and still need ugly sweaters.

Yes, I've got a collection to produce, but I have one more task to complete. It may involve the most important conversation of my life.

CHAPTER 26

ixon

THE LIGHT KNOCKING ON MY DOOR ESCALATES TO A POUNDING. IT
must be Brooks. I'm sure he's concerned. Without a glance in the
peephole, I fling the door open, and my bottom jaw slams to the
ground.

"Mia?" I ask. "What are you doing here?"

"Nixon, hi," she says. I've never seen her look more beautiful
or uncertain of herself. She's carrying a box, a rather sizable one.
"Can...may I come in?"

"Thought I was the enemy? Why would you want to come in
here?" I hear myself reply. I'm not sure where these words are
coming from, to be honest. I've never wanted to see, to hold, or
to be next to another human being in my life as much as I want
to be next to her right now. But a bitterness, an anger, wells
inside me faster than I can control it.

"I made a mistake. Can I please come inside? This box is
getting heavy."

"Here, let me help you with that." I relieve her of the weight she's carried here. Looks like a gift-wrapped box for copy paper. "Come in."

How could she possibly believe I'd ever betray her? How could she think I'd do anything to hurt the woman, the angel who brought Christmas back into my life?

Yes, I had a past, but I also have a future, and one need not look anything like the other. I'm capable of change, but she didn't believe in that. She didn't believe in me. So, right now, I'm not entirely interested in anything she's got to say. However, I concede to let her unburden herself if that's what she needs to do.

I step to the side and allow her in. Then she removes her coat and rests it on the couch. "Despite appearances, I won't take up much of your time. It's just my mom always taught me not to wear my outside clothes indoors."

"I see." I can't deny I'm a little disappointed on the inside. Outside, I'm a robot going through the motions. "Where should I sit this?"

"Actually, it's a gift for you. You could set it next to the tree."

"Should I open it?"

"After I leave. Please."

I offer her a seat and fill a space on the couch adjacent to her, crossing my arms over my chest, armoring myself against any additional pain she may inflict. "You've got something you need to say?"

"Yes, a few things." She wrings her fingers. She's never been so uncomfortable and nervous around me before. Perhaps she's afraid of what I'll say or do. Part of me wants to let her off the hook, release the tension in the room. Another part of me, the part that controls my mouth, expression, and attitude, refuses to give an inch.

"I guess you saw Dustin this morning. It seems everyone did."

"Couldn't miss him."

"I should've listened to you. I'm sorry I didn't."

"Regrets?"

"More than one, I promise you. I'm hoping this visit will alleviate some," she says. "I hope Christmas miracles happen every day."

"I guess."

"Anyway, I wanted to tell you I came up with an idea for the Christmas collection...well, we did," she says.

"We?"

"Us. You and me. Let's say you inspired me. Our game of Taboo. I pitched it, and the entire team is psyched up," she responds. "We've got a new, innovative campaign, and it's all thanks to you dissing me after I stole your parking spot."

With quick mental replay, I smile inside. On the outside, I offer nothing.

"Before I left the house this morning, I looked inside the briefcase you left. Why didn't you tell me?"

"Oh, I don't know because you wouldn't answer the door. Because you wouldn't answer any one of a hundred different calls I made. Because you refused to speak to me. Because you jumped to conclusions and made assumptions about me based on some nonsense in the past. Because—"

"I'm an idiot. But you're clearly not. Your Christmas campaign, the one in the case, was nothing short of amazing. Almost as good as mine. Almost," she says with a wink, so I know she jests.

"I developed it at Signed & Sealed," I reply. "Never pitched it. I was saving it for the right moment. There I was using my work to save your skin, and the fox was already in the hen house."

"Dustin."

"Now Renee and Regina have your old campaign and the old one we created for Sweet-Hart."

"If Dustin gave the campaign to them, why was he promoting Love & Kisses this morning?"

"One guess."

"Ugh," she groaned after a moment's thought. "I wonder if Cody and Tessa have figured it out yet."

"Well, they fired him, so they know something. Now they've got some hard decisions to make," I say. "But it's a good thing you came through with the new campaign."

"The best part is you were my inspiration. The thing is, I know I don't deserve it after I behaved so horribly, but I hoped that maybe we can start over again. I'll be your date to the Card-Fest Christmas Party and Winners' Ball if you let me. If you'll forgive me."

"I appreciate what you're saying, but I can't. Part of me wants to forgive you, but another part can't get over the fact that you wouldn't even give me the chance to explain."

"Nixon—"

"No, the thing is, I started falling for you because I thought you saw me differently. But when the chips were down, you treated me like everyone else. I want to be with someone who believes in me. It's obvious to me that you don't."

"Nixon, you're right, and what you're saying is fair. I made the mistake of trusting someone, once, who let me down. Unfortunately, he entered my life right before you. Judging you by his standard was wrong, and I can't turn back time and undo what happened. All I can do is promise you that someday if you forgive me, I'll make it up to you...because in my heart,"—she says pressing her hand to her chest—"I know you're different, and I do believe in you. That's why I recommended you...as the new Creative Director for Sweet Hart Cards."

"Excuse me?"

"I mean, obviously you'd have to meet with Tessa and Cody for approval, and you wouldn't even have to deal with me. I'd stay out of your way and let you work directly with Zeke and the rest of the creative team."

"Even after everything I said to you today?"

"I don't want you to work at Sweet-Hart Cards because you're cute...or because I'm falling for you."

"You're falling for me?"

"I want you there because you're the most qualified Creative Director available and, I know, because I've interviewed nearly every single one in the city. None of them hold a candle to you or your work. You could take Sweet-Hart cards to the next level."

"You really think so?"

"You don't have to believe me. Talk to Tessa and Cody. They'd like to meet with you today. But if anything I say still holds weight with you, I know you can do this job. You'll kill it. We need you. I need you."

She stands and puts her coat on to leave. "I promise I won't bother you again...at least on a personal level. You've made your feelings clear, and I want to respect them—and you." She opens the door, and I glance back at the tree and spot the box next to the tree.

"Did you forget something?"

She shakes her head. "No, the box is for you, remember? You and your tree. You've literally changed my life. You've been my inspiration. Maybe in some small way, I can do the same for you."

In an instant, she's gone from my home, from my life, and deep hollow pit forms in my stomach. I resolve to deal with it, to endure with this minor loss now and save myself a major loss later. I don't want to go through that pain again, not after losing my father. I'm not going to subject myself to it.

I collapse into the sofa, and my eyes shift between the box and the tree more times than I care to admit. At first, I'm determined not to open it, and then my curiosity gets the best of me.

After pulling the top off the box, I fall back into my seat, this time in disbelief. Mia's gifted me with several strands of multi-colored lights. The label says they twinkle. She's also given me enough of her homemade ornaments to fill my tree.

I don't think I've ever intentionally used the word dazzle, but that's the only word I can think of to describe them, except without a word, I'm smiling and happy again. She's created ceramic trees, ornaments, donuts, and coffee, everything that reminds me of my dates with her. They are memories of us to dangle from my tree.

Just looking at them starts my mental and emotional journey to places and times when Christmas filled me with life and joy.

After hanging them and giving life to my number two tree, I suit up again, this time for my meeting with Tessa and Cody. I've got something important to say something they need to hear.

"You've had a busy few days, huh?" Mabel says to me as I wait for Tessa and Cody to call me inside.

"This isn't supposed to be an interview, but it sure feels like one."

"That's because it's an interview," she says. "No matter how great and wonderful we are, we've got to prove ourselves over and over again."

"I guess that's Hart Enterprises."

"No, baby, that's life. Every day we recommit ourselves to getting life right from moment to moment. You're about to have a moment. Just remember that it was a blessing to wake up this morning, and the opportunity to get your moment is a gift."

I smile. She's right. Every day we wake up is a new day to get it right. That's exactly what my dad used to say. That's what life and death taught me.

A second after that thought passes, the Hart duo calls me inside.

They welcome me with warm greetings, and I take a seat. After we exchange some small talk about plans for the holidays, we get down to business.

"I think you know why we're here today, besides Dustin."

"Sweet-Hart needs a creative director," I say.

"And as we heard from Renee and Regina, both of whom I'll be dealing with very soon, you need a new job," Cody begins. "I assume you've seen the headlines over the past few years and the court battles between my sisters and me. I'm curious to know what motivated you to take a job with the publishing arm."

"This is going to sound crazy, but I've never wanted to work anyplace else. Devon Hart and Brian Sweet—they're legends in this industry. Early on in my career, I applied for Hart positions, but I was under-qualified back then. By the time I'd reached the level I needed to be, no jobs at my level were available. Then I got the call from Renee and Regina. It was a dream come true...until they told me about the assignment."

They look at me intently, as if they're sizing me up, trying to detect lies in my plea. They won't find any.

"I never viewed it as an opportunity to work for them, and despite appearances, I've only worked in the best interest of Hart. Rather than compromise Sweet-Hart Cards, I gave them a campaign I created for Signed & Sealed, hoping they would see my value. They didn't because all they wanted to do was take down the company."

"Mia gave us your work. I know we can't use it, but the campaign is as impressive as anything we've seen during our interviews. We'd like to have you at Sweet-Hart Cards if you'll join us."

This was the moment I'd been waiting for, one I've spent the better part of my life striving to reach. Everything inside me wanted to seize it and jump right in. But I couldn't. Not without doing the one thing I believe I've been destined to do since the magical seven minutes in which I fell for Mia.

"This is truly an honor, and, more than almost anything, I want to accept your offer and the position. But, uh..."

"Almost?" Tessa says.

"I will accept the position, but I do have one condition. If you can meet it, then I will start right now. But if you don't, I'm afraid I will have to walk away."

"Umm, okay? You have one condition?" Cody says. Tessa presses her hand against her heart before she can speak further. "What is it?"

I gulp hard. I'm sealing my future or my fate. The next thirty seconds will expose it all.

 ia

I'M HOME ALONE AND TOAST MYSELF FOR FINISHING THE CHRISTMAS collection. The all-night print job will be shipped off to the Sweet family bookstores in a day or so, and the entire line posted on the website. Now, I'm getting dressed to head into the Christmas Card-Fest part.

We submitted a selection of our cards in time to be hung at the tree lighting, on the Douglass Fir for the D.A.Ds (Deployed and Active Duty). Of course, I have no date. Doesn't matter, though. I did the right thing by all involved. After shooting down their ideas for months, we finally achieve success. Not just with any idea but the right one.

Sometimes you don't know how wrong something is until you find the right thing.

This is true of more than just Christmas card campaigns. It's true of people, too—men like Dustin and Nixon. Dustin turned out to be everything I believed him to be, and Nixon turned out to be everything I hoped he'd be and so much more. Before I can finish my thought, the phone rings. It's Sophie. I glare at the screen before answering.

"Morning, Chica! Any word?"

"Nothing. He's off the grid. Gone silent."

"Something tells me he'll come around."

"I dunno. It would serve me right if he didn't. Why couldn't I just trust him?"

"Your problem is never about trusting people," Sophie begins. "It's about trusting your gut. When your instinct tells you a person is good—or a collection is good—I hope from now on, you'll believe it, because you've got the best instinct of just about anyone I know, myself included."

"Ha. Ha. You're funny," I reply.

"Any more word on Dustin's fate?" she asks.

"Apparently, he's newly employed as the VP of Love & Kisses cards," I say. "Thank God, I had the foresight to tell Kyle to limit his system accesses. As a temporary employee. he never viewed or stole any sensitive data, like our Valentine campaign."

"See? Instincts."

"I suppose. It doesn't seem like it's going to do me much good without Nixon, though. Oh, well. You win some, you lose some. Anyway, are you and Brooks coming to the Christmas party tonight?"

"Of course, we've got to defend our record. Undefeated in the couple's ugly sweater category."

"Yeah, I was hoping Nixon, and I would give you guys a run for the money this year. I even special ordered from the Jingle Jumper."

"It's not too late, Mia. You never know. He may come around."

"I'm not sure if enough Christmas magic exists in this world. Anywho, I'm running late for work. See you guys in a bit."

It's cold and clear outside. Cloud puffs crowd the skies, but rays of sun pierce them like beams of hope. By the time I get into the office, they've already shut Dustin's' office all the way down. I hope they've fumigated.

My butt barely hits the seat in my office before Zeke pokes his head in my office. He's wearing a lighted elf hat and a candy cane on his sweater, which is Christmas ugly but not on purpose. Sadly, he's been thinking it's holiday stylish for the last two years.

"Cheer up! The holidays are upon us. You look like you got a lump of coal in your stocking rather than the woman who developed the Christmas collection with the highest focus group scores in the history of Hart Enterprises."

"Shut the front door!"

"Don't mind if I do." He swoops into my office and closes the door behind him. So have you heard about Dustin?"

"Love & Kisses. Vice President. Wish I could say I'm shocked, but I'm not."

"You might be shocked about this—apparently, Love & Kisses is under new management. Biggest industrial secret since the reason they avoid putting heads on greeting cards."

"First of all, that's not a real secret. Second of all, it doesn't matter. Tessa and Cody are a powerful combination. Third of all, we don't have to worry about anything except finding a new Creative Director."

Zeke jerks back his head as if he's in disbelief.

"I thought—hmmm. You may want to talk to Tessa." Clearly, I'm supposed to know something I have no clue about.

My eyebrows raise. As my curiosity piques, our conversation quickly comes to an end. I high-tail myself into Tessa's office for the scoop.

"Uhhh...anything you'd like to talk to me about?" I say after bursting into her door. The green, blue, gold, and red sweater lights up the ugliest Christmas tree ever weaved into a sweater. I fill with laughter, and it explodes from my gut.

"You guys are really gunning for Sophie and Brooks this year, huh? I don't know whose more competitive, but I know who's looking like a sure-fire winner."

"So, what brings you in here today, besides insulting my Christmas attire?" Tessa asks.

"The Creative Director position. I still need a new one."

Her eyebrows scrunch.

"We do need one, don't we?" I ask again.

"Ummm...not the last time I checked. I take it you haven't spoken to Nixon yet?"

Now *my* eyebrows scrunch.

"Nixon? I'm not sure...I mean, the way we left things yesterday, I thought he wouldn't...what'd he say?"

"He came in for his interview on time, as scheduled."

"And?"

"And...he killed it, thanks to you for showing us the collection he developed for Signed & Sealed. He was practically a shoo-in."

"Practically?"

"Well, he would only accept the job under one condition and, frankly, he required a major concession from us, from Hart Enterprises. If we refused him, he told us he'd walk away and never look back. And let me tell you, we offered every penny he was making at Hart Publishing and then some."

"So, what happened? He walked away?"

"I think he should be the one to explain," she replies.

"But he won't speak to me."

She shrugged and offered me zip, zero, nada in the way of consolation. "All I can say is you need to speak to him."

"But, Tessa, I thought we were besties."

"We are," she says. "And trust me when I tell you, my silence is for your own good. Now, let's talk about the party tonight —you in?"

"Fine!" I stand up to storm out—half playing angry and half-serious. "Yes, I'll be there. And I hope SoBro smokes you guys in the ugly sweater contest."

. . .

At home later that night, the party's about to start, and I'm still here. I've been stalking my phone, hoping it would ring, waiting for Nixon to give in and call. Instead, I sit in utter and complete silence—the loudest rejection I ever heard.

At the height of my despair, I realized something about him...about myself. If we're meant to be together, nothing can keep us apart, not today, tomorrow, or someday in the future. I'm a better person now, more confident in myself, and I'm stepping into the future a changed woman. The best part is I'm over Dustin and ready to trust and believe in someone new, ready to believe my gut when making the right decisions.

The matching sweater I bought for Nixon haunts me from beneath the tree even though I'm wearing mine—we could've won, but we won't because he won't speak to me. I suppose I deserve the silent treatment, but I don't like it. There's not much else for me to do. Before my Uber arrives, I pour myself a glass of champagne and toast myself for having the courage to attend another couple's party alone and single.

I glance down at my phone when the alert sounds. My Uber has arrived, so it's time to go. I slip into my coat, open the door, and off I go until...

NIXON

It was my gut, an instinct, an urge I can't quite put my finger on. For the first time in my career, I put everything, my entire future on the line. I was willing to give up all that I wanted for something bigger than me, for something that mattered more to me than my desires, maybe even more than what I needed.

My career had been a study in fierceness, pragmatism, ruthlessness, perhaps some selfishness. Rarely generous. Never charitable.

At Bartholomew & Fink, I engineered the sale of a subsidiary that cut the head off the beast—got rid of expensive, oppressive top management. Industry frowned on the move, but now, under new, progressive leadership, the firm thrives. We had to eliminate management everyone was used to, and that's painful; not everyone has the stomach to execute such an aggressive plan.

At Keene, I manipulated an Acquisition that eliminated a thousand jobs, eight-hundred of which were vacant positions. Yes, I was dragged through the press for that deal. However, with the reduction in overhead, the firm went from red to black in two years. Many were unhappy with my choices, thus the bad media, but I don't work for optics. I always do what's best for the company and the people.

I can't deny I had an ax to grind; so many had counted me out, called me a sham, the hatchet. I'd lost so many times I need wins, and I got them, but not without scars. Now, today, sitting before Tessa and Cody, I was primed to win, and I risked losing everything they offered. And, why?

For what I really wanted. For who I needed.

And when she opens her house door, in the moments before the Christmas Card-Fest Party, I'm filled with thankfulness, gratitude, and excitement because I fought for her dream—and won. And I've come bearing important gifts.

"Nixon?"

She pauses for a moment. I'm not sure how to gauge her expression. Her eyes look as kind as ever, yet her lips don't stretch into the smile I hope to see. She's not unhappy either, so I'm grateful.

Seconds later, I'm inside her house, standing at the door with a gift bag in my hand. Judging from her stunned silence and bulging eyes, she's in disbelief. My visit's unexpected. No one's told her. My news is a best-kept secret.

"Are you on your way to the Christmas party? You got a hot date?" I ask.

"On my own again. Besides, I save my best holiday dates for breakfast at home, tree shopping, chili cheese dogs, and s'mores. What are you doing here?"

"I needed to see you, to talk to you. I'm sorry for my behavior toward you, giving you the cold shoulder. I should've accepted your apology, but what you did...I thought I deserved better."

"You did. You deserved so much more ."

I remove my coat to reveal the sweater I picked up from the Jingle Jumper. I special-ordered it with Mia and her Christmas-crazy tastes in mind. I hand her the present.

"Nixon! How did you—the sweater. You're not going to believe this." She reaches under the tree and retrieves the exact same one—in my size. "Great minds think alike. The Jingle Jumper?"

"Of course."

"How did you know?"

"Hanging around the Christmas crazy lady."

She smiles. "Does that mean you're going to the party this evening?"

"As your date, if you'll let me."

She removed her coat, disappeared, to fully reveal her sweater. Funny how much alike we turn out to be.

"Horrible, isn't it? What can I say? I'm competitive. I wanted us to win."

"We did win," I add.

"Don't be silly," Mia says. "We've not even hit the party yet."

"No, I don't mean the sweater contest." I take her hand and lead her to the couch where I sit her beside me and cup her hands in mine. "I went to the interview today, and they offered me the Creative Director position on your recommendation."

"I was hoping you'd accept the position. I can't believe you'd turn it down."

"You didn't hear? I accepted it—but with one condition—that

they add a Christmas ornament line and that you design and curate it."

"Wait, what?"

"You even get to name it. I was thinking Christmas Mementos by Mia. Thought it had a nice ring to it."

"Are you serious? You must be kidding me."

"No, I'm not. Tessa was thrilled about it, said she couldn't believe she didn't think of the idea herself."

"You went out on a limb for me despite everything that happened, everything I did and didn't do."

"Mia, I believe in you. That's what you do when you believe in someone, isn't it? After all, I did no less for you than what you did for me."

She covered her face with her palms and then launched at me with both arms open. I folded her in an embrace. We pulled apart just enough to look deeply in each other's eyes, and before I slowed myself down to savor the moment, my lips covered hers.

The world disappeared, and no one remained but Mia and me, together in our ugly sweaters. Seven minutes to a lifetime in a matter of days. At this moment, I not only understood Christmas magic, I believed in it. I believed in her. Most importantly, I believed in us.

"Wow," I say. "Did the earth just move?"

"Yes." She says, smiling widely, then glances down. "Or, maybe no. I think that was my phone. It's in my pant pocket...vibrating."

She pulls it out and glances at her screen. "It's a text from Cody, corporate. He's calling for an emergency meeting with company leadership. Like right now."

"Does it say what the meeting's about?"

"No clue," she replies, and furiously begins to type. That's when my cell phone begins to vibrate. I glance at my cell.

"Same message. Direct from Tessa."

"Hmmm. You're probably not in the system yet. Tessa just

returned my text. She says they want to share some official news before the Christmas party."

"Official news? What's that about?"

"I don't know, but we better head over there now."

It's after rush hour, and I'm driving, so we're back at Hart Enterprises in no time. Both of us do double-takes on one another, realizing we're walking in the lobby together as if being coupled is second nature. We hold hands and weave our fingers together like it's a habit as old as we are. We smile and release one another before we enter the conference room. We may be ready for us, but we both realize that not everyone else will be.

We enter the room; Tessa, Cody, Mabel, and Kyle are already seated around the conference table. Mia and I find seats next to Mabel, and Cody dives straight in, with not a single word minced.

"I called you all here today because I wanted to give you a heads up on the latest news. We'll be making a few announcements tomorrow, and we want to make sure you're all prepared to answer questions. There will be many."

Tessa stands next to Cody.

"First of all, you should know that my sisters, Renee and Regina Hart, have tendered their resignations. Effective immediately."

There should've been more surprised expressions in the room; no one's shocked.

"You're all aware that we've had a mole in the company for some months now. When we first started experiencing intellectual property losses, I hired a private investigator to root out the source of the problem," Cody says.

"The investigator's been working for the past year since Hart acquired Keep It Real," Tessa adds.

"In his final act for the company, my father dictated, as part of the bylaws, that should any officer of this company acquire a controlling ownership interest in a competing entity, he or she forfeits his or her shares in Hart Enterprises; they will be immediately severed from the company," Cody says.

We all sat in stunned silence, digesting the news. He didn't come straight out and tell us what happened, but my lady speaks up. She, of course, never misses a beat.

"Wait a minute," Mia says. "Ownership interest. Love & Kisses? No!"

Cody pinches his lips and nods. His eyes flash with anger, so Tessa takes over.

"It seems they purchased ownership interest through a shell company. They've controlled it for a little more than a year. No one knew. They've concealed it well."

Everyone in the room gasps and groans.

"We've been firewalling Hart's Publishing and greeting card operations since the court battles, so they've never had the requisite system access to steal our most critical proprietary information. Still, they know this business, learned it from the best—our father's"—he glances at Tessa—"and they will be fierce competition."

"Any good news?" Mabel said.

"As a matter of fact, yes. First, we're all still here, and we've got each other. Second of all, we've got a Christmas line with the highest focus group scores ever. We're certain this will translate into sales once the collection hits the market."

There's applause around the room.

"We've also hired our creative director, Nixon McCloud, who we've got no doubt will maintain the exceptional standards set by Mia and raise the bar if that's even possible. His first strategy is to establish a new ornament collection curated by Mia. It will appear as part of next year's Christmas collection."

Mia and I glance at each other, then thank everyone around the table for the applause.

"Now," Cody says. "I don't know about you, but I could use a tall glass of holiday spirits."

"Amen to that!" Mabel seconds.

After a short meet-and-greet filled with forced smiles and handshaking, Mia and I escape the crowds and go into Hart's Executive Conference Center, where the party's already in full swing. The DJ booms Stevie Wonder through the speakers, our song, *What Christmas Means to Me* comes on.

Dimmed holiday lights shine, and Christmas disco balls turn as I two-step backward on to the dance floor and gesture for Mia to follow. Mia soul slides in rhythm with the beat until her hand is in mine, and her body bumps against me.

"You impressed me tonight," Mia says.

"Really?" I reply. "Who says there's no such thing as Christmas miracles?"

"If a little Christmas Magic can lead us to this place, right here, right now, then what will tonight lead us to?" she asks.

"Victory at the Winners' Ball?" I reply facetiously.

She nods and smiles.

"Also," I lean in and kiss her before adding, "if I have anything to say about it—forever."

CHAPTER 28

ia

Different Black Friday, different year. SoBro's hosting the annual; the kickoff to the holiday season, and this eventful year has led Nixon and me full circle. We're back in Georgetown for the party, and I've just turned onto their street. I'm searching for a parking space but, as per usual, nothing. Thank God there's no snow this year...but there's also no parking spaces. I circle the block for nearly twenty minutes before I'm competing with a stranger for the newly vacant spot in front of SoBro's house. I'm ready to lay my foot down on the gas when the voice of reason speaks.

"Ease up there, Maria Andretti. Have we learned nothing from last year?" Nixon says. He's the same...but different, too. His eyes are brighter. His smile seems wider. He's finer than ever, and he's dressed in a Grinch sweater that matches mine.

"Yes, I learned something from last year, thank you very much. I learned that I need to hit the gas pedal harder and really cut the steering wheel tight if I want to zip in there and steal a spot fast."

I glance at him, and his lips are pursed together. That's one of the things I love most about him—he does not even pretend to entertain my shenanigans and foolery.

"Okay, fine. I'll let them have the spot and drive around the block a few more times."

"That's my girl. And think of the bright side, the farther away you park, the longer we get to walk and hold hands."

Holding hands was among my favorite things to do, next to well...Seven Minutes of Christmas Magic.

Two spins around the block, and a space empties directly in front of SoBro's house. "Maybe I should keep driving so we can walk and hold hands."

"Woman, if you don't get in that spot, there will be zero minutes in heaven tonight!"

I pull into that parking spot before he put a full period at the end of that sentence—we've been together for an entire year— I know his threat was not an idle one.

"So, did Sophie tell you anything about this year's victims?"

"Not much," he says. "Not enough for you."

Nixon grabs the gift wine, and we head into the party. It's funny how one year could change so much. Last year, I dreaded this party. Last year, I arrived alone and maybe a little bitter, wishing I could crawl into a hole from Black Friday until the day after New Year's, fearing I'd be coupled to death.

This year, I arrive brimming with excitement about what this new year will bring and reveling in the knowledge that whatever it brings, Nixon will be beside me, enduring it with me. He's the light that gives me hope. He's become everything my life needed. Most of all, he's the family I longed for.

We knock on the door, and SoBro greets us. I've got one thing on my mind (except a possible trip to the Christmas closet), and that is to help coach this year's Mia and Nixon. The poor souls have no idea what's about to hit them.

It takes SoBro a couple of minutes to let us inside because they're entertaining folks. Still, we're patient, holding hands, and looking at one another with goo-goo eyes that have become customary in our relationship and draw admiration from our friends and loved ones. I love looking at him, but, more than anything, I love what he sees in me. He's a witness to my good side and my bad side, and he loves them both the exact same, with all of his heart and soul.

"Sophie! Brooks!" I'm excited when they open the door. They greet us as if we hadn't just hung out last weekend. A positive and negative aspect of this coupling thing has been getting invited to and attending more couples' events. We spend less time vegging out and doing nothing. Maybe tomorrow.

"It's good to see you two...again. Glad you could make it," Sophie says.

Brooks adds, "I see Mia drove today and got a spot right in front."

"Yes, but I didn't steal it. This time I got it fair and square," I say.

"I hope you're hungry," Sophie says. "I've made my world-famous beef bourguignon, and we've got a fridge full of jolly juice."

"Good," Nixon says. "We've had a long day. I've been looking forward to this since Monday."

"Need a little something to knock off the nerves, old boy," I hear Brooks mumble, but I don't pay him any mind.

"How's the new ornament collection coming along?" Sophie asks. "Knowing your talent, it should put you guys ahead of the game after winning Campaign of the Year at the Winner's Ball thingy last year."

"It's fantastic," I reply, "and we're in good shape this year. I finished two months early."

"She cheated a little," Nixon says. "I mean, she had ten years' worth of ornaments to start with. Didn't take long to figure it which ones to mass-produce. I can't wait for you guys to see how she's put it together, though. It's brilliant. She's amazing."

He's always prouder of me than I am of me, it seems.

"Our entire Christmas collection is phenomenal thanks to this one," I say, pointing my thumb at Nixon. "We're so lucky someone was smart enough to nab him while he was available."

As far as the pride and bragging go, I'm the same for him.

"Well, look at you two," Sophie says, beaming with pride. "Go ahead and get seated."

"Who's the new Mia and Nixon?" I whisper to Sophie. "I want to sit next to them."

"I think they could use your help," she answers. "You'll know them the minute you see them. They're the ones who look like gazelles on a lion reservation."

We swing around the corner, and the happy couples, all the usual suspects, except two, surround the table. SoBro positioned the last two empty seats side-by-side and next to the sacrificial couple who'd be targeted to fall in love this year. Their adorableness knows no bounds; they're young and fresh from J. Crew ads like the rest. There's enough brown wavy hair between the two of them to cause motion sickness.

"Get comfortable, everyone. My world-famous beef bourguignon will be on deck in just a few minutes," Sophie says. "Nixon, Mia, I think you know everyone here except these two—Bella and Drew."

"Nice to meet you," Nixon says, shaking their hands. He pulls out my chair so I can sit down after greeting them. The sweetness is too much.

"Very nice to meet you," I chirp. "Aren't you two looking Christmassy tonight?" I sit next to Bella; Drew and Nixon flank us on each side.

"It's so nice to meet you guys," Bella says nervously. "This party is so lovely."

"It's okay. I've been there," I say to Bella in a whisper and then slide her glass of jolly juice a little closer. "Nixon and I were you and Drew last year. The good news is Sophie's matchmaking record is perfect...the bad news is Sophie's matchmaking record is perfect." I say with a chuckle. Perfection sets a high bar. "Trust me, have two tall glasses of jolly juice and go with the flow. You will either be ready for everything, or you won't give a darn about anything."

Nixon pipes in. "Do you guys know SoBro from Georgetown U?"

"Yes," Drew says. "Brooks is my frat."

Nixon begins to bubble because that means he and Drew are also "in the club" together. Common ground.

"I know Sophie from work," Bella says.

They'd never even met one another before this evening, and their ugly sweaters coordinated to the thread—his ornaments to her trees."

"Word to the wise," I begin, "you can try to run, but you can't hide. Sophie is like a relationship pit bull. Once she sinks her teeth in, there's no letting go until you die...or fake your death. Been there, done that. Just be sure to drink up. It'll be over in a few hours."

I glance back at Nixon, and we laugh.

Bella whispers to me, "You, sound like a professional."

"Single three years in a row. Last year, I landed this one."

"Oh, are you guys married?"

I opened my mouth to respond, but Nixon beat me to the punch. "Oh, no! Not yet."

"Really?" I turned to him, and now I'm giving him a deadly squint. I'm in no way, shape, or form pressuring him to marry me, but he could've kept his trap shut. I mean, every time someone mentions the "M" word, he looks like an escaped convict with a US Marshall on his tail. It's not necessary, which he must realize when he sees my expression. Lucky for him, I'm fine with taking things slowly for another year or so. Then it's put up or shut up.

He puts his arm around me, trying to play it off. "I'm kidding, baby. Any man would be lucky to marry you."

The strength it took for me to clamp shut and resist saying, "Fool! That includes you!" could reduce the Empire State Building to rubble, but somehow I managed.

DURING THE POST-DINNER MINGLING, SOPHIE BEGINS THE GAMES FOR the evening. I'm smug in the belief that I'll get to watch Bella and Drew suffer. If I can make it to Seven Minutes of Christmas Magic time, I'm going to be dying laughing thinking about them struggling as Nixon, and I did. Then I remember the hard part was brief.

As a matter of fact, it wouldn't be a step too far to say I kind of fell in love with him in that closet...after we stopped plotting to kill one another.

At that moment, I wished the same for Bella and Drew, minus the killing part. But Sophie cuts my thoughts short with her first command.

"It's time for our first game of the evening. Seven Minutes of Christmas Magic."

My eyes widen, and my head jerks all the way back. What about Christmas Taboo or Christmas Carol Chaos. This isn't right. And it's most peculiar because the closet magic's supposed to be the last game of the night, not the first. Now Sophie's eyeballing me...not Bella and Drew as she's supposed to. What the heck is going on here?

"For the new people, the rules are as follows: Brook and I select two of our lovely guests or a couple to enter our well-ventilated closet," she says. "Inside the closet, you can exchange anything as simple as a Christmas secret or as sweet as a Christmas kiss."

I'm still smug because I know Nixon and I are off the hit list. It's Bella's and Drew's year to suffer. Sophie and Brooks whisper in each other's ears as if they've really got a choice to make, and then Brook announces the name of the lucky couple.

"Our first choice is Nixon and Mia."

"Excuse me?" I say. "It's someone else's turn." Last year, and for the previous three years, they've called a married couple first...then the victim couple. We are neither.

SoBro turns to one another and whispers again. My overconfidence returns because I know they are not insane enough to repeat this mistake three times. Then Sophie announces the revised names of the lucky couple.

"We choose Nixon and Mia."

"Really?" I say with equal parts bark and bite. I glance around the room and fire venomous glares as warning shots. Nixon just shrugs and says nothing. No argument. It's like the first time ever that he doesn't back me up. I know one thing— there will be no magic in that closet this year. I make one last-ditch effort by sending a subtle reminder to SoBro. "Do you really want a repeat of our performance from last year?"

"We'll take our chances," SoBro says simultaneously. Well, it's clear who has whose back at the party. Still, neither Nixon nor I budge.

"Do you really want me to make good on my threats to divulge your college secrets?" Sophie says, threatening us both.

Annnnnnnd...we're in the closet.

Nixon and me. Me and Nixon.

It's dark. I feel his breath on the high part of my cheek, and then it's gone. Only a tiny sliver of light seeps through at the bottom of the door.

"I forgot my phone," he says.

"Figures," I reply in my disgruntled voice. Then I remember I'm stuck in the closet with the man of my dreams, whether the game is rigged or not.

"Lucky for you, I have mine," I say, retrieving my cell from my back pocket. I turn on the light to reveal Nixon...kneeling with a ring box in his hand.

"Nixon?" I say with tears already streaming from my eyes.

In Nixon's hand sits a heart-shaped diamond ring. I'm stunned silent and can't speak. Luckily for both of us, he does.

"Mia, I've never known a love like ours before. I've never had someone to believe in, to trust, and someone who trusts and believes in me. You make me want to be a good person. You make me a better man. I want to be your family. I want to protect you and love you for the rest of my life. Will you do me the honor of being my wife?"

Without realizing it, I've dropped the phone, which darkens the closet. I nearly tackle Nixon into a hug before saying, "Yes, yes, yes," and then cover his lips with mine. We kiss softly at first and then deeply.

Seconds pass like hours when we hear taps on the door.

"Are you two okay in there?" Brooks whispers.

"She said yes!" Nixon replies.

We hear cheers and resume our passionate kiss. The noises we make, they're real this year.

"Your time's up," Sophie barks.

"Five more minutes," I call out as we crumble in laughter.

"Make that fifteen," Nixon adds.

Then I whisper, "Best Black Friday party ever."

"No," he says, "best life ever—and we're headed for a Merry Christmas."

"No," I reply, "the merriest Christmas ever."

The end and thank you for reading SEVEN MINUTES OF CHRISTMAS MAGIC. If you enjoyed this novel, please leave a review at your favorite review site. If you want to hear Mia's favorite Christmas tune, visit:
http://klbradyauthor.com/romance-novels/seven-minutes-of-christmas-magic/

ACKNOWLEDGMENTS

Thank you to Almighty God for giving me the vision and strength to finish this book in such a difficult season. I'm truly grateful and blessed that You have given me this gift. I'm so glad that You helped me make room for this passion, and that You allow my books to find the people that will find enjoyment in them.

To my family, especially William Jr. and Joshua, thank you for being so supportive and doing extra doggie duty with my Meatball so that I could focus my attention on finishing the books.

To the DJs of Instagram and social network (and their wives and families who support them), including DJ Jazzy Jeff (and wife, Lynette); D-Nice; Questlove; DJ Mos; and Mick, thank you. They don't know me from a can of paint and won't likely read this. But I can say, without question or doubt, if it hadn't been for the healing power of the music they played during the Magnificent House Party, Club Quarantine, and other DJ sets, I would never have finished my books during the lockdowns. They sacrificed a lot to help us regular people maintain some semblance of sanity, and I'm deeply thankful to each and every one of them (as also reflected in the amount of merchandise I have purchased).

Lastly (but not least), to my readers, thank you for sticking with me throughout these years. I know it's been a while, but I will never stop writing as long as the ideas come, and God gives me strength to type. From Day 1, I've said I would write for one person as long as that person showed interest; however, I've been blessed with so many more. Thank you for taking the time out of your busy schedules and hectic lives to spend a little time with my crazy characters. I'm genuinely grateful, and I hope they bring joy and laughter to you, especially at this difficult time.

ABOUT THE AUTHOR

K. L. Brady, a DC native, started her writing career in the pages of diaries when she was seven or eight years old. But it wasn't until her fortieth birthday and an Oprah "Live Your Best Life" moment that she finally answered her calling and wrote her first novel–The Bum Magnet. The originally self-published novel was picked up by Simon & Schuster in a two-book deal and K.L. hasn't looked back since, penning the follow-up, Got a Right to Be Wrong and self-publishing the first books in two young adult series and a spy thriller series based on her twenty-year career in the U.S. Intelligence Community.

A certified nerd girl with a love of all things Star Wars, Big Bang Theory and Star Trek, she has a B.A. in Economics and an MBA. She also holds memberships in the Maryland Writer's Association, Romance Writers of America, Sisters In Crime, and International Thriller Writers. She's addicted to writing and chocolate—not necessarily in that order—and currently, lives in the Washington DC area with her son.

Website link: http://www.klbradyauthor.com
Facebook link: https://www.facebook.com/KLBRADY/
Pinterest: https://www.pinterest.com/authorklbrady/
Twitter: https://twitter.com/KARLAB27
Instagram: https://www.instagram.com/klbrady_author/

If you enjoyed this novel, please stop by and leave a review at your favorite site. They mean everything to indie authors. And join my newsletter for news on the latest releases, chances to get free books and early review copies, and special contests for newsletter readers only! (Note: We never spam; newsletter issued once every 3 months.)

http://tinyurl.com/klbradynews

facebook.com/KLBRADY

twitter.com/KARLAB27

instagram.com/klbrady_author

goodreads.com/karlab27

bookbub.com/profile/k-l-brady

OTHER BOOKS BY K.L. BRADY
IN THE CARDS SERIES – SWEET ROMANCE

Love is in the Cards – A Novel (Clean, Sweet Romantic Comedy)

In this second-chance romance, a greeting card company owner's life is sent into a tailspin when her business is acquired by the ex-boyfriend who dumped her. (Coming November 2020)

Seven Minutes of Christmas Magic (Clean, Sweet Romantic Comedy)

Sparks fly when greeting card company executive ruthlessly steals Mr. Right's parking space before a Christmas party—and then steals his heart. They would be a match made in heaven…if he hadn't been tapped to steal her work and destroy her career.

The Christmas Card Wars (Clean, Sweet Romantic Comedy)

There's trouble in the cards—Christmas cards—when the Hart family goes head-to-head in the Card-Fest competition. Renee and Regina bitterly defect from Hart Enterprises to lead Love & Kisses Cards. They face Tessa, Cody, and the rest of the Sweet-Hart Cards gang to vie for first place at the Annual Winners' Ball. (Coming in October 2021)

Women's Fiction – Chick Lit

Got a Right to Be Wrong (Some Strong Language)

One week before her wedding day, a woman with a life-long struggle with trust issues finds out a life-altering secret about her fiancée and questions their future.

12 Honeymoons (Clean, Sweet Romantic Comedy)

After a nasty break-up that lands her court, a DC socialite, struggling to find her purpose and love, gets arrested (again) and is forced to perform community service.

More Christmas and Holiday Romance

Five Golden Rings - A Christmas Novella (Clean, Sweet Romance)

A.J. and Kristie serendipitously "fall" for one another at the National Tree Lighting in Washington DC As fast as destiny brings them together, Murphy's Law pulls them apart.

The 12 Daves of Christmas – A Novella (Clean, Sweet Romantic Comedy)

It's a comedy of errors when Dave and Gabby attempt to meet one another face to face after falling for one another due to a misdirected text.

The Bum Magnet (Chick Lit/Women's Fiction - Some Strong Language)

After a lifetime of bad relationships, a woman decides to go on an introspective journey to find out why she attracts to the wrong men—a journey hilariously complicated by a new love interest.

The 007th Day of Christmas (Clean, Sweet Romance)

Coming Soon.

Sincerely, Santa (Clean, Sweet Romance)

Coming in 2021.

The Playmaker Series – Sweet Romance

Her Perfect Catch (Clean)

A struggling sportswriter finds the story of her lifetime, and love soon follows, during a trip to the Super Bowl.

The Player's Option (Clean)

When sports agent Ty Baker and C.J. meet at a pro-football conference, sparks fly, and they can both see love in the end zone...until disaster strikes. Each learns the other is trying to steal their biggest client and cut-throat competition threatens to tear them apart.

The Eligible Receiver (Clean)

Jet Jamison is hot, successful, wealthy, and can have any woman he wants, the one he truly needs still eludes him, that is, until Veda enters his life. A chance meeting with Jet begins with a sparring match and ends with love at second sight. But she's got a secret that threatens to tear them apart.

The Playmakers – 3-Book Box Set

Her Perfect Catch, The Player's Option & The Eligible Receiver

Are you ready for some love and football? This funny and sweet box set contains heartwarming romances featuring sexy professional football stars who deliver hot, flirty days and cozy nights.

Young Adult - Romance

Worst Impressions (Clean)

In this modern retelling of Pride and Prejudice, shy, basketball loving, tomboy Liz Bennett meets star high school quarterback Darcelle Williams and sparks fly—and she'd like to set him on fire.

Soul of the Band (Clean)

A bullied, inner city teen gets a chance to start a new life when, after her mother's mental breakdown, she is forced to move to a small town in Ohio and joins the high school band.

Spy Thrillers – The J.J. McCall Series (S.D. Skye)

The Bigot List (A J.J. McCall Novel #1)

An FBI Special Agent and her partner are drawn into an unsanctioned hunt for an intelligence community spy when Bureau sources are killed, and an internal investigation threatens to land them atop the suspect list.

Situation Critical (A J.J. McCall Novel #2)

An FBI Special Agent and her partner lead an intelligence community task force ordered to find moles throughout the intelligence community, and its first case targets the White House.

The Shadow Syndicate (A J.J. McCall Novel #3)

The FBI task force heads to New York to shut down a sleeper spy funding network, landing them in the middle of a burgeoning war between a Russian organized crime organization with links to diplomatic spies and the Italian mafia.

SpyCatcher (J.J. McCall 3-Book Box Set)

The Bigot List, Situation Critical & The Shadow Syndicate

Read the first three J.J. McCall Novels in one great set!